THE LETTERS OF IVOR PUNCH

Colin MacIntyre is an award-winning songwriter, multi-instrumentalist and producer who has released seven albums to date, most notably under the name Mull Historical Society, so far achieving two Top 20 albums and four Top 40 singles. He has been voted Scotland's Top Creative Talent and has toured worldwide, including with The Strokes, Elbow and REM, and has played all the major festivals. He has performed live on BBC Radio 1, Radio 2, 6 Music, Radio 4, *Later with Jools Holland* and *The Jonathan Ross Show*, among many others. He is the co-author of a Radio 4 Afternoon Play, and has collaborated with Tony Benn and Irvine Welsh. His other musical project is Field Stars, an electro art-pop collaboration.

Born into a family of writers and storytellers, Colin, a descendant of the Gaelic warrior-poet, Duncan Ban MacIntyre, grew up on the isle of Mull in the Hebrides, where his 'Bard of Mull' grandfather, Angus Macintyre, was charismatic bank manager by day and published poet and raconteur by night. Colin's father was the much respected BBC Scotland Political & Industrial correspondent, Kenny Macintyre. Colin now lives in London.

The Letters of Ivor Punch is his debut novel, and won the Edinburgh International Book Festival First Book Award in 2015.

colinmacintyre.com

@colinmacintyre

facebook.com/colinmacintyreauthor

THE
LETTERS
OF
IVOR PUNCH

Colin MacIntyre

WEIDENFELD & NICOLSON

First published in Great Britain in 2015
by Weidenfeld & Nicolson
This paperback edition published in 2016
by Weidenfeld & Nicolson

An imprint of the Orion Publishing Group Ltd
Carmelite House, 50 Victoria Embankment
London EC4Y ODZ
An Hachette UK Company

1 3 5 7 9 10 8 6 4 2

A CIP catalogue record for this book is
available from the British Library.

978 1 780 22904 1

Typeset by Input Data Services Ltd, Bridgwater, Somerset

Printed and bound by Clays Ltd, St Ives plc

The Orion Publishing Group's policy is to use papers
that are natural, renewable and recyclable products and made
from wood grown in sustainable forests. The logging and
manufacturing processes are expected to conform to the
environmental regulations of the country of origin.

www.orionbooks.co.uk

For Pam

'People and things pass away, but not places.'
Daphne du Maurier

'And fuck.'
Ivor Punch

Prologue

2009

J ake sat down in the sand and breathed in the familiar sweet, heavy air. The next day he would return to London, but tonight he was here, and he held his uncle Ivor's letter in his hand. He could see the pale blanket of the Atlantic Ocean in the distance. It was getting late and the sun was falling off the horizon, its destination the sea. Here, on this island, on the west coast of Scotland, he was Jake *Punch*. There was no getting away from it. But strangely, he had no desire to. Only the swarms of thirsty midges could threaten his sanctuary. He had forgotten how persistent they could be.

It was late summer in the year 2009, but in his mind, as the night fell around him, it was 1978. It was the summer of 1978. It was seven years before his birth. He looked out as far across the land as dusk would allow him, to the attendant trees, the purple heather-strewn hills and, more immediately, to the flat familiar turf. It stretched out before him like a beautiful green sea below the lingering hills. Jake knew he was alone. Invisible.

He ran his hand through his jet-black hair and itched his sallow skin. Then he raked his fingers slowly through the sandpit. This was his second visit to the Games field that evening. It was here on this very spot, in that summer of 1978, that the father he never really knew leapt like an angel with wings into the local record books. That was before the bomb that killed his father. Before there was a him. Jake had never really thought much about the bomb. He had considered the plane, the fallen, even the point of explosion, but he had never imagined the finer details, the ingenuity of the technology required to bring down the plane.

He was now four years older than his father had been when he jumped. This was the first time he had been to this spot as a man older than his father. As Jake looked from the island to the darkening surrounds below the reddening sky, he took some comfort in the fact that this land, this Games field, this island, had existed not only before he had, but also before his father, before there were bombs, and planes. Jake had posted all of Ivor's letters tonight, except this one, the one addressed to no one. 'Dear . . .' it read. But Jake knew whom it was intended for. It was for his father. He of no fixed address. He of no physical grave, which rendered his father in a way un-bombed. Jake could only hope he was still floating in the sky, in the ether, careering through space, still jumping, his arms outstretched, his legs reaching for eternity as though a magnet were pulling him towards the ocean. This, Jake had heard, was the illusion his father created at this sandpit. If he were on the ocean, Jake imagined his father as a floating straw. Or was it, even then, to the sky that his father was being summoned? Jake opened Ivor's letter, reawakened his phone for light, and began to read.

Dear . . .

Well tonight the tubes finally unblocked. I haven't been able to shit for a week it seems, but the Gods have answered my prayers. Far from whistling as it came out, the damn thing near recited the alphabet. Anyway, despite this success, the body is breaking down. And fuck. You probably don't need to know any of this, but at least you never had to experience the humbling of the body's gradual decline. No. Small graces. And fuck. There is a rattle in my chest again; each cough is like the rattling of my soul. If I have a soul. If it wasn't stolen a long time ago by my father. Really, he and his fucking dovecote stole my childhood. I never talked to you much about that either. You were too young.

I can't make it far beyond the front door these days. You would hardly recognise me. I looked out of the window to the sea today. I've been looking every day of course, but not really seeing it. Since you were taken I have instead been more preoccupied with the sky. But this looking to the Atlantic got me thinking back to my time whaling on it. And you know – despite the extremities of its fury, I did also experience its calmness. And, as a result, I always viewed it as very definitely one thing, like a person, like an island. Like a son. And fuck. I see in the newspaper that today's quotation is from the man Benjamin Franklin. 'There never was a good war or a bad peace.' Well he should be alive now to have a word with my chickens.' And fuck. They don't know when a battle is won or a victory lost. At least I learned that as I neared retirement or, really, after I lost you. That is what you gave me, a relocation of my anger, because I couldn't blame my father any more. You gave me something else to blame. A plane falling out of the sky was my transformation. There have been times when I'm ashamed to say I could almost have thanked you. But maybe that is not what old Benjamin was alluding to. And fuck.

You never got to see this new President of America. A fine man. He'll have some trouble making this world a village, as is *his desire. I've told him so. Maybe a better place to start is an island. It still chews me up not knowing if you ever reached your prime. You never saw this decade or the one that came before, maybe just as well. You see – the plane is in the news again and this President is on the side of you and me – he is trying to stop the release of your bomber. I thought you should know. Yes Obama and Scotland are fighting over the fate of the Libyan culprit. The cunt.*

The past is catching up on me, and the anger stirring. And I promised myself you wouldn't see that. I don't know my reasoning for putting this pen to paper. Maybe it is because if I speak it aloud, well, only Gorbachev the chick will hear me. And he's a long way from giving me a conversation, let alone an egg. Or maybe that is just the vanity of an old man alone, stripped of his authority. But I am thinking back to that day, back when I could still piss in a straight line. It was just about the perfect moment. Your record long jump. And fuck. It was. It was one man's answer to the question posed, one man's conversation with the Gods. And the world knew it. And this land, and these trees, and that ocean, and this man, still does.

I must drop the pen. I am tired. I have gripped the hand of the past too tightly tonight. It has its effects. And fuck. My poor boy. I say goodnight to you. Sleep well.

Ivor

Jake looked across the ever-darkening turf and could almost see his silhouetted younger self, having taken leave of his violin and placed it safely to one side, attempting to re-enact his father's feat on this playing field. On those days and nights he would make sure his only audience was the midges, then lunge in wonderment, trying to replicate the jump he had heard so much about, to form his father's elegance, his body shape, to fashion the 1970s hairstyle, to suspend himself in air. Then he would top off the whole charade by imagining himself holding aloft the golden Games trophy that bore his father's name. And all, he now recalled, to the unlikely soundtrack of Sibelius's 'The Swan of Tuonela' on his walkman.

As Jake watched the film in his mind unspool, he smiled, his eyes filling up, and then he rolled to the side to prevent the boy landing on top of him. With this sudden movement Jake came to and shook his head free of the past. He looked around, slightly embarrassed, and then mildly spooked. He thought of the Headless Horseman, who was believed to lurk deep within the nearby woods, how it might be present. He was struck not only by how many times as a child he had tried to reproduce his father's jump, but also by how many times in adulthood he had willed the plane not to fall. He was struck too by how often he had willed his father to return from, what was it – the ether? And now he knew that Ivor had too. He brushed sand off the letter. As unlikely as it seemed, now he had written proof that Ivor shared some of his emotion. Jake looked in anticipation to the sky, to the amalgam of crimson, purple, yellow and green; it was as though the playing field and all his surrounds were reflected above.

He thought back to 1994, and that December evening which marked the sixth anniversary of the plane going down. He had been taken against his will on the Christmas fir tree hunt with Ivor and his friend Randy, and they had encountered a dead horse. All these years on and still Jake could feel the texture of the horse's skin, the firmness of the

5

beast's dead muscle echoing through his hands, and the foul smell of the men's cigarettes and boozy breath. Fifteen years on, whenever Jake thought about Ivor, an act of regression occurred. He was once again 'the boy'. He guessed he had known nothing at the age of nine, or maybe, he thought now, he had known everything.

He patted the sand off his clothes and took another long intake of breath; the same smell of the land, freshly cut. He would need to bottle it in his lungs, this peat-scented air, for transporting to the mainland, to the metropolis. He looked to the black outlines of galloping hills and into the darkness where the Atlantic Ocean rested. The view was the same, the smells and still of the evening familiar, the grains of sand beneath him unchanged. But the twenty-first-century world in which he sat, in which he had blossomed away from the island, was very different. He turned off his phone, took the fleece out of his backpack and smiled at the significant sky above, watching it move like lava. He buried the letter inside his fleece, lay back in the sandpit and let sleep overtake him. He was home. He was in the perfect moment, in the symphony of the unborn.

6

I

Out Stealing Firs

1994

Ivor Punch stopped in his tracks and dropped the rope that was dragging the fir trees.

'What the fuck is *that*?' asked his friend Randy, coming to an abrupt halt and looking ahead through the dusk. He tapped Ivor on the arm with his can of beer, having turned to make sure they were not being watched by the boy trailing them. Ivor shifted, as though the charade was unnecessary.

'A horse? Well ... well ... what the fuck's it doing lying alongside this track in the forest?' Randy's voice was more high-pitched than usual; he was doing his best to appear shocked. He took a gulp from his can.

'Fucked if I know,' Ivor said wearily, but stooped closer.

'Looks like it was hit square on the front,' Randy said, screwing up his face, warming to the charade and peering more closely at the animal. 'Reminds me of the wife.'

'But with a cock ...' Ivor wheezed, crouching to investigate the remains.

But with a cock, the boy replayed in his head.

Ivor shook off the cold by flailing his arms. He was known on the island as 'The Clock', because he had one arm noticeably shorter than the other. The boy knew that nobody dared call his uncle that to his face.

'It must have belonged to the Headless Horseman right enough, Ivor?' Randy croaked.

'And fuck,' Ivor confirmed, concluding his investigation. 'It won't win the Grand fucking National any time soon.'

It was becoming dark. Like everyone in their town on the island the boy had heard of the Headless Horseman, but had never seen him. He could hear his own breath quickening. He looked towards the rest of the world across the blackening waters of the Atlantic Ocean. 'The other world,' his grandmother called it.

'This'll do.' Ivor looked around and up to the sky. It was the 21st of December, but surprisingly mild in the woods. It was because they lived in something called the Gulf Stream, the boy's grandmother had told him. The men settled and the boy realised that was them for the night.

We're sleeping here – by the horse? the boy wanted to ask. The thing lay so still and hopeless it didn't seem like a horse at all.

'A dead horse? *Here?* What are the chances?' marvelled Randy.

'Fuck,' Ivor said, irritated by Randy's over-acting, 'whatever it was, the thing's taken a fair hit, the teeth are nearly up its arse. Okay.' Ivor got up off his lopsided haunches, in so doing taking hold of the night.

The sky was giving way to a black blanket and the boy looked up to the relieved, remaining trees, which had evaded capture by Ivor and Randy. There, in the hills, he and his friend had once seen what they believed was the Headless Horseman. He had never come so far through the peat bogs and forest since.

'As good a time as any for a draw,' said Ivor, bending to lay

8

out two cigarette papers on the side of the horse. He began rolling them and then looked at the boy through a drink-fuelled haze. 'You're my brother's kid,' he croaked. 'Despite the influence of Mozart and his pals, we'll make an officer of you yet.' The boy knew his uncle would give him this same talk again on Christmas Day; it had been the same each year since his mother and father died. 'And fuck, he's a quiet one. Did you get yourself a ride in the school yet?'

'Ivor! Come on, he's what, eight? He's only just off the tit,' Randy chuckled.

Nine.

'Old enough,' Ivor choked, gesturing to the boy. 'The bugger would sooner sleep with his violin. I curse the day he ever received it.' He sniffed. 'Whoever it was that sent it to the lad ... And fuck. What a racket he makes. It's no wonder the house is surrounded by cats' shit.' Ivor paused. 'Fucking Syphilis or whoever it is ...' he added, causing Randy to itch his groin.

Sibelius.

They rolled out their blankets and Ivor threw the boy an extra one; the men were now only distinguishable by their roving cigarette tips. It gave the boy the impression that their arms were moving like the orchestra conductors he had seen on TV. He liked the look of these people playing instruments in suits, the way they merged into one. There was something about their remoteness that drew him in and made him want to become one of them. The music, coming from a place called the Royal Albert Hall, seemed to speak only to him. And it was then, as he listened to that music, that he realised he was different from Ivor. He could smell the dead animal even more now the daylight had fully disappeared.

Randy switched on the torch. As he staggered, the light roamed like a lighthouse beam intermittently revealing the horse's coat, and the boy caught sight of the mane. Randy tied the torch to a tree.

The boy swigged on an old Sprite bottle that his grandmother had given him, which she refilled endlessly with water from the tap. She hadn't wanted him to go out, but his uncle Ivor had forced the issue. 'Anniversary,' Ivor had said through a whisky glass.

Ivor sucked hands-free on his roll-up; it died on him so he lit a match and reformed that protective lattice of fingers to provide shelter. The boy watched as his uncle's smoke drifted towards what Ivor called 'the inferior mainland' – these parts of his uncle escaping, leaving the island behind.

Randy looked to the boy. He leaned his mass of bushy hair into the light and his face became ghoul-like. 'They say the Horseman once knocked out a horse with his fist . . .' he whispered. 'Christ, maybe he does the same from a stable in heaven–'

'You have no idea of heaven, none of us do,' Ivor interrupted, and then choked on the thought. The boy looked up to his uncle and then to the stars, which twinkled like cats' eyes.

Heaven is where Gran says Mum and Dad are.

Randy jabbed the boy, making him his audience; his ash fell like glitter and his breath smelled of beer. 'The horseman's knuckles still held a big tooth; his fist could smile,' said Randy, wide-eyed. 'They say he's your ancestor, the same dark skin and black hair. "Duncan Punch" they called him. That's why you're all called "Punch". But I've no idea how he lost his head.'

'Enough,' instructed Ivor. 'We all know the story. And fuck. He's dead anyhow, just like . . . well.' He looked to the boy then took a dislike to the brief eye contact.

The boy noticed his uncle's eyebrows met at the middle. Then he saw an image of the plane's battered remains behind his closed eyelids. *Flight 103.*

Ivor looked to the healthy pile of fir trees they had stolen earlier from the Estate further out near Bloody Bay. He and Randy would sell them in the town. 'We've enough there to keep Father fucking Christmas going till Easter, the bastard.' He drained another can and rubbed his eyes.

'Can't say I feel much like one of Santa's little elves, right enough,' said Randy.

Each year the boy watched his grandmother cursing the needles that fell on the carpet in their front room, until January came and the space where the Christmas tree had stood returned to being worn carpet. Something was there and then all trace of it was gone, like his father and mother. To him it was always odd to see such a wild thing as a tree dressed and domesticated; it was a bit like seeing Ivor at the breakfast table, dwarfing the salt and pepper pots.

'We're late with them this year, some fuckers will already have a tree.' Randy lit a match and made the most of small piles of sticks placed within last year's circle of stones.

'Here, get this down you,' Ivor said, throwing a can of beer towards the boy. It rolled to his foot. The boy flinched but hoped the darkness had saved him. 'I had my first can when I was your age,' Ivor added, reaching for one of the fir trees and dragging it free from the rope and onto the fire. 'We can lose one,' he said, 'it's useless anyway, covered in lightning scars. Call yourself a forestry man, Randy.'

The boy winced. His father was a memory, less than a flame. His mother too, and he knew even less about her. Nobody seemed to really know where she had come from or anything about her family, even after the bomb. He smelled the dense aroma of resin as it arrested the evening air, spreading as though a reminder that they were there, the trees, living things after all. He opened the can and sipped it. Ivor smiled at him, his rotten teeth flashing like crooked piano keys.

'Poor kid,' Randy said, more solemnly, swigging from his hip flask and looking over his shoulder to where the boy sat. 'Your old man loved the Christmas tree run.'

'Err, aye,' Ivor countered, clearing his throat. 'Enough. I said enough.' The boy had never heard his uncle Ivor mention the plane that fell from the sky.

'Can you drink that fucking can or not?' asked Ivor.

'Leave him alone,' Randy said.

'I'll do what I like. The boy's my blood. All I have left.' Ivor gulped. 'And fuck. He'll know that in the years to come. He'll know . . .'

The boy's my blood.

Randy winked to the boy and then turned to Ivor's silhouette with a smile. 'I don't know the time but it must be late. If you'd stretch out your arms you could show us yourself Ivor! Go on – give us a chime!'

Ivor ignored the goading. 'I'm hungry,' he said. The smoke from the fire was now sky. The boy watched his uncle pull two knives from his bag.

'Let's eat,' Ivor decided, crisscrossing the blades. He motioned the handle of the knife towards the boy. 'Here, you make the first cut.'

Me?

'Come on. It won't carve itself.'

'Are you sure he's ready, Ivor?'

'Is there another way to find out?'

'Your father was a bloody good hunter, son, the best. I mean, especially for a man with brains,' Randy said. 'And he was a fine fucking athlete. He could jump over this horse where it stood – the cunt had springs, not legs. So you'll be fine, just fine.'

'How will that help him now?' asked Ivor. He looked to the boy, his voice breaking. 'I'd start above the thigh. Good meat there. I'll get the china set up.' Ivor pulled a newspaper from his bag and scrunched the pages into plates. 'You'll need this.' He handed his nephew the other blade.

The boy considered how different from his father Ivor sounded. He took a sip from the can and held one of the blades more tightly; he looked at the other on the ground beside him.

'Maybe he's not–' Randy started.

'He's ready!'

The boy realised he had never cut into anything, apart from the time he had made a little slice in his forefinger when pressing too firmly on his violin's rough strings. Even then, he had hated the sight of the blood. The thought occurred to him now that the plane must have been full of blood.

'You'll be okay, son. Just ... here, let me help.' Randy slid closer to the boy and took the can from him. 'Bring the knife up and come down hard into it, with both hands.' Randy lifted the boy up onto his knees. He held one of the blades above the boy's head. Ivor busied himself at the fire. The boy's arms were static in the air, his eyes closed. There was a pause and then the blades came down with all the weight he could muster into a surface that felt like the earth. There was a sound unlike anything he had heard. When he opened his eyes he saw blood. Randy slumped down on his backside.

'You fucking helped him!' Ivor shouted.

'I did not!'

The boy's hands were still attached to the knives, and the horse.

'Well ... what are we waiting for – a fucking napkin?' Ivor motioned to the big blades. 'Here, hand me the cutlery and I'll cut us some dinner.'

The boy was woken by hunger and cold. A sweet smell came from the last cuts of peat on the fire. His head hurt and the air felt heavy, like part of him that he couldn't shake off. He could see his uncle Ivor was sitting up, his back straight, his thighs at his chest; his shorter arm was more noticeable now. He had never seen Ivor so peaceful and he kept silent to enjoy that for a bit. Randy was lying motionless on his back, his eyes closed, his big, square head resting on his forearm, a can of beer still clutched in his hand. And beyond Randy the boy could see the missing chunks of land that had fed the fire. The land now looked like a carcass too, like it did in the photographs he had seen of the blue and white nose of the plane in the field.

'Are ... are you okay Uncle?' the boy asked, getting onto his elbows. 'Is everything okay?' In the half-light he thought he could see a secret door to where he imagined the Headless Horseman might live. The soft wind rattled the trees as though there were other voices out here whose language he didn't speak – could Ivor be one of them? Maybe his uncle was now a ghost, like his father and mother.

'I've never liked that bastard.' Ivor nodded in the direction of where Randy lay. 'Uncouth. He'd stick his dick in that fire if it would make him come. And fuck. I have seven years on him and you wouldn't know it. Look at the silly big skull he has. It's a wonder we ever see the fucking sun.'

'Or the moon,' attempted the boy.

'Can you believe he's just about to start a job driving the island's bank van?' asked Ivor.

'Is he?' The boy looked to Randy's greying blond hair.

'Aye, the bugger's fifty,' continued Ivor, 'clearly the Forestry Commission is not good enough for him now. And fuck. That's how he knows all the nooks and crannies out here. He's trading in his steel toecaps for brogues. You know his real name is Archibald? Thick as a tree trunk. Not like your dad.'

The boy remembered now that last night the men had cooked and then actually eaten part of the horse. He had wanted to be sick.

'I had a dream,' Ivor said. 'It woke me; the fucker.' He moved to flick off the torchlight and rubbed at his thin, greying beard which, despite its fragility, always managed to join up his ears, nose and Adam's apple. The boy looked to the big bones in the fire.

'I dreamed I was with Pavarotti,' Ivor said. 'And we were walking around a supermarket.' He shook his head.

'Pava-ro-tee?'

'But,' Ivor straightened his back, 'we don't even *have* a supermarket?'

'Who is Pav–?'

'He's a singer, fat like the Pier Master.'

'Oh,' said the boy.

'Your grandmother likes his voice. Not the Pier Master's.'

'Does she?' the boy asked.

'Just one Cornetto, or some fucking thing. Bastard ate a few anyway ...' Ivor looked, frustrated, to his nephew. 'You don't remember the World Cup? Italia '90? Gazza crying? Ah, you're too young.' He turned away in disbelief. 'Four years is clearly a long time.'

But it had been six, since the plane.

'And fuck. I just don't understand it,' Ivor went on, reaching for an abandoned can.

'I never understand my dreams,' the boy said. 'I had one about my dad.'

'No, well ...' said Ivor, now sobering up and ignoring the reference made. 'But, I mean ... I've never even met the man?'

'Gazza?'

'No!' Ivor tossed the can away. 'Pavarotti!'

'Oh?' The boy looked to the ever-lightening sky. 'So have you met Gazza?'

'Eh? No. No.'

'I never met my dad really, did I?' asked the boy.

'So where the fuck did that come from? Pavarotti?' Ivor shook his head.

'Or my mum.'

'Italian he is ... right enough. Can hold a tune.'

'Maybe you were still hungry, and that's why you dreamed of a supermarket?' the boy offered. 'Was my dad there, in the supermarket?'

'What? Hungry? No chance, I ate enough of that horse to give me a fucking gallop this morning,' Ivor said. The boy laughed. 'No,' repeated Ivor. 'And shush. You'll wake that cunt.' Ivor looked down towards his best friend whom, the boy realised, his uncle didn't even like. 'More chance of getting a sentence out of the horse right enough. Although, a sentence is just what Randy fucking needs.'

'Can I ask you something?'

'Well, I'm awake now, might as well,' replied Ivor, looking around to survey the early hour. His eyes settled on the carcass. 'You should have tried it you know. Tasty. Like venison but tougher.'

'Uncle Ivor, how can you wear the police uniform on nights like this?'

'Eh?'

'Don't you feel, eh, funny about it?'

'Call me Sergeant when I'm in uniform – okay?'

'Yes, Sergeant. But—'

'Look, you can go back home if you want. And fuck. You're starting to sound like your father ... I recognise his conscience.'

'What d'you mean?'

Ivor looked to the piles of captive trees and sighed. 'Maybe I shouldn't have brought you. I was going to put a stop to the tree scavenging, but well. That bastard who runs the Estate – he's away. I should fucking arrest him for being a curmudgeon alone. Owns the land all the way from here up to Bloody Bay, the fucker.'

Ivor coughed again. 'This fucking chest of mine,' he said, 'it'll get me in the end. Well, it wasn't like any supermarket I've ever heard of. Not that I've ever been in one, mind. I'm not sure there was even such a thing when I was last off the island. No, I'm just fine with the produce from my chickens. That is, when the little fuckers behave.' Ivor produced a roll-up as if from nowhere, lit it and took a long draw. He looked to the boy. 'I should never have let him go. I remember the day he left for the business college,' said Ivor, 'a Punch going to college, Christ ... And it was the first time he'd ever been off the island. And fuck. Looking back at us, at my father and mother – your grandmother and grandfather – you know, he told me we were just dots on the pier.'

The boy wondered if this was how astronauts saw the earth, morphed into something so small they could cup their hands around it.

'Don't you stay,' Ivor said, with a pained smile. He worked the horsemeat from his teeth with his tongue, his sallow skin turning grey. 'Other than a bit of training for the force I only ever really left the island to hunt whales. And then I found what I considered a more honest profession. Or so they tell you. I've hunted all my life, one thing or another. Mammals in the form of whales, disguised as drunks. And now Christmas trees.'

The boy looked at Randy's body. He still hadn't moved.

'Uncle Ivor – is he ... *dead*?'

Ivor sat forward again; he was looking to the ground. He spoke more slowly: 'Aye, he's dead lad.'

'What d'you mean! Have you killed him?' The boy jumped to his feet. Randy stirred. 'Bloody hell!' The boy moved to the side.

'No! No. I thought, I thought, you meant your father ... Sit down will you lad. And fuck.' Ivor shook his head towards Randy's body, which was still once again. 'What a bloody commotion over a drunkard. No, *he's* fine. He has more lives than a cat's litter. Just ask the bank.' Ivor looked away for several seconds and then he croaked, 'I'm worried it has come for me.'

'What?'

'Pavarotti. Death. Fuck knows ...'

'What do you mean?'

'I've stayed the same too long. At least your father upped and left ... and well, he was on his way to ... America – do you know? And with your mother, too. Poor lass.'

'Yes,' nodded Jake, 'Gran told me, and I saw then on the news.'

'He was handsome, and surprisingly good with his brain. Although he didn't always like to show it. But he was clever. That's what got him into trouble. Otherwise he wouldn't have been bothering New York for a work trip. And the woman your mother with him! And fuck, it was Christmas in only a few days, just as it will be now. She was an American. They would have been back on Christmas Eve – to our little island. Bloody New York! For just two days! Christ!' Ivor shouted. 'Cagney and fucking Lacey.'

'Who?'

'He said one thing to me,' Ivor went on, 'your father ... the last time I spoke to him, back when you all still lived in Glasgow.'

'What? What did he say Uncle Ivor?'

'He said, "Get me a good fir." A good fir! What do you think he meant by that?'

'Maybe he wanted you to know he would be alright? And that he wanted a Christmas tree, for us.'

'And fuck. He was the best athlete I ever saw, better than any of us. You know that?' Ivor flinched, as though he was catching up with the past travelling through his body and flashing behind his narrowed eyes.

'Yes. That's what everyone says.' The boy smiled. 'Did you see his record long jump?'

'See it? I fucking nearly arrested him for it! In those amateur conditions it was, it was beyond human. Beyond . . .' Ivor rubbed his eyes.

Randy groaned and turned over. The boy was startled to see that Randy's ankles were handcuffed.

'You know I often wonder what the pilot of the plane must have been thinking . . . one minute flying through a beautiful sky, the next up in smoke. And your dad . . .' Ivor's voice failed him; he looked away. 'They say one of the passengers hung from the gable end of a house in the town, you know, still strapped in her seat.' He recovered. 'She was hanging like a headless angel or some mad fucking Christmas decoration!' Ivor looked to the boy, his eyes widened, his expression more desperate. 'Headless!'

'Uncle Ivor, did you know my mother?'

Ivor shook his head. 'No lad. We didn't really know anything of her. What a cunt of a thing.'

'Do you miss him?' the boy asked. He watched the shape of his breath stay out in front of him; he wondered if his father could still dream.

'Call me Sergeant when I'm in uniform, what did I just tell you?' Ivor sniffed heavily and then shook his head from the past.

'What did Randy do, Sergeant?'

Ivor's voice was now more assured, he sat straight up and looked down to the body beside them. 'Randy was talking about going back to steal another horse from the Estate. I had to arrest him for his own good. Not to mention the horse's.'

'Uncle Ivor – did Randy kill this horse?'

'Aye. Randy shot it the other day and we had to come out and kick it in the face to make it look like a car had done it, in case anyone came along and wanted to make a fuss. You never know out here. And fuck. It's not often you get a chance of some decent meat . . . but one horse was enough. I was so deep in my thoughts last night I'd forgotten all about the thing till we stumbled on it.' He looked to the boy. 'Good powers of deduction, lad. Must be in the blood.'

'Why did he . . .?'

'. . . He sells the meat to the factory ships. Foreign fuckers love the stuff. Even though I've warned him against it. Better that we spoiled it, to keep the silly fucker out of jail. Otherwise he'd be back out here tomorrow with his frying pan faster than Delia fucking Smith.' Ivor looked to the coast and now the boy could hear waves.

'The Atlantic's waking,' Ivor said. He saw the look on his nephew's face. 'Here,' he tossed the boy his coat, 'put this on. I don't want grief from your grandmother. And anyway . . . it's only death; as my father used to say: "mortal as a heartbeat, but fearless, like the sea". Despite the fact he was a shit, it can't be denied he was good with a word. Aye he was good with a word. I took that from him.'

The boy saw more clearly the pile of trees, and his uncle's glistening badge. 'Are we criminals?' he asked.

'I prefer to think of us as tree scavengers.'

'Santa's helpers?'

'Aye,' said Ivor, standing up. 'Something like that.' He lowered the trousers of his uniform and began to piss on the carcass. 'I better spoil the fucker good and proper. In case

Randy wakes up and requests seconds; or thinks about selling the stuff from the bank van.' He sighed with relief. 'Ahh . . . see if I can get the badness out.'

The boy shuffled backwards. 'What's going to happen to Randy?'

'Anyone asks, then you weren't here – okay?'

'Yes, Sergeant.' The boy smiled.

'You're a good lad Jake,' Ivor said. The boy had never before heard his uncle utter such a thing. Ivor zipped up his fly, sat down and, in the absence of speech, shuffled his bum cheeks close to his nephew. He placed a hand on top of Jake's and the boy felt the fish-scale roughness of his uncle's skin. Ivor let go and opened a final beer. Jake watched the can become a spiritual thing as it caught the shards of winter light; he wondered who it was that had just taken his uncle's place. *You're a good lad*, his uncle had said; and the fish-scale lumpy palm, which Jake knew had once held the measuring tape at the end of a record-breaking long jump, had held his own. Even at this age, Jake was certain this moment could never be taken away from him.

'Now sleep a bit more,' said Ivor, smiling to his nephew. 'We'll need all the strength we can muster to drag that bastard thing further into the woods. And I don't mean Randy.'

2

A Curious Life for a Lady

1861

'Everybody must believe in something, and for me it is travel. You must find your own passion, my dearest Hennie,' Isabella, her sister, the esteemed travel writer, had said before taking off on another voyage around the world, leaving Henrietta Bird alone, in the biggest village on the island.

They had moved to the island from Edinburgh two years before, where they had given up their house. Now they were here for good, except, given the regularity of her sister's worldly excursions, Henrietta knew that really it was just she who would permanently reside here. She had no idea what the locals made of them; 'hoity-toity', they no doubt said. But she was not hoity-toity, she was lonely; and most appallingly, she believed in nothing other than her perennially absent sister. Each day that passed Henrietta felt that there was somehow less of her. But something had changed recently. A new presence was making life a little easier for Henrietta as she became resigned to the fact that she now shared her sister with the national newspapers printed in London, where it was said even Queen Victoria herself read Isabella's travel books. 'Celebrated Isabella goes where no western woman has ever gone,' one recent headline had exclaimed.

She doubted the village had noticed her beyond a faint

impression, but she adored her adopted landscape, its openness, and the island's beautiful coastal walks. The air was so much fresher than the thick Edinburgh smog, and the sounds of birds in her garden so much prettier than the grinding, heavy racket of street trams and pitiful cries of the city's beggars. She sat in the front room of the house, and waited. He would come soonest. The force.

Her corset dug into her sides and she regretted getting so dressed up; pathetic it was, all for a glimpse of a man who cared not a jot for her; a man whom she had never heard utter a single word. The irony wasn't lost on Henrietta that he carried so many words in his satchel on his postal rounds; indeed, each of her sister's letters – these internationally published letters – had been delivered by this man they called Punch.

Henrietta wondered if he knew the significance of the letter he had delivered only days before her sister last took off, which carried the postmark of 10 Downing Street. But this man Punch had not made any fuss of the delivery; he had thrust it through the letterbox as though it bore the address of the island's bank manager and not that of Lord Palmerston. *Miss Isabella Bird*, it had said on the front, in what must have been the Prime Minister's very own hand. On her return, her sister was appointed to visit the great man in Downing Street. Henrietta powdered her face and checked the results in her hand mirror. She too had longed to travel, but somebody had to make a house a home, her sister had said, and this was indeed what their late father, an esteemed medical man, would wish they do with his legacy.

She heard the faint sound of a bell and rushed to her familiar position at the front window. She pulled aside the curtain slightly and through the white netting that remained, she saw him on his horse, turning the corner, where the hill became steeper. She wondered what he called the horse. She had seen it pulling carts full of peat slabs, fir trees at Christmas and, on more sombre occasions, even a coffin, which her sister had told her he made with his own big hands. Today the horse was fulfilling its role as the postman's mode of transport for his weekly mail run. It was her sister who had said he went by the name Punch. A simple man, she thought, living on this Hebridean island they had found. She wondered who or what it is that really decides your fate.

Isabella watched the horse make its final ascent of the hill, obeying its master's turn; its hooves almost seemed to be dancing above the dirt on the ground below. She wondered if this man paid any attention to the postmarks on Isabella's letters, from America, the Sandwich Islands, and today, she anticipated, Japan. He was the final, if unlikely, link in a chain of hands that had enabled this delivery from the other side of the world. The bell sounded much closer now and so Henrietta let go of the curtain. She stood with her back to the window and tried to control her breathing. To help calm herself she stared blankly at the house's plain interior, which was dotted with her sister's mementoes from around the globe, and included carvings in dark wood brought back from the tropics – it was then that the bell stopped. She rushed upstairs to the top window; from there she could look out to the island's shores and the unimaginable places that lay beyond, to where her sister travelled. The farthest Henrietta had gone alone was Shetland. Now she looked down below, standing on her toes to catch a compromised glimpse of the man and his horse – this, her weekly desire for greater height. She knew that Mr Punch was not married. He was a mountain of a man, and only a little older than she, perhaps in his late thirties. She was startled by the sound of the flap on her front door. Was it the motion of his usual delivery or, more than that, a knock perhaps? But he had never knocked. She froze with a mixture of excitement and fear. Then she heard the distinct sound of a fist on wood.

She stood for a second more, then rushed to the mirror by her bedside and fixed her hair. She rearranged the collar of her dress and put on shoes; she must wear her finest shoes. Then she stepped slowly down the stairs. She could hear the horse blowing heavily and collected herself. '*You are really the strong one, my dear,*' her sister had said, and so now she must become that person. She released the two bolts and opened the door. There he stood in breeches and with a string instead of a belt around his waist. She was embarrassed by her wandering eyes. Henrietta took the letter from him and briefly saw his handsome face. He said nothing but seemed to speak with his eyes. She bowed her head and began to close the door, but it jammed. She looked down and saw steel toecaps, then glanced up at their owner.

'Would she know the man Darwin?' Punch asked the earth, and then cleared his throat, adding, 'ma'am.'

'I'm sorry?' Henrietta gulped; her mouth was dry. She had not expected to greet him and now this, a doorstep conversation? 'Yes, my, my dear sister I presume you mean?'

'Aye.' His voice was deep, as if coming from his soles. His head hadn't moved.

'Well, yes she does know Charles Darwin; Mr Darwin,' Henrietta nodded, opening the door more fully. 'Our father and Mr Darwin were fond acquaintances during their time at Edinburgh University. We were much younger at the time, but Isabella has kept up the contact, so to speak.'

'Aye, well,' said Punch, dragging back his boot.

'Why, may I ask–' Henrietta began.

'The man's a liar,' Punch interrupted, moving his head to the side, and then, 'excuse me.'

'It's – quite all right. How has he offended you Mr–?'

'I've seen the outside of his letters, you know, to your sister, Miss Bird. The other Miss Bird. His postmark is not something a man would miss. I had a mind to throw them in the harbour, but, well, I have a job to do.' Punch turned to check the status of his horse; he had dropped the reins on their arrival. It was said that horses didn't disobey him, her sister had reported. His techniques apparently included punching the poor beasts on the jaw; it was by this action that he had been locally rechristened.

'She has corresponded with him, yes. But they are merely acquaintances, in ink,' Henrietta informed him, 'nothing much more.'

'His fancy ideas . . . Thinks he's God, pardon me.' This time he said 'pardon me' to the skies, which had now clouded over, chasing away the brief sunshine of the morning. 'He wouldn't last long with his ideas around here, not in our kirk.'

'No,' Henrietta said, stealing a glance at the man's fine cheekbones.

'I should like to see him explain his ideas to the local minister,' said Punch, screwing up his face. 'You know him?'

'The minister?'

'No, Darwin.'

'Oh, yes, yes I do – if only, nowadays, through his correspondence with my sister.' Henrietta was alarmed at her growing desire to ask him in. She held her sister's latest letter by her side and wondered if Punch knew these letters were now bound in books and sold the world over. But had he not referred to her sister as 'the *other* Miss Bird'? For the first time in her life it had been implied Henrietta was the foremost Miss Bird.

'I did my own test,' Punch said, playing with the chain that escaped from his waistcoat. Henrietta noticed that there was no watch at its end.

'You did, Mr . . .?' Henrietta stopped. Did he prefer to go by his nickname or by his birth name? Punch didn't offer a solution.

'My test,' he went on, 'was to kidnap a snail.'

'I see.'

'Yes. I ordered one of Mr Darwin's books. It cost me six weeks' peat supply. My mother was not best pleased with this arrangement. I sat the snail in the middle of the table . . .' Punch looked down to kick the dirt. He turned to his cart and Henrietta saw an axe propped against the rail – for cutting peat, she hoped.

'And what then, Mr . . .? Em.' Henrietta felt such a fool; she had done it again.

'Call me Punch, they all do now.' Punch rubbed at his scarred fist. She'd heard his knuckles had once held a rogue horse's tooth for an entire postal round, giving the impression that his fist could smile.

'Of course, Mr Punch.'

'Yes, that'll do,' he nodded, 'been called worse.'

Henrietta laughed nervously. 'And the snail? Mr Punch?'

'Well, I didn't give it a name,' replied Punch, looking confused.

'No,' Henrietta said impatiently, 'what was your experiment?'

'Well I sat it on my bench in the workshop, you know, where your sister came to have the horse's shoe repaired?'

'Yes, I remember.' Henrietta had wished to go too, but couldn't summon the courage on that day. Now she was reminded that she must visit her horse, kept nearby in a field that came with the house, but she had been much too tired of late; perhaps it was the effects of her solitude, for it could seep under the skin. She had heard Isabella talk of the man Punch's mother, who was partial to sitting outside the cottage she shared with her son, busy working knitting needles, her bruised, heavy legs streaked with blue and purple veins, which her sister said gave the appearance of an ancient map of the Ottoman Empire. *Cailleach Taigh Geal* they called her, 'old lady of the white house', so named because of her son's regular upkeep of the outside walls.

'And I put Mr Darwin's book on one end of the bench,' Punch went on, 'and my copy of the bible I positioned on the other end.' Punch looked back in what was the direction of his house, his workshop, then turned and caught a glimpse of her fine neck; the whole village was talking about her. 'And do you know what happened?' he asked.

Henrietta shook her head.

'I set the snail on the bench, positioned right in the middle between the bible and Mr Darwin's book – and asked it to decide. *It.* And do you know what it chose to do? Every time it moved in the direction of the bible. Every time. Slow bugger right enough.' Punch advanced his big fist in a slow, concentrated fashion, to signify the snail.

'Oh? I see,' Isabella said. His demonstration was somewhat lacking authenticity, she felt, but no matter.

'Yes. Every time it made the right choice. Proof enough for me, Miss Bird.'

Isabella wanted to offer him her Christian name, but to do so would invite suspicion; it was not proper for a single lady to be talking to a man like this at her door. Her sister would not approve.

'And will the snail be joining your congregation?' Henrietta smiled.

'Eh, no. We'd be waiting all week on it to find a pew,' replied Punch; his serious face was unchanged; his head remained perfectly still.

'Indeed,' said Henrietta, smiling broadly enough for them both.

'Have to hand it to the man Darwin though, his books burn better than any slab of peat I've seen,' Punch said, looking questioningly to the mainland, and then in admiration to his horse and cart.

'Really?' said Henrietta; she had attended the local church briefly and only once, having slipped out before even taking a pew; she didn't like to arrive on her own.

'Anyway, I must get on. Not every letter I deliver has waited since leaving Japan to arrive, but still, they're all equally important.' Punch bowed clumsily and touched his head; as he did so beads of sweat escaped from his leather cap and gathered at his muddy brow.

'Good morning to you, Mr Punch,' Henrietta said, and returned inside her house. She leaned her back against the closed door and it felt like his snail was moving across her and inside her dress.

The following week Isabella heard the bell and ran up the stairs to her usual vantage point. The bell stopped and then the post flap sounded on her front door. She ran downstairs, having already prepared herself, and unlocked the bolts. But he was not there. She could faintly hear the bell and turned to see Punch and his horse retreating, descending the hill. She stood for several seconds in the morning's cold air and then went back inside. She picked up the letter; her sister's last parcel from Japan had included sketches – the very first ever to be made of the reclusive Ainu people in the region of Hokkaido. She took the letter opener from her bureau and sliced the envelope open. But there was nothing inside. She checked and there was no postmark on the outside. The handwriting on the front was vaguely similar to her sister's, but there were spelling mistakes that her sister would never make. And after every single word there was a misplaced comma. She held the letter to her chest. It was the most precious, grammatically incorrect thing she had ever received.

A week later there was another letter; once again Punch did not knock. She was dismayed to see a foreign postmark and found enclosed a letter from her sister and more sketches, with a note for them to be sent to the engraver in Edinburgh. She was elated. To complete this task she would need to hand the mail to Mr Punch.

The next week she heard the advancing bell and the horse's hooves on the road. She remained downstairs and re-leased the bolts before she heard the horse's bell stop ringing. Punch pulled up the horse.

'Mr Punch. Another fine morning,' Henrietta said quickly,

opening the door. It was warmer and she noticed his sleeves were pulled up, revealing his black, hairy forearms. There was sweat on the horse's flanks.

'Miss Bird,' Punch touched his cap. 'Aye, indeed.' He was embarrassed to have brought another fake letter and didn't know what to do now that she had emerged unannounced from the house. He felt stupid to be playing these games. Punch wished now that he was carrying something from the famed scientist; he'd even retract his own theory, as proven on his workbench, just to be spared this humiliation.

'Nothing today from your friend Mr Darwin?' Henrietta offered.

'Eh, no, Miss Bird. I believe I've silenced the man.'

She watched as Punch smiled for the first time, a painful operation which forced his cheekbones to take the strain from his dark eyes that she now saw floated like coal in oil.

'Will you post this for me please? And I do hope this will cover the charge?' Henrietta offered the letter along with a guinea.

'Oh? Aye, of course.' Punch was relieved to have this genuine task, and in his eagerness he very nearly took the little woman with her letter. 'I'll make sure it goes in the week. I'll be certain to do that.'

'You'll be thankful it is not another of Isabella's letters to Mr Darwin.'

'Eh, aye.' He placed the letter into his satchel on the cart.

'For that purpose I imagine you might employ the snail, Mr Punch!'

He kicked at the ground uncomfortably.

'Thank you, Mr Punch. Will you have a refreshment for

your thirst – and your horse?' She had prepared lemonade.

'Eh, well, I'm fine, but,' Punch turned to his horse, 'Seamus – he'll take a sup of water, I'm sure.'

'Oh? Yes, of course.' Henrietta disappeared into the house and returned with a bucket.

'Here …' Punch moved quickly to take the weight from her. She was a weakling it appeared.

'Oh, thank you. You are most kind.'

Punch laid the bucket in front of Seamus and he dipped his big head and slurped loudly at the liquid.

'He learned his manners from me,' Punch said, turning away. Henrietta giggled and hardly recognised herself.

The horse finished too soon for her and then Punch made off; she gave the bell every chance to ring all that week but there was silence, interrupted only by birdsong and the occasional sound of cattle being herded past. The loneliness set in once again. It was then she realised that when he had come the previous week he had been without a letter to deliver. Her spirits lifted.

The following week she prepared sandwiches and hot tea. It was colder and the sea mist was doing that thing of rolling up through the village and disappearing into the trees in front of her house. In the past she had been grateful for its powers of camouflage but not now. At the first sound of the horse's bell she charged around the front room making final preparations and then made sure to straighten out her hair and powder her nose. She stood on the inside of her door and as she heard Mr Punch approach the flap on the outside she undid the two bolts. The door swung open and Punch nearly fell onto her.

'Oh, I'm sorry,' he said, collecting his balance. He had

touched her breast with his hand, he was sure. He knew he couldn't blame that on Darwin.

'Thank you, Mr Punch,' Henrietta said, bending to retrieve the letter from the outside step. Punch was upset – it was his job to make sure a letter correctly crossed a threshold, even if he had never done so with a wife. Henrietta looked at the letter, which would soon find its way to a printing press. She quickly placed it on the bureau by the door and did not give it, or the postmark, a second glance.

'Will you repair inside? There's just a touch of lunch ... nothing too ...'

'Eh? Well, I have one more letter to deliver, but ...' Punch turned to his cart.

'Oh? Well maybe you will not want to ...' Henrietta looked to the mist coming off the sea behind his shoulders, which looked like it might engulf them both. She could see fishing boats coming in to shelter and then the Pier Master's warning bell sounded.

Punch turned sharply. 'I had better not, Miss Bird.' He nodded to the busy sea, as if he had received the message personally. 'There could be trouble, you know ... And I hope there won't be call for a coffin, my supply is low right the now.'

'Oh, of course. Well thank you, thank you for posting the letter.' Henrietta moved inside. She felt like such a fool for believing in anything.

The next week there was no mail. Henrietta stayed one full day in her nightgown. She was more frequently of a mind not to eat. The last letter from her sister had remained unopened. She questioned now whether her sister really loved her at all. Was it merely the business of housekeeping for Isabella that she was in, to be administered always with efficiency and a side-plate of decency. Henrietta felt herself disappearing and regretted selling the house in Edinburgh. To her, this island and its folk increasingly resembled the icebergs Isabella had reported seeing in the North Atlantic – they were impossible to penetrate. But halfway through the next week, not on post day, she heard not the mail bell but the sound of a cart rattling. She arose wearily from her pillow and saw the clock hands showed midday. She dressed quickly in yesterday's clothes and then stood at the top of the stairs. Her hair was not tied, something she realised too late, because the door had sounded. She moved down the stairs, opened the door and felt the cold rush in. There was Duncan Punch standing with his fearsome axe in hand. She looked beyond him to Seamus and the cart, which was stacked full of what looked like slabs of earth. The cold light of day made her squint and forced her to look away.

'Afternoon, Miss Bird, I thought you might need these, what with the weather going the way it is.' Punch moved aside nervously to fully reveal the peat cuttings. He could see that she was shockingly unkempt.

'Oh? Why . . .' Henrietta squinted.

'I thought seeing as there's been no letters then your sister must be soon to return and you'll both need a winter's supply.' Punch stepped back and put an apple in Seamus's mouth.

'Thank you Mr Punch, that is most kind. Can I offer you both some refreshments?' Henrietta had nothing prepared, but there was yesterday's soup, which she had not touched, and had kept overnight in her garden cooler.

Punch glanced quickly between the stacked peat and the opened door. He didn't speak, but he took part in the industry of nodding his head and tapping his cap.

Henrietta closely observed the power in the big man's responses to events as they were unfolding; it was as though he had planned each of them.

Punch felt he had seized something that hung before him, an invisible strand, an opportunity, which might never present itself again. He felt he had lived too long in that place of labour, of duty.

'Aye, well, something wet might help us with the journey home. I'll load these first though.' Punch propped the axe and strode to his peat cart.

Henrietta watched as he walked in the usual way, with an exaggerated overstep, as though he were pedalling an imaginary bicycle. He had engineered over the years for one shoulder to become permanently lower than the other, it was his favoured side for cradling lumber and supporting his cart before he had the horse. He repositioned his cap using both hands – one at the front and one at the back. It was a graceful but deliberate action, as was everything the man did. This grace could even be found in his overstep, thought Henrietta, if she looked closely enough.

'You'll want them out the back?' he asked.

'Yes, thank you, Mr Punch.' Henrietta looked suspiciously at the big axe head. 'I ought to help you?'

'Eh, no. No need,' Punch said; he knew she would only be a nuisance and was not rigged out for such work.

He unloaded the peat and then returned to the front of the house where Henrietta met him again, having prepared herself.

'Please, come in,' Henrietta smiled. Punch flexed his knuckles and looked back to Seamus, a look that unequivocally said 'stay'.

'You'll not mind if I take this inside?' Punch asked, as he clutched the axe. 'It's a handy tool.'

'No, no...' Henrietta said, although the presence of the axe in her house made her feel slightly odd and – what was it? – vulnerable. The implement now carried even more menace than it did before. She watched as he placed the axe against the door and then kicked the soles of his big boots against the base of the door frame. When no mud fell, he crouched to remove them.

'Leave them!' said Henrietta, louder than she had planned. 'Do not worry about that.' She moved further inside and he followed. Punch hadn't the usual amount of muck on his face, she had noticed, and he smelled sweet, almost perfumed. His cap was now removed and revealed his hair to be jet-black and combed to the side. He had something else in his hand, in a paper bag. Henrietta noticed how each of the cuts of peat, now stored in her garden shelter, looked as though they had been measured to the exact same dimensions, such was the order and homogeny of their form.

Punch followed the small bundle of woman through to the kitchen; he knew the layout from the previous occupants, a family who had moved back to their people in the farthest of the Outer Hebrides, the distant isle of St Kilda. It was said they had webbed feet and now he found himself looking at this lady's shoes; they were unlike anything his mother had ever stood in. Henrietta's eyes were fixed straight ahead on the back door. Her hands moved swiftly to grab at the apron which she had left on the kitchen table. She applied it around her waist but the garment fell loose. She was embarrassed to have to step out of it as though it were an under-garment. She folded it less neatly than usual and looped it around the

37

steel bar on the front of the stove. She was doing more than necessary to appear normal, and to act as though the sight before her was normal. She pretended the whole world was normal still. She was immediately embarrassed by the presence of the framed letter from Mr Darwin above the sink.

She could smell fish. She looked to Punch and there was the usual deep, swirling fluid evident in his dark eyes, which could make him appear vulnerable, and reminded her of his horse. Punch tapped his leather cap quickly on his upper thigh several times, which Henrietta seemed to know was a motion to substitute speech. She nodded her head in acknowledgement. He then turned and moved quickly to the side with a broad step to fully reveal the paper bag he had placed on the kitchen sideboard.

'Thank you again, Mr Punch. You didn't have to do that with the peat. How very neatly you stacked them.' It occurred to her that all that was missing were his beloved commas, which could have been placed between each slab. Would this be a good time to offer him a lesson on the correct use of the comma, or would that only serve to patronise him? Was she in fact of a mind to unsettle him? And, if so, why? She wondered if her mind were playing tricks on her? Henrietta knew that only her sister would be able to tell from the tone of her voice, from the high pitch, that she was intensifying her gratitude. But it was not premeditated. Her big sister called her sincere. It had something to do with the shape of her face, the hang of her head, and the way her body and mind moved singularly for the benefit of others; even her father had expressed as much when he was alive. It had been part of her undoing. Henrietta knew that now. Life to her was something that passed by, like the sound of a tolling bell.

'Here, sit here, Mr Punch.' Henrietta pulled out a chair from under the kitchen table, the one she seldom used. Within the confines of domesticity, Punch's eyes became a swirl of chaos. If Henrietta looked too closely she felt seasick. Punch too was on unfamiliar terrain. With each step he took she watched as the kitchen shrank. He made his way to the table. As he sat down the feet of the chair screeched on the stone floor. He looked embarrassed, as he had done when clunking his boots against the door frame.

'So I have lentil already prepared.' Henrietta became aware that she was speaking in a teacher's voice, which embarrassed her. She placed the soup, a spoon, a knife and some bread on the table.

'Ehhh,' Punch cleared his throat with a sawdust cough and looked up to the framed letter. 'Darwin, I see. The man is persistent, I'll give him that.'

'Oh.' Henrietta wished she had thought to remove it.

'Will she have met Dr Livingstone, our man in Africa?'

'I believe they have corresponded.'

'Aye, well. I have no quarrel with him. Nor does the Kirk.' Punch reset the chair by lifting it slightly, therefore silencing any further betrayals from the stone below. He was more used to stone and timber obeying him. Within these four walls Punch was sure he now heard the woman's accent somehow more distinctly, the English twang.

'I make wooden swords,' he said abruptly. 'You know, for the local children.'

'Oh? You are quite the local Leonardo ...'

'Who? Well, anyway, aye, I make swords. I do that.' It was odd for Punch to find himself reduced to a scene of domesticity; here he was propped next to a young woman and salt and pepper bowls, rather than vices, peat cuttings, coffins, wooden swords and clouds of dust. Even his mother, on every day other than the Sabbath – when he would wear a decayed suit jacket that belonged to his father on top of his overalls – fed him in his workshop. His nail bag remained tied to his waist, momentarily redundant. He lurched towards the sideboard to retrieve the other thing he had come to deliver.

Up close Henrietta saw that his big hands were rough, with lots of tiny cuts, like fish scaling. Punch caught her looking and then his own eyes darted away.

'The peat can be hard on the hands, especially in the winter when it doesn't want to tear so easily from the land.' Punch inhaled with some authority. 'In the winter the land doesn't want to let it go.'

'Oh?' Isabella looked away and then back again. His swollen palms made the cutlery look like parts of a child's teaset, and quite inadequate for the eating of soup.

'What have you there?' Henrietta looked to the paper bag. The big man almost fell off the chair in the act of retrieval. It screeched once again. It was strangely powerful, thought Henrietta, how a worshipper of silence could influence the words of others around him. Did Isabella know that?

'Scallops. A gift, or payment in kind, from one of the fisherman, for a repair I performed,' Punch announced, placing the bag on the table. Occasionally they would bring him thick ropes, fishing nets, or lobster creels, in need of attention. 'Unlike prawns, which come from the mud, lobsters enjoy a coastal habitat, and the crevices in rocks can be hard on the creels.'

Henrietta smiled.

'Yes, the fishermen do not always have time to perform

40

such repairs themselves during the season, which seems to be never-ending. Mother hates the prawns,' Punch finished with a slurp.

'Very interesting. Some of them cannot swim, I have heard?' Henrietta offered.

'The prawns?'

'No,' Henrietta laughed. 'The fishermen.'

'Oh yes, such is their confidence in the sea. My father went that way. My mother insisted I make a living on dry land, which I have done. She calls it, in English, "brash reckless-ness" – this thing the men who take the wave have in their bones.' Punch nodded approvingly at his words, momentarily feeling like an equal.

'Well, this is very kind,' Henrietta said. 'Will you have more soup, Mr Punch?' She heard that the tone of her voice had changed. It sounded more open, more relaxed, as though she were talking to another version of herself.

'No. I better go. The man Darwin is not the only one with work to do.'

'Thank you again, Mr Punch.' Henrietta cleared his bowl from the table.

'Duncan,' Punch said, as he walked along the corridor. He replaced his cap, picked up the axe and opened the front door. Once the door had closed behind him, Punch stored the hair clasp he had taken from the bureau in his nail bag. It had 'H.B.' inscribed on it. Reaching for Seamus's bridle, he re-membered that she hadn't had any soup herself. Something was amiss with the woman Bird.

'That was … nice,' Henrietta said out loud, returning to the dirty dishes. 'Duncan,' she repeated to his empty bowl. 'Why, Duncan!' She laughed. The sound of the cart faded.

She reapplied the apron to her waist, fixing it into place, restoring the common order. Despite the continents which separated them, Henrietta felt the disapproving tug of her sister's shame, for she had had a local and single man in their home. But as she stacked the dishes, Punch's voice echoed in her head.

She did very little for the remainder of the week. Punch did return, and on this occasion he came without his horse, his letters or his axe. After his visit, Henrietta was enthralled to feel the most wonderful glow and, surprisingly, not an ounce of shame.

But her excitement was soon dimmed due to lightheadedness and frequently occurring headaches, and so she was bedridden for several days. In the weeks that followed, when she was not enduring severe bouts of vomiting, she felt pangs of shame rising within her and so kept her worsening condition to herself. She took to lying on the floor of the front room, on the very spot where he had laid her down on his suit jacket, imagining her head still in his big hands. She would stand only occasionally, steadying herself to gaze out of the kitchen window in loving admiration at the fussy piles of peat in the shelter; despite her discomfort, she marvelled at these tidy, unseasonable stacks of earth which had been arranged so perfectly and with such care by the very hands that had held her flesh so tenderly, and as no other had done. '*My dear Hennie, anyone would think you had seen slabs of gold,*' she heard her sister say in her head on one of those mornings. Then she fell to the stone floor.

3

The Unknown Sailor

1966

Alexander thought of his grandfather, Fingal McMillan, as a kind of fisherman, but his grandmother would often say that her husband was afraid of catching too many fish, of emptying the sea. Alexander wondered if that meant his grandfather was lazy, but he knew his grandfather was not afraid of the sea. In all weathers, Alexander watched him row his old wooden boat skilfully through the lines of moored craft. Sculling to the northern entrance of the village harbour the old man then slipped between the battered sea wall and the dark rock promontory. He fished around the edges of the Hebridean island on which they lived, and often continued out to the beginnings of the shifting Atlantic tide. His working life had been in crofting and pig-rearing, but it had failed him, he told his grandson, and so now it was to the sea he escaped.

Eliza was the name of Alexander's grandfather's boat, which he had recovered as a ruin and fixed up himself, and it was not much longer than he was. It was named after Alexander's mother. She had fallen seven years previously from the brooding grassy headland next to the harbour and died on the rocks below. It had happened in 1959 when she was only nineteen and Alexander was one. On the black granite rock facing below the point where she fell, where it reared up from the sea just above the high water line, there appeared the words GOD IS LOVE painted in bright white, six-foot letters. No one knew who put the words there and they could only be seen from the sea. Alexander had never set eyes on them.

Occasionally Alexander would be allowed to sit in the boat on the shore prior to his grandfather setting off, but the old man was not keen on having company while at sea. It was as though he liked to be alone with *Eliza*, and Napoleon, his dog. 'He might be small,' he would say of Napoleon, 'but he can bark an order. He must be learning from your grandmother.' Alexander liked sitting in the boat. It was as close as he could get to his mother.

One bright morning Alexander's grandfather was making his way down to the boat and the light on the sea was blinding. Alexander screwed up his eyes and followed his grandfather eagerly, just far enough behind, trying to walk like him in long grey shorts and black Wellington boots that jarred at his knees. He noticed how his grandfather always leaned forwards as he walked and wondered if his arms were heavy. Fingal walked as if he was entreating the world to become vertical and rise to him. Alexander smiled at the sound of his grandfather's dark blue oilskins, which squeaked like an army of mice. He was at first a spectator of the rudimentary tasks his grandfather always undertook: packing his lunch, boxing the bait, preparing his rods and bailing the rainwater that had fallen overnight. Alexander's grandmother had once said that his grandfather was protecting himself by thinking that if he maintained these rituals nothing could get to him. But it already had.

'I'll try a creel,' Fingal said, as he tied one onto the back of the boat, '... see if the lobsters are interested.' Alexander looked to the large fishing boats going off in search of bigger catches. Occasionally they would sound their horns and his grandfather would raise a hand just long enough not to miss his stroke. The *Daisy Bell*, the *Dawn Breaker*, boats of red, blue and black paint, which during the off-season would be propped like rusted nautical dinosaurs on the shoreline to be repainted for another year's assault on the sea. Not that the off-season lasted long for these hairy men who marched in packs – morphed into a single, bushy mass of eyebrow and roll-ups, blowing the smoke towards what they considered the inferior mainland. Alexander was only eight but understood his grandfather to be always in their wake, their wave even.

'Get in,' his grandfather said, straightening his deerstalker then rubbing his beard.

'Eh?' asked Alexander; he felt his heart thumping; he was accustomed to being told to get out at this point in proceedings.

'It's time you felt the sea underneath you,' his grandfather said, his Adam's apple moving violently as if to applaud the rare occasion of his words. Alexander couldn't believe it. His grandfather passed him a life jacket. 'Here,' he motioned, his beard encrusted with bacon fat. Alexander inspected the bright yellow jacket. 'It'll be a wonder if the fish don't see you coming.' Alexander let his grandfather tie the life jacket around him and felt his body shake with excitement: he was going to the sea! His grandfather let him stand up to undo the rope from the railings near the old clock, in so doing disconnecting them both from the island. It was the first time Alexander had left.

'Okay sea, here come two fishermen,' his grandfather said, releasing his grip on Alexander's ankles and taking the oars. Alexander had never seen his grandfather this excited. He turned his head and watched wide-eyed as *Eliza* left a V in the water behind them, and the big clock became smaller and smaller and he knew they would not hear it chime even if it tried. He turned beaming to his grandfather but the old man never returned his smile. Alexander was old enough by then to have heard various family members, including his grandmother, mention that his grandfather seldom spoke because of that day when Eliza died. She was only a name to Alexander, like a character in a fairy story.

The old man knew the real reason for his own lack of engagement with the world, and it had nothing to do with his daughter's fall, but instead the thing that had been done to her, which could never be undone, that only he knew about, that made her jump.

Alexander wished his grandfather would tell him more about fishing and hoped this trip was his way of finding out. His grandfather always kept a bible in his top pocket but never talked about that either. As Fingal McMillan rowed out into the bay, Napoleon sat diligently, his foul morning breath only partially disguising the old man's bacon farts.

He was in his sixties by then but Fingal could still row like a man half his age. He often credited his enduring lung capacity to playing the pipes before and then during the Great War. But he never played now. Not since. As their village became smaller Alexander realised his grandfather wasn't wearing a life jacket over his oilskins. He took that as a sign of the old man's connection with the sea, with Eliza.

'Right,' was all that Fingal said when they had reached

a position far enough out where one of his buoys was bobbing, the elements over the years having turned it from red to pink. Alexander looked back at the island in the distance; it was the first time he had ever seen it in this way and he felt a sense of pride in the lump on the horizon. His grandfather usually took a small radio with him and when Alexander couldn't hear the radio static from the shore, he knew his grandfather was no longer of his world. It seldom seemed to be tuned to a station at all. But now here he was, part of that other world, and his grandfather hadn't turned the radio on. Alexander hoped this meant his grandfather would rather hear him. The creel was not granted any launch more ceremonious than a kick from his grandfather's boot.

'I hope the sea is hungry,' the old man muttered, as the rope uncoiled quickly after the creel.

'Ha!' Alexander leaned over to watch it disappear into the sea and felt a violent tug on his belt.

'Here! Careful with that leaning. This is a boat not a bloody hobby-horse,' the old man said, re-fixing his hat. Alexander sat back fearfully, and watched his grandfather apply the worms to the hooks. His fingernails were bruised with peat. The first rod was cast and then the second.

They bobbed for an hour and nothing was said. Alexander dared to peek over the side of the boat at his reflection in the sea and waved. He had been told that his father had left the island as a young man, when he heard the news that Eliza was pregnant. His grandparents had decided it was better left that way. '*The truth would only lead to shame,*' he had overheard an uncle say.

'You hungry?' the old man finally asked. Alexander nodded, his knees tucked into his chest. It wasn't a cold day but winter was pulling on summer's tail, as his grandmother had said. Each of Alexander's grandparents had a form of poetry about them: his grandmother with her words, and his grandfather with his lack of them. The weather was turning for the worse, erasing his reflection. There were greyer clouds hovering above and Alexander felt light rain on his face. But he didn't mind, he was in awe of the water's expanse. All his curiosities were being answered.

Alexander's grandfather unwrapped the lunch which he'd made himself. He removed his boots and Alexander saw the old man's woollen socks had expanded to make his feet look like a giant's. He watched his grandfather look back to the island, at the murky outline almost lost to the low-hanging clouds, but still it commanded the gaze: it was part of something, but at the same time as distant as perfection. 'It might not be much more than a baby's fist of land,' said Fingal. 'But it's our island, God's earth.' Alexander looked to the mainland, which had now emerged as a faint, lumpy expectation on the opposite horizon. Fingal had only ever been there on his way to serve in the war in Flanders, being recruited a year younger than the required eighteen. As a result, his memories of the mainland were mostly stained with blood. Even on the peace of the sea he could hear shelling.

'See that rockface halfway between the village and the lighthouse.' The old man chewed, motioning over his shoulder. Alexander turned around to face their island and nodded.

'I can't hear you,' his grandfather said.

'Yes, Grandfather.' Alexander chewed more quickly to clear his mouth of bread and ham.

'Skipper, call me skipper on this boat.'

'Yes, skipper,' Alexander managed.

'And the paint on it, can you see the letters?'

Alexander squinted; it was impossible from this distance to really make out anything.

'I painted that after your mother fell, my daughter,' his grandfather announced to the distance. 'Those are my brushstrokes on the rockface. She was picking daisies; she got too near the edge. You were just a baby, back with your grandmother at the croft. The croft was a proper one then, deserving of the title. It should have been me that fell.' He employed two fingers to flatten his moustache and then fiddled with a rod. 'Fuck. It should have been me. Anyway, I painted that.'

'What does it say?' Alexander asked. He had never heard his grandfather talk like this. The old man gulped; his hairy Adam's apple danced, a traitor to his emotion.

'It says: "God Is Love",' replied his grandfather, placing one of his big hands on his breast pocket. 'He gave us three more days with her. She should by rights have died instantly. I've counted – she fell 120 feet onto the rock below, but still kept her pulse. That was miraculous.' He nodded. Alexander winced, not at the fall, he couldn't really feel that, but because his grandfather had.

'But why I like it out here,' his grandfather went on, now taking one oar and manoeuvring the boat ninety degrees, 'is because if you look just above the rock you can see a light . . .' He paused. 'So I'm asking you now if you can see the light – or is it just me?' His voice was pitched higher than usual, sounding almost desperate. Alexander looked to the sky directly above the point where his mother had fallen, above the black rock cliffs; the painted letters were still a blur. Fingal asked again, more impatiently, 'Can you see the light, son?'

'I can, skipper.' The rain had stopped. In reality he couldn't see any more light there than he could see elsewhere above their heads, but he wanted more than anything to see it; he wanted his grandfather to know he had seen it.

'I can touch it,' his grandfather said, raising his free palm. 'Some days on the way back to shore I look round and I can clasp it in my hands. It means everything to me. It's her. That is why I brought you here. To see the light.'

Alexander wiped away his fringe and looked harder.

'Okay, enough,' his grandfather said, reaching for his boots and pulling from one a bitten sandwich. Alexander was disappointed; he had never before heard the full story of his mother's death. When he was a younger child he had believed his grandmother's explanation that angels had carried his mother away. He wondered now, given the bible in his grandfather's pocket, if God also had something to do with it.

'Well,' Fingal said, taking a final bite, 'she'll be in a place now where better things happen to people and where, well, people do better things. And where flowers grow. She still held them in her hands,' he nodded, 'lying on the rock.' Alexander could see the tears in his grandfather's eyes, but he turned away so the old man couldn't see him looking.

For the rest of the expedition they checked and rebaited the lines. Before they left, Alexander's grandfather tied the creel line to the buoy and pulled up one he had set the previous week. His face creased with the endeavour. Alexander saw sweat gathering in the dirt grooves on his grandfather's forehead.

'She's heavy,' Fingal wheezed, flashing his rotten teeth, the only time he had ever nearly smiled at his grandson. The creel emerged from the water like a sea goddess who had held her breath for a thousand years – and in it, beneath the seaweed, was a large lobster.

'Look!' Alexander shouted. He gasped in awe as his grandfather pulled the creel fully on board and leaned down to look the lobster in the face.

'Reminds me of your grandmother,' the old man said, 'similar claws.' Alexander giggled and his grandfather poured a measure of whisky from a bottle he kept on the boat. He gave his grandson the only glass and swigged several times from the bottle. Alexander couldn't coax the foul liquid beyond his lips and his grandfather looked at him, knowing that. There was silence. 'You could have called me ... By rights I'm your ...' the old man stopped.

Alexander wasn't sure what his grandfather meant. Napoleon had slept for the past hour but now sat up and barked; as if he too felt the significance of the words nearly said.

'Ah, the little dictator.' Fingal had named the dog after a character in that book Eliza used to read, *Animal Farm*. He'd leafed through the pages, but it sounded like no farm he had ever been on. Still, he liked the name. He corked the bottle and began working the oars. Napoleon barked again. 'He calls for home and defends the woman he loves,' said Fingal McMillan. 'I used to get more sense from my pigs. Still. We should get you back.'

They approached the island, following the same route that the bigger boats would later take. Several fish had been caught and they glistened like strips of silver in the bucket, some still wriggled, their eyes desperate and bulging. They too appeared disturbed in some way. Napoleon was allowed one and immediately tore the stunned head off. As they neared the island's coastline, and the lighthouse became commanding once more, Alexander could now read the very neatly painted letters on the rockface, each one a capital and twice his size. He recalled seeing two paint pots hidden in the barn where his grandfather used to rear pigs – one marked 'Boat' and the other 'God'. And beside them lay a stack of long rods that looked as though they connected to each other. At the time he had wondered if it was his grandfather's job to paint the sky. He couldn't stop himself peering for signs of his mother's fall on the rocks below.

As they turned into the bay and approached the moorings, Napoleon barked and jumped off to swim ashore. Alexander's grandmother was waiting, sitting on the steps of the clock with a woollen shawl around her shoulders. She smiled at Napoleon's emerging wet coat; the dog at least was happy to see her. The boat came within ten feet of the shore and they gently bobbed until the sea's depth could be measured in inches.

'Here,' the old man took Alexander's elbow and forced him up, 'you can travel on foot for the rest of the way. I need to go back, I've forgotten something.' Alexander looked down at his grandfather; he was quick to follow the order, but didn't want to leave *Eliza*. 'Take this to your grandmother,' Fingal said, untying the creel and placing it in the boy's arms. Alexander waded towards the island's sandy shore. When he looked back, his grandfather was already twenty yards further out and rowing more freely, almost joyously. Napoleon barked and Alexander looked up to his grandmother who leaned down from the white railings to take the creel. He heard the clock chiming.

'Well, what a gift,' she smiled. Then she turned for home and Alexander followed. 'Silly bugger. No doubt he's going back for more.'

Two weeks passed and Alexander's grandfather had not returned. And then it was four weeks. The fishermen worked their boats as rescue vessels in search of Fingal McMillan. The notice board outside the ironmonger's carried updates on the search, but the local newspaper held off printing an announcement. Alexander and his grandmother were comforted by their extended family. It became two months. Alexander's grandmother had stared to the waters in expectation, which became hope, then longing, and finally wonderment: at the sea, the mainland, to the direction in which her husband last rowed. Each hour that passed she missed her husband less and her daughter more. Every morning Alexander walked down to the seafront at dawn in his yellow life jacket to undertake his own private search, his knuckles gripped and turning white on the railings above the shore. In the evenings he lay in his bedroom, which had once been his mother's, in a shape he hoped was her own with a pool of tears gathering in his ear. He had never even seen a picture of his mother. Unbeknown to him, a dead pig had been clothed in this room.

His grandmother stared at the sideboard, at the only photograph she had of her husband – a war portrait, taken before all the mess, before the real pain. Alexander didn't know what to do but try to escape the hushed adult voices around him.

Napoleon was the only one who didn't seem to grieve; it was as though he had known in advance and was keeping some form of pact with his dear departed leader. One day, a month or so later, there was a knock on the door and the dog barked. Alexander opened it to see one of the local fishermen standing in orange oilskins; the man looked the same as they all did, his face an ageless mask above the fluorescent uniform.

'Here,' the fisherman said, 'give this to your grandmother.' He turned and squeaked away. Alexander took the note. His grandmother was sitting in her usual place, her false teeth now removed permanently in grief and distilled in a glass of whisky, giving Alexander the impression he was alone in a house with an aged, Hebridean glove puppet. She took the piece of paper from her grandson and unfolded it. A tear fell from her cheek as she nodded quietly.

'What is it?'

'It's his final position when last seen,' she replied. It had been written by hand, by those hard men of the sea, in keeping with a tradition they upheld when they themselves lost a man overboard. 'It's what they call a Recognition Notice. They finally consider him one of their own.' Alexander's grandmother pulled out a tissue from under her cuff. She stood and rummaged in a drawer, then taped the notification, the writing facing outwards, to the window of the front room.

'The highest of honours,' she managed, as she smoothed it to the windowpane. 'He has been acknowledged by Longitude and Latitude,' she announced to the light coming in over the failed croft. 'He is immortal now. He's got what he always wanted, he's one of them, the pitiful old sod ...' She broke down. Alexander opened the front door and what was left of the croft, the world even, smelled different; he leaned out to gaze at the note from the outside. Sixty-six years seemed like forever. His grandfather was as old as the century.

One morning several weeks later, not more than 400 yards from that black granite rockface with the white letters which had barely faded, the empty grave Alexander's grandfather had instructed be dug in his memory was cut into the earth. The inscription on the gravestone was the one he had wanted, which he paid for posthumously with the proceeds of his few remaining cattle. 'The Unknown Sailor,' it read. His instructions for the cattle sale and the wording on the memorial had been found by Alexander in the barn on the croft, written neatly on a page torn from a bible.

After those that had gathered for the service departed, Alexander looked to the sea and wondered: *Skipper, are you still out there?*

'With each ripple from the old bugger's oar he has sent back the makings of a legend,' said one of the remaining fishermen in attendance, over Alexander's shoulder. Alexander enjoyed the feeling those words gave him as he looked down to the grave of his mother in the next plot.

'They are together again.' Alexander's grandmother had returned for him. Her pride in her husband's new, elevated status competed with her anger at the nature of his sudden departure, and at what he had done to their daughter all those years before. Despite what her husband might have thought, she knew, she knew what had happened, in the way only a mother does. 'He has gone to the sea. It understood him better than I ever did,' she said through her whisky-scented teeth, wrapping an arm around her grandson. The last mourner remaining apart from them, the island's young police officer, Ivor, now moved to place a heavy hand on Alexander's shoulder.

'Not good,' the officer tried, removing his hand. 'If we find so much as an oar you'll be the first to know, lad. And ... eh, look after your grandmother.' He tapped his helmet at his waist and walked off.

Alexander looked to the sea, and to the blanket of sky above the bay – it was *somebody*'s canvas. He saw a beam of light pierce the clouds and felt his tiny Adam's apple jump as his grandfather's often did. He couldn't tell his grandmother what the light meant, or what his grandfather had said. He feared if he did then it would break a spell that had been cast out there on the sea, in the beginnings of 1966, between a grandfather and his grandson.

FINGAL McMILLAN

56 37 N, 06 05 W

24th AUGUST 1966

AGED 66 YEARS

RIP

4

The Knicker-Knocker

2009

'Oh – hullo?' the man said.

'Yes. Hello,' said Tom; he stopped walking along the beach, looked up to the man then quickly averted his eyes. He was slightly irritated by this interruption and transferred the shrimping nets to his other hand. He repositioned the newspaper under his arm; he was relieved not to feature in it.

'Fine day,' the man said. Tom stole another look at him, incredulous now, and figured the man was in his eighties. He was tall but very thin.

'Pardon?' Tom shivered, looking up to the thick density of dark grey cloud enveloping the island. 'Well, for December I suppose it would be. I better be off. Thanks.' It was the tail end of August.

'You'll not catch much more than a cold with them.' The old man nodded to the coloured nets on sticks.

'No, I suppose not … look I had really better get on …'

'Aye. Right enough, off you go. No, in December we'll have sun. Nothing surer.'

'I'm just going down to my children …' Tom motioned towards his two daughters who were further across the beach; he dropped his newspaper and it was taken by the wind.

'Ah! A *Telegraph* man!' the old man said excitedly, raising a chorus of squawking seagulls.

57

'Mmm ... yes.' Tom dropped the nets and chased the newspaper for several feet as though it were an escaped emu, then reached to fold it into a manageable bundle. He wondered if it would be better if the paper blew away, taking the day before yesterday's news with it – to where – the mainland?

'The *Daily Telegraph*. Me too,' said the old man, effortlessly moving his right wader to entrap the last rogue page.

'Eh – you are?' Tom bent to pick up the page; he heard how his voice had risen; he sounded like a snob and knew it. 'Thanks.' But then the thought quickly followed: would even this man, on this remote island, have read all about him and his pathetic world? This shitty, economically collapsed new world which he had created for everyone.

'Aye. I've never read the thing though.'

'What ... do you buy it for then?' Tom asked, sounding relieved, and trying to replace the Sports section. Even his beloved Arsenal were in trouble again.

'For the squirrel,' the old man said, nodding back in the direction of the big village, 'I keep a red one.' He bent down for the nets and handed them over; Tom noticed how remarkably sprightly he was.

'Eh, thanks again. Thank you. Righto ...' Tom clamped the nets and newspaper between his legs, and pulled his pink cashmere jumper up and around his shoulders, tying the sleeves around his neck as though he had just bowled an over.

'Aye,' the man nodded, brushing his wader over the sand, 'I buy it for the squirrel, right enough.'

Tom now needed to know: surely, he had every reason to assume the world's squirrel community were unaware of global news. Surely they did not hold the knowledge that he had brought a world-renowned bank to its knees in their pea-sized brains, transporting it up and down trees.

'Your squirrel can read?' Tom had to ask.

'Oh now, that would be silly!' The man chuckled.

'It would.' Tom nodded quickly. 'It would. Yes, of course.'

'But that *Telegraph* fits the floor of his cage perfectly. Snug as a rug.' The old man smiled his glassy eyes to reflect everything around them.

'Oh, I see.'

'Aye, I'm sure the people actually print it to the dimensions of my cage. It's very good of them if they do. I even wrote to inform them. I change it every two weeks, like the bed linen. But still I've never read it, mind. Looks all too serious.'

'I'm afraid it is.' Tom sighed.

'The squirrel does the crossword for all I know.'

'Ha!' Tom didn't know what to feel. At least here was the possibility of a person in the UK who might just be unaware of what a cunt he was. 'Look, good chap, I better ...' Tom motioned once again in the direction of his children who were paddling in the Atlantic.

'Aye, of course. Nae bother. John the Goat they call me.' The old man brushed his silver-haired chin with his hand. 'The goatee beard – it used to be more impressive.' He reached out his hand to Tom.

'Tom ... Bywater,' Tom stumbled over his own surname; he still struggled to say it in public; when ordering pizza he now used his mother's maiden name. He let go of the bony hand; he could have crushed it.

'Well, your squirrel obviously copes well with being two days behind.' Tom was relieved the old man's face did not register his name.

'Behind what?'

'The news. Your papers are two days behind.'

'Or maybe we're five days ahead. That is possible of course.'

Tom paused to look beyond his children to the ocean.

'You know we have a lump of rock out there? An island in fact, some say ...'

'What?' Tom managed disinterestedly.

'... and folks here believe it exists, but there's no mention of it on any map they've ever bothered to bind. Nothing surer. But it's out there – The Looming, they call it. We call it.' The old man sniffed authoritatively.

'Look, well – *ciao*.' Tom stole a glance at the ocean then chose the direction of his wife.

'I saw you talking – were you on your bluetooth? Which fucking bank has fallen now?' asked Zoe, sipping at a plastic cup. She fidgeted with the collar of her dress and looked to their children who were busy digging up sand. They were, it occurred to her, changing the shape of the island, even the globe.

'No, you know there's no signal in this place – just as well. No trace. Isn't that why you wanted to come?'

'Then you've started talking to yourself? It's come to that? Good grief.'

'Look Zoe – I was talking to the old man. Leave it out, love. Maybe you should have some water with the wine? It's early, even for you.'

'... ish. What old man? We're alone on this beach, or hadn't you noticed?' She looked to the sky with a grimace then pursed her crimson lips; she had taken to wearing a lipstick that matched red wine. 'Even God has put away his bucket and spade.'

'Him – the old geezer ...' Tom dropped the nets and looked

back expectantly in the direction he had just travelled. But he could see nothing other than an empty expanse of sand. 'Fuck? Where has he gone?'

'I watched you, Tom, you were on your own.' Zoe tilted her head back down to her book. 'Shit!' she rose quickly and attempted to save the wine. 'Lucky,' she said, pouring more into the cup.

'Clumsy, more like . . .'

She lay back down with her book. It was a relief to read about something other than her husband being Public Enemy Number One. Maybe the effects on him were more serious than she had imagined. She had just about started to feel as though her marriage was not in crisis, as though the failing economy was not resting on her family's shoulders.

Lucy came running towards them and nearly tripped over her Wellingtons. 'Mummy!'

'Hello love. Did you catch anything?'

'No, I had the nets, remember love?' murmured Tom.

Zoe took her youngest daughter in her arms; she was a welcome warm bundle that smelled of insect repellent and the sea. Her daughter was changing, becoming too big to hold, to suffocate.

'Amazing,' Tom said, now taking solace in his phone.

'What – that there's signal?' asked Zoe.

'No. Well, yes, albeit weak, but it's remarkable – that she travelled all over the world exploring, and it says she lived here . . . she lived in our bloody rental house.'

'Language,' cautioned Zoe. 'Who are you on about now?'

'The woman whose name is on the sign by the front door. Isabella Bird. I've found her Wiki page. Just imagine she did all that in the nineteenth century.'

'Who?' asked Lucy. 'Mum?'

'Of course,' agreed Zoe, lifting her head up from her daughter's hair to blow a sarcastic kiss to Tom. Despite the sea air, Tom could smell the wine fumes.

'I'm hungry ... frightfully,' Lucy croaked into her mother's chest.

'Ah, lost the signal.' Tom said. 'But apparently she was the first woman to be elected a Fellow of the Royal Geographic Society; books titled *Journeys in Persia and Kurdistan ...*'

'May be just as well the signal's gone.' Zoe groaned.

Tom put his phone away, put on his glasses and resumed his inspection of the beach. 'Binoculars would help,' he muttered, and then: 'Lucy darling, did you see me talking just now? To a man? An old boy!' It occurred to him he would never have said 'frightfully' at her age.

Lucy shook her head, and then smiled up at her mum. Zoe recalled Tom as he was on their last night in London, before this attempt at a holiday; a desperate man he had been, terrified even to go to the end of their leafy street, let alone an airport.

'I saw the fucking man! Look, he was John the ... fucking pig or something. I was talking to him!'

'Language, Tom!' Zoe shouted, and then mouthed, *fucking hell*. She took her hands off Lucy's ears and said quietly: 'Dad's just under pressure, love. Again. Although, personally, I'm starting to wonder if this Isabella Bird ever existed ...' Zoe knew her husband was secretly delighted to have found somebody connected to their rental house, to this island, someone who was potentially more noteworthy than he was.

'He was maybe eighty? Tall and he, well, he has a squirrel, a red one. But it wasn't with him.' Tom scoured the horizon

62

but he could only see his other daughter, Philippa, and a general merging of sea and sand. It wasn't necessarily beautiful to him, it was just emptiness, void. 'Look, he was . . . wearing a flat cap . . . and bloody hell?' Tom spun around in bafflement. 'He must be sprightly . . .'

'I didn't see a red squirrel . . .' Lucy whined.

'He had a roll-up behind his ear, I saw that.'

'The squirrel?' teased Zoe.

Tom frowned.

'Love, nobody else saw any of this.' Zoe looked up to her husband, who she could see was becoming desperate again. She noticed how, with his glasses removed, the combined effect of his round face and big lips made him look like something you would find on a Victorian jug. His face was more aged; the etching at the bridge of his nose ran deeper, his chin was unusually unshaven. It was becoming impossible for her to look at him – this man who once claimed to have followed Roxy Music on their European tour – without hearing Elgar playing in the background.

She knew what he was looking for. If only he could magic this old man into existence then maybe it would mean his bank did not collapse, and he was not in fact a failure – or 'a cunt', as her friend Sadie's husband had said. If he could find the man, they would no longer be 'BIG SHOTS WITH OUR MONEY POTS', a headline one tabloid had spent a long time, and no doubt the educations of several Oxbridge alumni, devising. It could even open up the possibility of play dates for their children. But she wasn't about to forget what he had done to her either. Like the pillow Tom travelled with, which he maintained remembered the shape of this head, she would not forget.

Tom looked down to his wife's pale skin, almost the same tone as the sand; only her long brown hair, its familiar strands stuck to her cheeks and arrested in the corner of her mouth, and her red wine-inspired lips, saved her from disappearing into the beach completely. Her head was tilted gracefully. Even now there was something about her he could never reach, this woman from accounts he had discovered in the 1990s when it was all going so well and John Major was secretly fucking Edwina Currie. Zoe dropped her book to the blanket and hugged Lucy more tightly. After a few seconds Lucy silently released herself and jogged off to rejoin her sister.

'Mum. You smell of wine again!' Lucy shouted. 'If I see the mystery man, I'll shout – okay Dad?'

'Thanks love.' He turned to his wife and pinched his nose. 'See – I'm not the only one who says it.'

Zoe didn't react. She watched as the initial enthusiasm of her daughter's gallop was downgraded to a heavy trudge. She could see how Lucy walked with that familiar swinging right arm as though she were whipping a horse; it was all Tom. Silly little bitch. Zoe then stared up at her husband as he put his glasses back on, becoming the photograph that had been running on TV news. She rose from the blanket and walked over to him, in conciliation; she smiled as if she were in beautiful pain. 'Oh Tom.' She put her arms out to him.

'Look, I'm sorry,' Tom said, taking his head in his hands; in so doing he let go of what he now understood to be squirrel carpeting. 'Thanks love – for everything.' He felt patronised.

Zoe put her long arms around her husband, careful not to spill from her plastic cup, and felt his soft body quiver. He was like a bundle of overgrown child. She wondered if this was him addressing what commentators had called an absence of remorse. They held each other for several moments. She could feel his heartbeat on her neck.

'I preferred you as plain old Tom anyway – who needs the knighthood. Fuckers.' She ran her fingers through the fuzzy mass of blond hairs now turning white on his neck; they were like bits of candyfloss, fallen and forgotten.

Tom looked out to the sea, to the world baying for his blood. 'Fuck. And now I'm seeing mirages of old men goats? Honestly, just fucking take me to the nearest asylum and throw away the key. Bad bloody show all round.' Tom breathed in heavily. 'Look, didn't you see him though ... he had waders on?'

'Tom, drop it. Let's go before the girls get hypothermia. Somebody's forgotten to invite summer up here.'

'But you were looking down, love – you were reading?'

'I was.' She waved her book without turning around to him. 'And even Salman – the king of magical fucking realism – Rushdie, didn't mention this man-goat.' Zoe turned to the overbearing landscape, the Atlantic Ocean centre stage. She took a breath of the beauty before her but still she could not feel it. Looking at their place in the world from this distance had made her even angrier, but still she loved him, despite the mess, the debris of shame he had tipped on their family. Maybe this was a charade they were playing now, just for the kids' sake. Or perhaps it was a sitcom they now inhabited, or a post-watershed news exposé.

She watched her children play. Lucy's red hair shone like a beacon against the white sand. They were dressed for the height of winter. But they looked so content playing together, a world away from the school run traffic in Islington, not expectant of the sun, and better natured than their parents. They had been so excited to buy their Wellingtons and fishing nets. Zoe remembered her own childhood, the family holidays in Devon, the mysterious little crabs in rock pools escaping her evil prods; she wondered if even then she was evil. She would never have guessed that her parents were soon to divorce. Maybe her father was a cunt too, back then, and she was blissfully, evilly, dutifully, unaware?

'You think we have *enough* clouds?' Tom asked. They both laughed. He had wanted to go abroad, to some place where nobody would recognise him, but the authorities wouldn't allow it as long as the investigations were 'ongoing'.

'And still no sightings of Hamish Macbeth.'

'Wasn't he on the *mainland*?'

'Hark at you and your local buzzwords. I haven't seen his dog either . . .'

'Well now we base our holidays on the lives of fictional characters,' continued Tom, 'damn it – we could have visited Stuart fucking Little in New York!'

Zoe smiled. She noticed as Tom laughed that he had re-introduced the snort he would make through his nose before the crash. As though it were the engine of the whole act of laughing; that if he were not to snort he would extract no pleasure from the joke. He stood before her, appreciating only his side of the joke and in the manner of a pig. She ran her bare toes through the escaping sand. She looked back to the carpet of grass between them and their hire car – this grass was called '*machair*', according to the sign; it was apparently becoming extinct and needed to be protected. Then she saw a tall thin elderly man in the distance. He was wearing waders and a flat cap. And then he was lost to the dip of the land. *Good*, she thought, he's gone.

Tom kneeled down beside her. 'I'll go and check on them.'

He turned on all fours, and reached for the fishing nets.

'Leave the nets. It's time to go,' said Zoe, scrunching up her cup. 'And don't go talking to yourself again.' She ground her teeth and watched him become smaller as he progressed down the sandy path; he hadn't laid so much as a finger on her since all this started a year ago. She had hoped that maybe this island could reignite their sex life. And that if it did then it would reinstate her power over him. She watched her husband walk with the nets by his sides positioned like skiing poles, which reinforced her sadness that they hadn't been to their chalet in Switzerland either since it all began.

Her husband had defied her. He had reached that stage of middle age when a man can become too powerful, too snorty, she thought, and he had tried to do something almost illegal about it. Now Islington, all of North London and indeed the world knew – and everything he had was gone. She could tell just from his walk that he missed his uniform of briefcase and BlackBerry, suit and tie – what they stood for. There were still reporters raking through their bins, she was sure; the police had been no better. He'd failed. They'd failed. He had turned them into goldfish. She looked behind her once again for the old man. Yes! He was well gone. Now she felt powerful – more alive – evil, even. She drank the remainder of the wine.

That night, after the girls had gone to bed, Zoe went out to the back garden to check on the clothes she had hung on the washing line. She had enjoyed the feeling of control while pinning up her family's clothes, something the staff would never allow her to do in London. Wilma Flintstone flashed through her mind. More fiction, she thought. As she un-pegged the clothes Zoe noticed several items were missing.

She looked around the garden in case the wind had blown them off. She put down the basket and checked in the foliage beside the peat shelter but there was nothing there either. Three pairs of her underwear were missing. She had been thieved on, again.

'Everything okay?' Tom asked, standing at the back door.

'Yes – I'm just being a good little wife.'

'A good wee wife, I think you meant love.'

'Yes.' She looked into the basket and once again to the garden. She felt herself tingle, becoming wet.

'Come in. Let's try the wine. I'm not expecting much from it . . .'

Zoe stood at the back door and waited for him to go back inside. She took a final glance into the dusk for some form of explanation, to the lane that ran alongside the end of the garden. She had the strong feeling that another lady had once stood here, from another time, watching. *I am here because of somebody else*, she thought, *another woman who used to live here.*

As she was closing the back door she noticed a creature, a lizard or something, crawling on the windowpane. She laughed out loud, and then turned back to make sure Tom wasn't there. She looked out to the darkness again, gazing curiously, wondering whether a normal woman would call the local police or tell her husband about the missing knickers. She smiled; somebody had noticed her.

She looked closely to the small animal again. 'What do you live for?' she asked it. It was her question and it had come right out of her mouth. Nobody had asked her or told her to think it. It was *hers*, not Tom's, or to do with the fucking bank: it was her own private question to the world. It was her discovery. To the creature she had found.

The next morning they were going to tour the island's historic sights – there was a castle in which Oliver Reed had filmed and inevitably fucked that Tom was eager to see. Before they left, Zoe pinned more clothes to the line. She had hand-washed the girls' underwear and also two of Tom's shirts, one pink and one yellow. She imagined if those didn't scare away whoever it was who had taken her knickers then nothing would. At the last minute, as a test, she pinned a pair of her own worn underwear.

'More laundry, hun?' Tom asked as they drove through the winding roads of the town, intending to take in the island's Atlantic coastline. Zoe had noticed him getting out of bed last night for what seemed like an hour but could well have been just a few minutes.

'Well, it doesn't do itself, Tom,' said Zoe with a smirk. She felt her excitement at the thought of her underwear in somebody else's hands.

'I have a surprise for you all,' announced Tom.

'Oh no ...' mocked Philippa, their eldest, from the back seat.

'We don't need any more surprises,' said Zoe.

'I made a call to the island's Historical and Archaeological Society,' Tom chirped. 'I spoke with a charming fellow called Pluto. He has offered to meet us at the town clock for a little tour of the island. You know, to get us into the swing of the place.'

Zoe cupped her hand around her mouth. 'Will he show us a replica of Oliver Reed's cock?' she whispered.

Tom nodded in exaggerated fashion without taking his eyes off the road.

'*What* Mum?' asked Lucy.

'Nothing.'

'Well, at least they're not *spelling out* words any more ...' moaned Philippa.

'Will he have Daffy Duck with him?' asked Lucy.

'We can but hope ...' said Zoe.

They drove along the colourful seafront and Tom pulled up the car alongside the town clock near the old pier. 'There,' Tom announced, self-congratulatory, 'he's waiting for us. Goodo. I do like it when a plan comes together.' He opened the door excitedly.

'No Daffy I'm afraid, Lucy dear, oh well ... clearly the man dressed in the dark though ...' Zoe said, as she watched Tom positively run to meet a curious-looking man who was sitting on the town clock, apparently in fancy dress. She could tell from Tom's demeanour that the success of their holiday, the happiness of their family, the possibility of an economic recovery, and the staving off of global recession, was resting on the success of this tour. She and the girls reluctantly unfastened their seatbelts. 'Let's wait here until we know what's happening, girls. Clearly we're under-dressed.'

'Hello!' began Tom, extending his hand and nodding. 'I'm *Thomas*. So you must be ...'

'Tom, am homour. Yesh, my fwiemd, I am P'uto.'

Tom shook his head questioningly, he looked the man up and down. It was instantly clear his host's decision to wear a tie with his tracksuit was ill-thought-through, if not a full tactical collapse.

'Oh bugg'r! I cwean fo'got!' Pluto groped around in his pocket, then turned away to the clock – *to do what*, Tom wondered – prepare a magic trick?

'My teeth! Now that's better, sorry my friend, I sometimes forget!' Pluto now flashed ill-fitting teeth that, in their migraine-inducing whiteness, could only have been drawn by Walt Disney himself. 'I only now picked them up from the Mobile Bank. They were doing me a favour. Anyway, Pluto is at your service. Is it just yourself?'

Tom turned to his family who had not left the rental car. They were used to more spacious vehicles and looked like caged gerbils. 'No, we'll be four. That okay?'

'More the merrier, I say.' Pluto turned back to his visitor. 'Tell me, what do you do Tom?'

'Oh,' Tom shifted uncomfortably. As he stalled for time he noticed Pluto wore a badge saying I.H.A.S.. The 'A' had been added haphazardly with a black marker. 'I'm an ... designer, mechanics and the like. Interiors mainly. Yes.'

'Really?' fizzed Pluto. 'You know,' he turned to make sure he was not being eavesdropped on, 'maybe you are just the man to ask.' He smiled, nodding, as though his life's desire had been to engineer this moment. 'I've always wondered: in your honest assessment is there much advancement still to be made with the common household toilet flush?'

'I'm sorry?' Tom screwed up his face, barely concealing his disgust, then remembered his charade, 'Oh ... well ...'

'It's just something I've always wondered, you know, when I'm doing the necessary ...' said Pluto, squatting for effect.

Tom watched as the man righted himself. 'Well, I guess it has somewhat reached its peak. You know, the force of the, the flush ...' He looked to his car. 'Look, I'd really ...'

Pluto put on the glasses which had been hanging from a string around his neck. 'Ah, there's kiddies too! Just as well I washed my mouth out with soap and water this morning eh?

Well, it was for the new teeth, but still ...'

'Erm. And would we commence here?' asked Tom.

'For what?'

'For the tour?'

'Oh yes! Well, we *do* ... but as charming as I may seem, there is, eh, a small matter to take care of first ...'

'Which is?'

Pluto kicked the heels of his black brogues, which Tom noticed not only because of their clash with the tracksuit, but because they had white laces. 'This attire does not come cheap my friend ...' hinted Pluto proudly, putting his fingers through the red whiskers populating his chin and his throat. Tom now saw the medallion around Pluto's neck, which read: 'World Stone-Skimming Champion'. There was no mention of the year, and 'World' had been drawn on rather crudely, with what appeared to be the same black marker.

'Oh, yes. How much am I due you?' Tom felt he couldn't turn back.

'Eh, fifty pounds per person, and I'm afraid we don't do any discounts, you know, we have import tax ...'

'Really?'

'Yes, my friend, and we take payment in cash, in advance. And a little for the petrol too ...'

'Well,' Tom took his wallet from his back pocket, 'here you go then.' He handed over £220 in twenty pound notes. And then realised he had left himself short. 'A Mobile Bank you say?' he asked, looking around.

'Yes, but you've missed it for today, my friend,' said Pluto, fingering the notes. 'Thank you.' Tom watched as Pluto put the notes into ... were they in fact, *pyjama* bottoms not tracksuit bottoms?

'Tom!' Zoe yelled from the car. Tom turned to see his wife shaking her head and drawing an imaginary horizontal line below her chin to signify 'abort'.

Tom turned back to Pluto. 'Look old boy, maybe this is not such a good idea, you know, I think the family had set their heart on a trip to the beaches, you know, what with the weather looking up and all ...'

'Well, seeing as you're here, and you've already paid, can I at least tell you about the clock on which we stand?'

Tom looked impatiently to the car. Zoe had started the engine. 'Well yes, Pluto, but just a line or two?'

'It was built by a Spaniard. Did you know we have a Spanish Armada ship sunk in the bay here?'

'No, I didn't,' said Tom, edging away. He now wished more than ever that he could have taken the girls to Disneyland; at this rate it would have been cheaper.

'Oh yes,' confirmed Pluto, and then, cupping his hands to his mouth, he whispered, 'that's why I like to be careful of anyone listening in, the Inquisition, so to speak. Yes, the walk to the lighthouse, where I point out the exact spot where it is believed to have been sunk is often referred to as the high point, if I might say, climax even, of my tour, especially the sombrero. The ladies can't get enough of that; you know my moustache takes me damn near half the way across the Atlantic already, don't you think?'

'But I'm sure I read somewhere that the clock's origins were completely different?' asked Tom, glancing to the car. 'Something to do with the Bird woman.' He turned back. 'Anyway, I thought you said Spanish, and not Mexican?'

'Oh no. You have been misinformed there, Tom. No, the clock is Spanish, Tom. I'd bet my engagement on it. Look, you can all but see the nachos floating on the bay? Look? Anyway, you'd better be off.'

'Yes,' Tom turned back towards the car. 'Thanks, I think I better . . .'

'And then I take you to the WWII Memorial,' Pluto went on, 'do you know we have a man walking about here, still living and breathing, whose name is on the bloody memorial?'

'Really?' asked Tom.

'Nothing surer. Salutes himself, along with the others, every year . . .' Pluto nodded with growing authority, a smile broaching his crimson face.

'Well, I should make tracks . . .' Tom edged further away. 'Okay. Thanks again. Goodbye . . .'

'Adiós, my amigo,' smiled Pluto, mimicking the flushing of a chain with his hands and flashing his new teeth. 'Toodle-pip.'

When they returned to the cottage later that afternoon Zoe moved quickly through the house to the kitchen. She looked out of the back window and her heart raced: everything was still there, even the girls' underwear, but not her own.

'You might at least have closed your door,' Tom said, putting down the carrier bags. 'Should we trouble that wine again? Wasn't too bad I thought . . . or did you have enough at lunch? I can go out and get more later?' He was keen to make the world, her world, a better place, however much red liquid that required, especially given the disaster of the historical tour.

'What?' Zoe quickly turned.

'The car. You left your door open? One of the local fellows stopped to wait for me to close it. Nice enough chap; didn't understand a word.'

'What did he look like?'

'Why?'

'Just . . .'

'Look, he was like them all, hairy, bad teeth . . .' Tom briefly suspended Zoe's glass between them before relinquishing it. 'Are you *sure* you want more?'

'Thanks.' Zoe grabbed the glass. 'Funny though . . .' she took a sip.

'What?'

'But I didn't hear a car.' Zoe shouted to the other room: 'Girls! Did you hear anything outside?'

'Look. Zoe – what in fuck's name?'

'Well, it's just – you know, after yesterday and the invisible man and now, well . . . I suppose it could have been your new friend Pluto . . . Are we relying on Walt Disney now to make it all up for us . . .'

'Look, it was hazy at the beach, Zoe. Hazy. I'm not sure you were best qualified to judge . . .' Tom snorted and put down his glass.

'It was fifty-five degrees Tom! There was more chance of having a conversation with a fucking polar bear.' She detested it, but in actual fact wished him to keep up his tendency to begin every sentence, every argument, every point of view with the word 'look' – because then she could hate him even more for it. She knew, even if he didn't, that it was borrowed from Tony Blair.

'Anyway, do you want to talk about it?' asked Zoe.

'About what?'

'About last night.'

'Look. What about last night?'

'Nothing. I suppose they took *themselves* off the washing

75

line...'Zoe walked towards the girls, leaving Tom exasperated.

That night Zoe sat up alone. Even though the afternoon's theft had occurred while he was with her, she decided she would set up as gatekeeper at the bottom of the stairs, next to the Victorian bureau with a mirror she could not bear to look into. She hadn't heard any noise coming from the top half of the house, but just after the distant chimes of the town clock at 4 a.m. she heard a sound at the front window, put down her wine glass and moved across the room to separate the curtains. She slowly opened the window and stuck her head out but there was nothing evident, just the stars in the dark sky accompanied by the distant sounds of the boats colliding gently at the moorings.

In the lights at the seafront she could see the outlines of fishermen going about their honest work. She could hear the water and the ropes taking the strain of the boats. It was a sort of symphony. She pointed her phone to the sky and took a picture of the moon. She texted it to her sister. There, she thought, she had given her sister a moon. She drew the curtains then lay down on the sofa and put the bottle to her mouth. Were there other women, she wondered? Other women whose underwear was being taken? Who felt themselves getting wet? Were those trawlers stuffed full of knickers? Deftly, as though there was someone to conceal the act from, she removed her underwear. Then she quietly opened the back door and walked through the garden in her bare feet. The grass was wet and the evening dew refreshingly cold underfoot. She passed the shelter where the rental lady had said there were slabs of peat *if they fancied the full island experience*, and then she looked up to the darkened bedrooms at the back of the house. Was it Tom taking the underwear, she wondered? She turned to the washing line and noticed its straight lines formed a square in the dark sky as though marking a boxing ring for what – the moths and bats? She quickly pinned her dirty knickers to the line and returned indoors. She turned to where the lizard had been earlier and whispered: 'I know the answer now: it is to experience the thrill of defying.'

On the way back to the front room she stopped to drain her wine glass and then noticed all the family's footwear stacked neatly in their correct pairs. *Cunts*, she thought. It had to be the work of Philippa, her eldest, who was like him in this way – always drawn to order. Zoe walked to the matching pairs and, just as methodically as they had been placed, she disrupted the order. 'There,' she said softly, smiling. 'Still prodding.' She remembered when Philippa was younger, a baby, and the anxiety she had experienced with her first child, how she could mistakenly hear Philippa's cry in the sound of the washing machine cycle, or in the murmur of the freezer making ice, in the groan of the household's dirty water escaping through unseen pipes, or even in the singular pitch of a crisp falling onto a china plate. Did she care more then? Had she become the world's least attentive mother? Had he stolen that from her too?

For what was left of the night, Zoe slept downstairs on the sofa, her head facing the staircase so she could catch her husband red-handed should he choose to transgress again. She slept lightly, waking to the sounds of the boats escaping the island or to take a sip of wine.

The next morning she was woken early by the sound of Tom rattling through the kitchen drawers; now he was standing above her with a mug of coffee and a smile.

77

'Sorry love,' he said, 'it's not a latte from Paul, but still, at least it's hot.'

'Thanks. Sorry, I stayed up with a stupid film. I must have ...' Zoe manoeuvred herself to a seated position. 'The girls?' she asked groggily.

'Still rallying – behind schedule as usual – the sea air will not be helping.' Tom's attention had been hijacked in the kitchen when, through the clearing condensation on the glass of the back door, he had noticed the re-emergence of letters that read: TAKE MINE. It was not Zoe's usual free-flowing hand but unmistakably a representation – here in a kind of finger-breadth penmanship – of her accountant's tendency to slip unnecessarily into capital letters. He had no idea why she had done that. Tom sat opposite her on the other sofa and fingered his iPhone. Zoe noticed he was wearing a tracksuit for the first time in years.

'How's the wifi?'

'It's better here by the window.'

'Have you started training for 2012 or something? And God, the new trainers are a bit white, no?' She narrowed her eyes to counteract the glare.

'Have you borrowed them from Pluto, Dad?' asked Philippa.

'Okay – come on, get your sister, like I said, we're getting your mum some hot Scottish scones from the seafront.' Tom rose to his feet. 'But first, we're going to take a walk.'

'Lucy!' shouted Philippa. '*Pluto's* here again! Come, Dad's got his tracksuit on!'

'Ouch ...' said Zoe, putting her hands to her ears.

'Good work with the flip-flops Philly ...' teased Lucy.

'Pardon?' said Philippa, looking puzzled at the incorrectly ordered line of footwear. She crouched to begin her repair.

78

'Leave them!' shouted Zoe.

'Easy love,' said Tom, putting his hand on Philippa's shoulder.

'Make sure you tell them about the lady Bird who used to live here,' Zoe said, reclining on the sofa. 'And be careful on your walk.'

'Ladybird?' Lucy asked.

Tom looked at his phone. 'I was just checking ... bloody hell, it says here that Darwin once visited.'

'I should think he had plenty to study on this island,' Zoe replied.

'The sun has got his hat on – hooray!' Lucy opened the front door and stepped out.

Tom and Philippa followed. As he closed the front door behind him and his two daughters, his attention remained on the phone.

Zoe dozed for several minutes and was awoken by knocking at the door. She opened it to reveal an old man in a flat cap sporting a declining silver beard.

'Hello?'

'Hullo. Good morning dear – I'm not disturbing I hope?' enquired the man, removing his cap. He was tall and very thin.

'No. But can I help you?' Zoe rubbed her eyes awake.

'Well, I hope I can be of help to *you*. Here, I brought your man a fresh supply.' He handed the lady two copies of the *Telegraph*. They had clearly seen better days; the front page of one was covered in holes and the headlines were missing; she thought how happy that would make Tom, given his usual front-page billing.

'Oh, well, thank you – he'll be ...'

'Aye. I suspected he'd be missing the cricket news or such. A nice fellow,' said the old man, flashing his gums. Zoe watched him nod his approval as though he had hit a boundary himself. 'I enjoyed his craic on the beach.'

'Oh?' said Zoe, realising who this was.

The man moved uncomfortably, and then quickly shuffled his arms under his coat.

'Are you alright?' asked Zoe. She thought it best to keep him on the outside. As the man's eyes fully opened they looked like black olives glistening in brine. He had the peachy, remarkably unblemished complexion of a ventriloquist's dummy.

'Yes, I'm fine. It's just Malcolm.'

'Malcolm?'

'Aye – my squirrel.' The man opened up his coat to reveal the head of a red squirrel poking from the inside pocket.

'Oh!' Zoe smiled nervously, and rested her hand on the door frame.

'It's good for him to get some exercise, you know . . .'

'Indeed.' Zoe smiled.

'I brought them to the island, fifty years ago.'

'What?'

'Red squirrels – we had none before that. I was the man to introduce them to the island.'

'How wonderful.' Zoe beamed. 'He is very cute.'

'It happened after the war, and to settle a bet. I was told it couldn't be done but I did it, right enough. I took them back in this coat. Devils ate half my insides.'

'I'm sorry?'

'Sorry myself dear – when you get to my age you realise you start a story somewhere in the middle. You see I went to the mainland, to source two squirrels – and I brought them back on the ferry. The bastard Pier Master damn near ticketed them. Can you imagine the cheek? Excuse my language.'

'No ... no that's fine.'

'And now we have hundreds of the little buggers. I, eh, let nature take its course.'

I should be so lucky, thought Zoe.

'Yes, for a long time they called me the *Feòrag*, the squirrel. That was before I grew the beard. Those more kind called me a magician.'

Zoe looked down the hill, to see if her husband and the girls were still in sight. She didn't really want Tom to see the old man now, to solve his puzzle, while confirming her to be the evil bitch she knew she was.

'It's John the Goat they call me now. You can call me John.' He looked down. 'Okay Malcolm, back in you go, enough sightseeing.' The man closed up his coat.

'It was a pleasure meeting you. And eh ... Malcolm.' Zoe rubbed the sleep from her eyes.

'Mrs, um ... before you go, do you mind me telling you something? Well, it's the real reason I'm here.'

'Oh – what?'

'You'll be unaware of the finer mechanics of our island, but you see, all public notices are posted on the ironmonger's notice board ...'

'Yes?'

'And we have a problem.'

'Which is ...?' Zoe opened the door fully. She saw his singed eyebrows were greyed and escaping from his brow like strands of Brillo.

'Well, we have, what would you call it, a series of

unexplained *incidents*. But there is a common factor. You see – it has involved the same item of clothing, every night.'

'Frankly Mr ... Goat, I'm at a loss. I'm not sure what it is you are talking about?' Zoe wanted to get inside, to run a bath, to ... and then it hit her.

'Somebody is stealing women's underwear, straight off clothes lines!' John the Goat's eyes widened to as yet unchartered territory. 'There is a sign notifying the womenfolk to be diligent. It's like wartime all over again. Some are even suggesting a curfew.'

'Really?' Zoe's heart raced, but she did her best to appear surprised, despite the frankness of his delivery and the staring fix of his eyes.

'And, the thing is, your husband is new here.'

'And?'

'Well, people here talk. I, of course, found him to be a nice lad, especially given the problems he's got himself into, that can't be easy – but I can't vouch for those on the island who have not spoken with him. Or do not know the obvious stress he is under. You see, I'm not a man to judge, my banking has always been done in carrier bags in the space under my bed ... even the Mobile Bank I consider a modernity.'

'I'm sorry – I really don't know what you're talking about.' Zoe closed the door.

'Goodbye, my dear,' she heard from the outside, and then, 'Apologies, Malcolm has clearly lost his tongue.'

Zoe rushed to the kitchen to pour herself a glass of wine. Then she ran upstairs. She upturned all the mattresses and found nothing. She rummaged through Tom's suitcase. Nothing. In her heart she knew her husband was not to blame but somehow needed to go through with this charade. Once again she felt excited. She rushed back down the staircase and leafed through the files in the kitchen, which the renter had said contained local phone numbers. She dialled the island's police station. Now she would get the bastard.

'Oh, hello. Whom am I speaking with?' She listened. 'I see. Sergeant, I wish to report a crime. Yes, it is my husband ...' She spoke for several minutes, providing the sergeant with the necessary information, and then put down the receiver.

She needed to calm down so decided to google the name 'Isabella Bird', the famous inhabitant of this house, this room. She lay back on the sofa with her phone suspended above her, and read more about the lady and her sister. She pressed on link upon link, revealing a labyrinth of twenty-first-century tunnels of Victorian-era information about these, what were they – her alter egos? She heard a key turn in the front door and quickly placed the empty wine bottle behind the sofa. It clinked on another. She wondered – did the police keep keys to all of the island's houses? She sat upright and watched as the door opened to reveal a blonde teenage girl.

'Oh?' the girl said as she looked up from her phone. 'I'm sorry, I was told it was empty. That you had, eh, *vacated.*'

Zoe heard the girl's East European lilt, which she suspected was of Polish origin. 'And you are?' she asked, now bolt upright.

'Adrianna.'

'And you have a key?'

'I'm the cleaner. My summer job. Is everything okay?' The girl noticed how the lady's hair looked like a bird's nest, and how there were dark marks around her eyes.

'Shall I go?' asked the girl.

'Yes.' As she watched the girl turn to leave Zoe shouted, 'No!'

Adrianna turned sharply. Now she could see one of the woman's hands had become a clenched fist hanging from her side, and there were red stains on her shirt. She hoped there were none that needed cleaning on the sofa.

'I – I didn't mean to do it,' said Zoe. She was now talking to a space beyond her visitor, as though this young girl were a bright light she could not look at. 'It's just ... he stole other people's money. No, no. Worse. He *borrowed* it; you have to laugh don't you? Borrowed it. Implying he knew best, that *only* he knew,' she thrust her chest forwards, now macho, 'what should be done with it, what they should *allow* him to do with it. Fuck, he might as well have taken the knickers.' Triumphantly she held her other hand in the air as though holding an imaginary glass.

'I'm sorry?' gulped Adrianna. 'The w*hat*?'

'With what?' Zoe said exasperatedly, and then paused to look at the light. 'Are you *Isabella*? Have you returned home?'

'Who?' asked the girl nervously, now eager to leave. 'I should go and come back another day?'

'Don't ever steal.' Zoe leaned impulsively over the sofa then remembered the bottle was empty. She looked to the girl. She was a beautiful angel, in a way.

Adrianna blushed deeply and put her phone into her coat pocket. 'I'm sorry you are feeling bad. I sometimes feel bad. I better go now.'

'You do?' Zoe put her head into her palms; now she was dealt the indignity of this girl pretending to sympathise with her.

'I ... have done a terrible thing,' Adrianna said. And then she laughed loudly, more nervously.

Zoe observed how the girl's laugh caught at the back of

her throat in mid-flow with an infectious hiccup; it was a momentary pause for thought, no, delirium. It was a laugh that enjoyed itself, despite the girl's revelation. Or was the girl just trying to make her feel better? She should laugh more often, Zoe thought. She remembered how her own girls, especially when they were younger, liked, no, *had*, to tell her the truth. They needed to be rid of the thing they felt, or had done, no matter how good or bad that thing was. And even if it were not the truth, but some detail of their fabrication, they needed to share it with her, like a jail door that needed to be locked. No matter if it were imagined, it was still their truth, for that second, and it needed to come out. She could only marvel at their joy in this act of sharing. Was that what Zoe was doing now, she wondered, by heaving her truth upon this teenage girl?

'I go,' said the girl, closing the door behind her.

Several minutes later there was another knock at the door. Tom had evidently forgotten his keys. Zoe put down the glass of imaginary wine, took a sharp breath and opened the door. 'Oh!' She stood back. Standing there was a tall young man with an eager stance, wearing a policeman's helmet and uniform.

'Morning ma'am,' he said, removing the helmet.

'Please – *please* Sergeant, call me Henrietta,' said Zoe, smiling serenely and fixing a clasp into her hair.

'I think we should stick to "Mrs Bywater" ma'am.'

'Yes,' said Zoe, 'whatever is best.'

'I need to come inside.' He held up his badge and she ushered him in. 'I'm sure this is a difficult matter for you, but you did the right thing in calling.'

'It's not my husband,' Zoe blurted out before the man had

sat on the very spot where Tom had been not half an hour earlier, and where her dear Isabella had sat. Her heart was thumping.

'It's me,' said Zoe. 'It has been me, *Henrietta*, all along!'

'Now, now. Settle down. That's good of you ma'am, to try to take the blame, to protect your man – but I must take your original statement.' The young sergeant noticed the wine glass. 'Where is your husband? I must warn you this is now a criminal investigation.'

Further round the coastline Tom and the girls had found a beautiful walkway that apparently led from the seafront to a lighthouse. The sun had burnt through the cloud cover and the girls wanted to stop for a rest. Earlier, on his way around the town, Tom had passed the local church and asked the girls to sit on the wall outside while he popped inside. It was an unusual urge for him but he had a feeling inside the small kirk, a brief moment of complete peace away from the glare, that made him feel a significant moment in his life was about to occur, perhaps a release of sorts. Strangely, he saw a likeness to John the Goat in the stained glass depiction of Christ.

'I'll go a little further,' said Tom excitedly, 'to see if I can't spot that sunken Spanish ship. Just sit here girls. God, this beauty takes your breath away.'

He walked on purposefully out of sight of his girls, but then needed to pee. He meandered off the path and onto the sharp descent towards the cliff's edge, crossing in zigzags until he found a good spot where he was clearly out of eyeshot. The Atlantic Ocean swirled and frothed below but was not yet visible. The sense of anticipation Tom felt was like hearing an orchestra rehearsing as he approached the Royal Albert

Hall, or the roar of the crowd just as he reached the top of the stairs into the Emirates stadium, back when he could still go. The cliffs rose majestically to his left and then fell in fits and bursts of green, yellow and brown. Here he was, world-famous failed banker, risking being done for public urination – even here, in this remoteness, he could not feel secure. He was hopelessly revealed to the watching mainland, below marshmallow clouds and an increasingly charcoal sky. He closed his eyes, emptying his bladder onto the peat.

He was at the mercy of the elements and briefly felt equal to them, despite the sound of nature's warning swirling below. He finished and stepped further out. Now he could see the ocean galloping, the swathes of brown seaweed gathering in the froth, clinging to the rocks like the discarded sashes of mermaid beauty queens. He understood at that moment what it was to be a visitor in this place, what a privilege it was to stand here. His cheeks were as red as a post box and he felt completely naked in the world.

He could smell the flowers and taste the sweet sweat coming off his body. Looking to his side, he saw something odd on the black cliff face. He walked further down towards the jutting edge, careful of the sheer drop. He got as close as he could. Now he could see what it was.

GOD IS LOVE

Tom could not be sure the letters were real. Was this the Kirk at work? Was this the hand of John the Goat even? He was immediately struck by the philosophical question posed – the necessity for proof, which had warranted this confident statement in paint. It was a stand-alone statement of joy, an answer even, the confirmation of someone's void filled? To his eyes, the cliff was beyond human reach. But if he could reach to touch the letters, might his void be filled? How succinct it was. Something here was both posed and answered by the surrounding landscape. And so now Tom asked the elements, 'What is God?'

He felt the letters calling him, offering him salvation, an un-fucking-up of sorts. *Tom*, they were saying, *come to me*. He knew, however dangerous the proposition, that he would have to attempt to touch the words, to reach 'GOD'. But first he would get closer to the land, and so he lowered his body and removed his socks and trainers. He burrowed his head into the grass. He felt as though he was standing up, such was the incline. To him, faith had been belief without evidence. But here, somebody had seen, somebody had been affected enough to make this mark. That made a lot of things seem possible. As he lay, Tom felt very small, and waited for his heart to slow; he was ready for something better. He closed his eyes and smelled it – that thing the land offers: the airy scent of freedom, of inhabiting a new space. He curled up and, with his fair skin reddened by the weather, opened his big, brown eyes as wide as they would go. He brought his arms to his chest and nestled his hands under his chin, thinking how visible these letters would be from the sea. He smiled to the sky and wondered if anyone had ever felt as he did now. He knew it would be okay. He imagined himself viewed by the watching world as a positive thing, an exclamation mark of sorts – perched here, stripped of honour but free, ready to reach out and touch GOD on an island inhabited by the world's most well-informed red squirrels.

∞ 5 ∞

The Looming

1976

I remember the evening in 1976 when Charlie and I were each seventeen and illegally driving his brother's Vauxhall Victor on the west coast of the island. The sky had been the same murky grey since morning. It was raining like falling spanners. I will never forget that night.

'There! Alexander ... I can see it!' Charlie shouted, facing the Atlantic Ocean, his mouth open wide. He was at the wheel and paying no attention to the road; I put my hand on the wheel too. We were very close to the verge. The drop was only several feet away and fell straight from the rock cliffs to the sea. He knocked my hand away. 'Look. It's the island! I'm sure!'

'Here! Watch the verge Chas ...' I said, taking the wheel again, but he paid no attention. 'Anyway, you can't really see anything through the rain.'

'I can see it. It's fucking there!' The sound of the Bay City Rollers from the tinny stereo did nothing to add to the sense of mystery my friend was trying to create. I looked out through the misty rain to the west, where I imagined people lived in distant places like Iceland and Greenland. But I couldn't see a thing.

'I'd rather you watched the road. There's nothing there,' I said, '... wish there was, but I've given up looking.'

What Charlie thought he had seen was The Looming. It was believed to be a small island which sat just off our own on the west coast of Scotland, nothing more than a lump of rock. According to local lore, it was only visible through the sea mist twice a century. There wasn't a known map in the land that documented it. Even the local fishermen, who had detailed maps of the sea confined within their heads, argued over its authenticity. I had never seen it. I couldn't tell Charlie that I sometimes wondered if that's where my grandfather had rowed off to ten years before. Several times I'd cycled the thirteen miles to this part of the island's coastline in the hope I'd catch a glimpse of his deerstalker or his boat, *Eliza*.

'What the fuck?' Charlie hissed, slowing down the car. The rain lashed the pot-holed tarmac. Through the wipers we could now see, intermittently, a figure out in front of us. It blurred then reappeared. 'It's not . . . is it?'

I said what I knew he was thinking. 'The Headless Horseman?'

'No. Look there's a head.' Even though we were old enough to know better I could tell from Charlie's movement that he was as relieved as I was. 'Or if it is he's wearing a dress.' I could hear our wheels turning more slowly, splashing, and the engine now sounded different, almost alien to our time and place. We tentatively approached the figure in the rain.

'Pull up – or you'll hit it,' I said.

'It is a bloody woman you know . . .' Charlie said, as he turned off the engine. The music was abruptly silenced. 'Shang-a-fuck-ing-lang . . .' he added, slowing the car to a halt.

'What's she doing out here?'

'I'll leave the lights on. Get the back door for her,' Charlie instructed, as he pulled on the hood of his parka and opened the driver's door. The rain was instantly upon us and the wind nearly took the door from his hand. The ocean roared close by.

'Wait!' I shouted, but he had already gone. He was always first. I wrestled his door closed and then reached back for the rear door handle on the driver's side, preferring to stay dry. I watched my friend approach the figure. They lingered for several seconds, and then together they walked to the car. Behind them, the road went on forever into a dark void. I pulled down the visor, wet my fingers and fixed my hair and sideburns in the mirror. I was immediately disappointed with my failing moustache.

Now I could hear Charlie's voice getting louder over the elements. He opened the back door.

'In you get, it's cold!' Charlie shouted. I could tell he was trying to sound older and more authoritative than he was. She seemed a lot older than we were, but now looking back I realise she would have been in her mid-thirties. I'd never seen her before, but this end of the island had a lot of visitors, mostly hill walkers, that we would never see in the big village where we were from. Her hair didn't seem to move.

'This is Alex,' Charlie shouted through the rush of noise. Now I was the abbreviated 'Alex' – to be perceived as older because then my friend must be too. Charlie smoothed down his garden-hedge moustache, moved away from her door and closed it behind her. The car became instantly dark.

'I know,' she replied, settling into the back seat. There were just the two of us now; Charlie was kicking the tyres. She didn't make a sound as she moved. I'll never forget how I felt not the cold, but instead a warmth rush in. I wondered why she was in a summer's dress, in winter, and in such an

out-dated style. She made our flared jeans seem inappropriate.
She knew?

'Hey,' I said, turning back, trying to sound older and for some reason more Californian. She had dark hair and smiled like the Mona Lisa. Somehow she was serene despite having emerged from the chaos of wind and rain. Charlie now jumped into the front and slammed his door closed. I remember the ease with which he manipulated the doors, given the mighty force of the wind. Despite the turn of events, I was still in awe of his prodigious strength. His coat squelched on the plastic of the driver's seat. The space inside the car felt very different now, as though it had become bigger. I could see nothing but outlines.

'Ffff . . . colder than I thought,' Charlie shook, pushing back his hood. 'Tyres are okay.' He hadn't heard what she had said to me and was already outside our pact. 'Were you waiting long?' he asked. 'You must be bloody freezing in that.'

'No,' she said. 'I knew you'd come.'

Charlie looked to me, puzzled. 'Ha!' He clapped his hands together.

We definitely didn't know her. Her accent was local but more refined; her voice sounded older than she was.

Charlie turned the key in the ignition and we were deafened by the Bay City Rollers. We both reached quickly to turn it off, embarrassed by our musical taste.

'What odd music,' she said. I looked back to see the smile I had heard.

'Eh, it's my sister's car.' Charlie was trying to redeem the situation, nodding towards the cassette player. 'Not to our taste at all . . . we're more eh . . . Pink Floyd men. Experimental.' I was glad it was dark. My face could never lie like his could. He didn't have a sister, he only had his older brother.

'*Men*,' she said.

'Did you break down?' Charlie asked, looking ahead and then scanning his rear mirror for an abandoned car we might have missed. I turned and caught her shake her head.

'Can we take you to—'

'... anywhere?' I finished, surprising myself with my eagerness. Charlie looked at me competitively, agitatedly. He was always a ferocious competitor, but this surprised me.

'Where were you going?'

'Oh, we were just out and about ...' Charlie said, beginning to drive off slowly, our headlights forging two tunnels through the darkness; the raindrops glistened with fine definition like diamonds falling. It was exciting now to be three, and to have a girl, or a woman, in the car. She smelled fresh, of rain or sea, but was somehow separated by more than the seating arrangements. Something was amiss.

'Out and about,' she said to the side window, in the direction of where we believed the mysterious rock to be.

'It's getting wilder. Just as well we found you now.' Charlie nodded continuously; I could tell he felt more important than I did about the rescue. To me, it didn't seem to be one at all.

'Would you like the heater on?' I asked.

'No, I'm okay Alexander,' she said. I turned around and she smiled at me. I turned back to face the road. I could still feel her smile on the nape of my neck.

'Yeah, just as well. There's not much around here. Were you lost?' Charlie asked, as he peered through the rain.

'No,' she said. 'Found.'

Charlie looked to me. 'We were looking for ... eh, a lump of rock ...'

'The Looming,' she said.

Charlie turned quickly to me again; his face was like a newspaper headline. Despite his authority, I knew that I should help him out more. I knew all of his looks, I realised then.

'Were you driving?' I asked, staring ahead; for some reason I thought we might meet another figure on the road. The possibility of there being a Horsewoman now entered my head.

'No. I don't know how.' She laughed softly. 'Certainly not a modern car such as this one.'

'Nor does Charlie,' I said. She giggled again. I could tell we laughed at the same things.

'Well I know where the verge is, and the sea,' Charlie said, making a mock right turn. It would have drowned all three of us.

'Do it,' she said. 'Drive over the edge.'

I turned sharply to her. I was worried that Charlie was so desperate for a screw that he might just do it. 'No!' I shouted, embarrassed by my lack of adventure and the high pitch of my voice.

'Ha! I like her,' said Charlie, thumping the wheel, and then looking into his rear-view mirror. He was always the thrill-seeker. 'You,' he corrected. His hair was long in a way that girls liked, especially older ones. His face was handsome, not beautiful, like Elvis some thought; his jet-black hair only added to the effect.

'What gear would you choose?' she asked.

'Huh?' I turned to Charlie.

'You mean for going over the edge?' Charlie asked, smiling.

'No.' She looked down and I noticed how beautifully her hair covered her eyes. 'I meant for the sea.'

'Well . . .' Charlie was a bit stumped, I could tell; he sounded like he used to when he was bluffing an answer so that he could get to gym lessons more quickly.

'Eh, so what gear would you recommend?' Charlie asked. I heard how his voice rose climatically; clearly he was pleased with this question, this alternative to an answer.

'Well, I've never been in a car,' she said, 'but I'm glad to be in this one.'

'Haven't you?' I asked. I looked ahead into the rain; the windscreen wipers were now squeaking as though the car had a soul. I had a soul I'd realised recently; my grandmother had confirmed it while holding my face in her cold hands. I'm not sure what I did to acquire one. I'd been having feelings that I knew would take me away from this place, far away, perhaps beyond The Looming to another continent even. Charlie's fate was harder to imagine. At seventeen he already had a certain duality: he knew the sea as well as the land, but his body, and – despite his reluctance to show it – his brain, had outgrown our school. As if to keep the fate gods even further at bay, he was tarnishing his good looks by growing his eyebrows. He was hoping they would meet in the middle like those fashioned by the island's fishermen and by his brother.

'No. This is my first time,' she said, sounding more sombre. 'So, don't go over the edge.'

Charlie looked to me as if to ask *what the fuck*? His eye did that thing of half closing, like Columbo's. I knew he was upset that she had used my full name earlier and not his.

'Are you brothers?' she asked.

95

'No,' Charlie shook his head.

'Best friends,' I said, too eagerly, 'blood brothers since we were seven years old.' I was immediately embarrassed.

'That's nice,' she responded. 'That makes me happy. It's important to be consciously happy, at some point in your life.'

Charlie laughed out loud. 'Sorry,' he said, still chuckling. 'You're a right one though, right enough.'

I looked at him angrily – partly because he was older, more athletic, and becoming a man; I wondered if this was what we were supposed to be like by now. Judging by the way the woman sat, and by how composed she sounded, it was as though she already knew the answers.

'Did you travel far?' I asked, and instantly regretted it. I had made it sound as though she was on holiday and I knew she couldn't be. She had nothing with her.

'No. Just a lifetime,' she giggled, as though she were saying more than she should. 'Just along the road. The long road. I'm here to make sure you're okay.'

'Oh?' I said. Charlie had gone quiet in the way he could when you least expected him to. 'A lifetime?' I shook my head. 'That's a while.'

There was silence for a mile or two and then she spoke slowly: 'Hours – like cars – collide.'

Charlie shook his head and then circled his finger at his temple. He still liked to pretend he favoured the actual to the lyrical. The rain. The road. The sea. The air. He loved to feel the air. I could see he was frustrated; even the usually dependable pleasure of the steering wheel on his flesh was now eluding him. Though he was a very different specimen, he reminded me now of my grandfather who, before he rowed off out of my life, would sometimes sit at the bottom of my bed in his pyjamas, which were more often than not a pair of waders and a T-shirt. He would shake his head at my grandmother's poetry books on my bed, envious of their words, I realise now – and perhaps even their increasing hold over me. I was discovering more and more of them back then, devouring words, just as my grandfather used less and less of them. I looked out to the ocean and knew I could never forgive my grandfather for rowing off. Maybe that's where he went – in search of words? But I knew from that day on I could never have chosen the sea as a workplace.

'"Hours – like cars – collide,"' I recited. 'I like that.'

'It can be arranged,' Charlie said, breathing heavily through his nose. He veered the car towards the verge.

'Fucking hell!' I yelled. Then I turned sharply to her. 'Sorry.' She looked more serious now. She made me think of my grandfather for a moment. Despite the pain he had caused me, he was a fading memory from the previous decade, fighting to stay alive in this one.

'Days – like hills – subside,' I said. There was more silence, but I could hear their brains ticking. I turned back, to her.

'Roads that don't come back.' She spoke with smiling eyes. I laughed.

'What do you think Charlie?' she asked. 'Of our verse?' I couldn't remember if we had told her his name, maybe he had on the outside. Charlie drove faster; he was always the fastest; he was making sure we knew that despite his silence and our verbal musings, he was in charge. He could do that without even uttering a word. He held the steering wheel like it was the wheel of a fishing boat. She seemed able to communicate that we appreciated his role without actually

97

saying it. It was the slant of her head, the tone of her voice, the shape of her hair.

Charlie slowed down again. He looked to the sea. I hoped he wasn't going to drive us into it.

'Hands – on clocks – unwind,' he said quietly, surprising her I could tell, but not me. Charlie looked to me sheepishly, briefly catching my eye. Despite the advanced growth of his eyebrows, he still looked like the seven-year-old blood brother I remembered. I turned back to her and she nodded. 'We *are* like brothers,' Charlie finished. Looking back now, I realise he said that as much for my benefit as he did hers. We travelled a little further along the coastline and nothing was said for several minutes.

'This will do me here,' she said. 'I have to go back now.'

I knew both Charlie and I were disappointed. He pulled up at a clearing in the overgrowth and even though we couldn't see it we knew the Atlantic was still out there, with nothing much between it and us. I remember now that the evening had become more open and forgiving, and had somehow taken on a more enriched life of its own; an impression that it might go on for ever. There was some form of truce in the air, and a new spirit in the darkness, one that was growing and unopposed. It might have been the stirring of what the older people called folklore.

'Thanks for the lift,' she said, 'and to you Charlie for driving us so *creatively*.' She looked to me and her voice broke for the first time. 'Look after ... *him*.' With that she opened the door just enough and quickly closed it behind her.

'You'll die a death in that outfit!' Charlie shouted, winding down his window and screwing his eyes into the wind and rain. 'Where do you come from?'

I realise now he was taking an opportunity for both of us, for me really, one which might never present itself again. He usually showed his courage when he needed to. I thought she replied 'the sea', but by then the sound of the wind and the rush of the ocean was louder than she could ever be. She raised her hand behind her as she walked back in the direction we had travelled. Soon she was lost to the shapes of the night. I immediately regretted not saying goodbye.

We sat in silence for several minutes until Charlie moved us off. We were no longer boys. Something had shifted.

'The Looming, I bet you,' he said.

'What?'

'That's where she came from. The Looming. You can forget any other post code.'

'I . . .' I realised I had nothing to say. No way of reaching her.

'Was she a mermaid?' Charlie fiddled with the cassette player. 'To think I nearly screwed a mermaid.'

Despite the inappropriateness of the sound, I welcomed his decision to fire up the Bay City Rollers. I pictured them on stage, not unlike fishermen, with musical instruments instead of creels. I concentrated on their jaunty melodies, which I knew, in times to come, would sound hideously dated – like my grandfather, had he given himself the chance. Neither of us wanted to speak. We each needed to work it out.

We pulled away from the coast in high gear, further inland where the wind was tamed. We were relieved not to have been caught while driving without a licence, despite having passed the house of Sergeant Punch and pulled up shortly after it. I think our intention might very well have been to get arrested, to do *anything*, just to shift our mood from the shadows of the sea, from the spirit of the evening that held us captive. Charlie killed the Victor's engine outside the house of his brother's neighbour; the rain was lighter now, nothing more than transporting mist. Somehow we weren't fearful that his brother would see the lights of his car, for which we had not asked his permission, returned to the wrong house. I'm not sure why we pulled up outside this house. Maybe we needed to see another living soul one step removed from us, to more gradually entice the world as we had known it back. We sat in silence and only then did I realise what it was – what was wrong with her, what had become wrong with *us* on this night when logic had briefly leapt from our island; yes we were still blood brothers, but we were older, and in the company of a spirit. It was a knowing moment that only the two of us could ever, would ever, be able to share. I needed to say it aloud –

'She was bone dry.'

'What?' said Charlie looking straight ahead. He switched off the lights.

'She was. *Bone dry.*'

Charlie turned to the back seat. He reached quickly and wiped the plastic. I heard the dry scuff of his hand on the seat. 'I knew it, I knew something was odd, but ...'

I didn't need to feel the back seat. I shook from a nerve or whatever it was running up my spine. Charlie looked as confused as I felt. He gazed out as if to make sure nobody could hear us; or perhaps he was searching for someone to tell us it hadn't happened – to tell us The Looming was a hoax and, like the myth of the Headless Horseman, we were stupid kids for believing otherwise. He switched the headlights back on but not the engine. I knew what he was doing. I too needed to see the neighbour's grass, the familiar clothes line, the stacked creels that never seemed to leave the side of his house, his Ford Capri – these items that confirmed our normal world, as it had been, as it would be again. Except it wouldn't be. We had become other people. We looked out to the neighbour's garage door. It was a dependable sight and revealed by the headlights to be the same blue we both understood.

'I can still smell her,' I said.

6

The Letters of Ivor Punch

Saturday 8th August, 2009

Dear Mr Obama,

There were six eggs in the chicken coop this morning, two more than yesterday and four more than the day before. It's official: you can tell your men the recession is showing signs of recovery.

In fact, I remember I was eating an omelette last year when I saw your speech on the night you got elected. After you knew you had won. I hope you will not be offended but I watched with the sound down, I prefer to watch folk's faces, and to read eyes. I saw your fine-looking family behind you. Big smiles and truthful stares. I never had a family. It never happened and it won't now. Or it had better not. And fuck. Seventy-two is too old to be doing with others. Now I am best alone; I sometimes see it as my gift from myself to myself. You get to thinking a lot about your death at this age, and you develop an art of becoming open to talking about it in the way others speak of life. It would be awful to trouble a wife or children with such macabre discussion. But I don't fear death as much as I once feared the notion of a wife. And fuck. It just never happened. There was once a girl who I did not so much put on a pedestal but during one fateful summer in my own way I crowned as Mary Queen of Scots. And fuck. 1958 it was. I loved her too much, I can see now. But she was too young. My mother used to say we are each and every one of us

God's children, but not Mary, she was of a higher power. I never listened to my mother when it came to Mary. My mother never saw her mantra disproven in the way I have done. She made the mistake of marrying my father. And together they banished the young girl back off the island. Just about the only thing they ever agreed on. And fuck. You see the girl was a mainlander, not one of us. She was visiting a cousin on the island that summer, when, well, it happened. I never forgot about her. Anyway.

I can hear the wind breaching the imperfections in my windowpanes. I have got to thinking that it is the unseen in life that causes most of the damage. I distrust the wind, always have. There's not a chance I won't be turned to wind, given to the elements. I expect it. Want it. It has happened to my family before. You see, I have a ghost in my family. And fuck. I live here on the island in a home that houses a bloody ghost: a memory of a person who died too young. I am writing about the plane that fell out of the sky. And I am writing to you sir because I appreciate your support of my cause, so to speak, which is to block the release of the Libyan bomber. You see, my younger brother, his beating heart, was in that plane. And fuck. I am writing to you good sir because a man must suffer for this act, and I had not intended it to be me, or the memory of my brother. That is, if a memory really lives and breathes in the way I hope it can. I'm sorry – I am forcing on you too many serious fucking thoughts on an evening when the wind is trying its damnedest to blow them away.

But I have enjoyed putting these words down. I am tired. It is late. 'The Clock' the local bastards call me, and I am not a man for sharing his emotions in the way I suspect you are. It is nearly midnight and I must listen to the shipping forecast. Old habits die hard. We're expecting your rain off the Atlantic. I used to hunt whales through it. And fuck. Back when I whaled – before I joined the ranks of the police here on the island – the waves could rise higher than the house I am listening to now. And fuck. Waves become oceans, like boys become men. They say you are a man of Hawaii and so you'll know that whales do not randomly wander through the oceans sir, they have a plan. In their migrations, these big buggers I used to hunt follow well-used vast waterways that stretch around the world underneath our waters. They are hidden. Much like the truth. And fuck. There is not a day when I don't wish I could bring all those big lunging beauties back to life, as I wish I could the doves. I agonise now at the thought of all the things I could have done, and said, to protect nature, instead of inflicting more harm. But that is another story. I was not so fortunate back then as to have David Attenborough whispering in my ear about the cruelty of man.

I should say I nearly cried – watching your victory speech. I respect your decision to not have. I remember the night well; I'm an old foolish cunt but I recall how I placed out a straightened hand to my forehead, put each of my feet in their slippers, and stood to salute every, what do they call it, square on the TV set in front of me. And fuck. You'd think it was the head man of the Scottish Constabulary standing there in front of me himself. My cleaner, Miss McBeth, thought your wife's dress not the most flattering. This is not an opinion I sought, you'll understand, it was offered to me as she made the best with my house. And fuck. The way her arse is growing I'm not sure Miss McBeth is in a position to comment on such matters. She has left me a supper of toast; well, I should say it is bread not so much toasted as had hot breath blown on it. I'll trouble it with butter and see if I can resurrect my failing appetite. She is a woman some would

perceive as quiet, but I know her to be, what is it they say now
– passively aggressive? You know, in the way quiet people with
confidence can be? You'll have encountered a few dictators with
similar traits, no doubt.

Yours aye,
Ivor Punch

PS: It is very late now but I couldn't sleep. I wrongly omitted
'Sir' – he is of course Sir David now.

Monday 10th August, 2009

Dear Mr Obama,

Now that I have put pen to paper to you I woke up in the middle
of the night with a familiar dream. Or should I say, a nightmare.
But was it because I mentioned the plane or was it the doves,
Mr Obama? My bed sheets were soaking, and I thought at that
late hour, well, this is it, I'm to drown to death in my own piss. I
believe Miss McBeth has been waiting for such decline so as to
close the lid on me, her recompense for all I have done. But she is
not the worst.

This dream makes me waken because I am choking. It
has always been the same. Fucking odd how we can sense an
injustice even in our sleep. I once saw the old political man Tony
Benn on the TV saying that old people should be wary of pains
in the middle of their chest, and that is what I had. He is a man
worth turning the sound up for. And fuck. I saw the giant dove
again. Except that last night, when I felt myself approaching
unconsciousness, the dove had become a giant plane. It was
then the pains on my chest started. You see, I feel the weight,
Mr Obama; I feel the weight of the fallen, the falling. As I'm

sure you do. And then that had me thinking all through the night about my father. My mother called him a shit of a man. I hear from Miss McBeth that your father left you when you were a tot. Well, in those fortunes of parental attendance, I have been luckier than you. But I am not sure it has done me any good. I have never been Head of State, like yourself, indeed on some mornings when Miss McBeth shimmy-shammies around me with that bastard Hoover that bleats like a demented lost lamb with its neck in a vice, I feel I am not even master of my own front room. She is older than her years. And fuck. Not the Hoover. I know it is more than the memory of those doves that keeps me awake, but still, I am ashamed of my part in their decline. At my father's bequest those birds stole my childhood, I realise that now.

You see – my father had a dovecote built onto the side of our house. I was only a child, small enough that an army of midges could have bowled me over. The Clock was my given name even then, given to me by my own father, the bastard, but he was not so keen on helping me in the dovecote. He was afraid of any sudden movement – I believe even a murmur from his bowels would make his wits scarper – and with the addition of years he only became more nervous. But the doves, what can I say? I did not know I was transporting them to their death. I am ashamed of my part in nature's demise. I never used to think like this. And certainly have never written anything like this down, other than an arrest ticket. No I never used to talk like this. I used to be more of a shit.

Anyway, I managed a few extra hours of sleep this morning without pissing myself. Miss McBeth will be happy or sad at that revelation; she is herself a hard bird to read. And fuck. I must shit soon, I used to be like clockwork – they weren't wrong

there. More trustworthy than Greenwich Mean Time. I am
definitely carrying extra cargo. It keeps me awake. You'll have
trouble sleeping I expect. This war. Your mind will be in a
jam-jar over it. I read in the local news that we have a lad from
this island in Afghanistan: a local boy, an army photographer.
I'd urge you to think of these young boys going to war as I do of
those doves I sent into my father's cote, unknowingly, for them to
multiply and meet their death with an air rifle my father loaded
for me and told me to shoot; he was not a man I could disobey.
And I feel them on my chest. You see – a plane fell out of the
sky. And fuck. If a man has a soul – and back then as a boy I had
reached the age when I began to notice its existence as a sort
of fluid inside me, even if I wouldn't have known the name for
it – from that same place, I lied to myself, because as time passed
I knew the impact of the misdemeanours I was carrying out
on behalf of my father and I hated it, but I carried on doing it,
watching those white champions fly, glide even, to their deaths,
like my brother in that plane – who'd have thought a journey to
the end could carry with it such beauty?

And fuck. It was not even the doves that were of value. It
was their manure. Shitty work yes. But enough of this for now,
it's nearly lunch and I don't want to put myself off it or further
block the tubes by thinking about muck. Miss McBeth will no
doubt have the local plumber look at me. She will catch me at
this table one of these days and think I am writing her a love
letter. Again. I must wash this weight off my body. I had hoped
these nightmares had become extinct. Things do. I've seen it.
But the events of this week, the news that the Libyan bomber
is to be released, have tickled a feather so to speak. They have
wakened the dead in a way that I did not want. If I thought
I could walk far enough I'd visit the local Highland Games

playing field again – it is on the hill nearby. I always felt better up there. You see, that was where he took our breaths away, my brother, with his record long jump. But seeing the field and the sandpit now would only be a disappointment. I am crippled with illness, and while I still have a brain that functions, I'll give it the best chance to remember a world as I choose to remember it; just as I chose to change. It is often the case that landmarks and significant things are better left in the imagination, where reality cannot apply its cold stare. If only you could do the same with your Bay of Torture that I read about. You must do something about that soon.

I see you're greying. Not to worry. It will add greater authority and gravitas to your statesmanship. I watched our Pier Master go through a similar transformation. Use it wisely. You can go a long way with a good-shaped head lad. They used to say the same of me.

Yours aye,
Ivor Punch

PS: They say polar bears are next – to be extinct.

Thursday 13th August, 2009

Dear Mr Obama,

Tonight a startling thought came into my skull. A terrible oversight of mine. I am of course not addressing you properly. I remember when I became the island's only police sergeant and one day I was without the uniform and one of the young local lads did not realise I had authority over him – I was surprised by my reaction. I punched him on the nose again and again until he bled for mercy; you see my family had a particular *reputation historically in this activity of punching to upkeep. My ancestor, the first man Punch, An Gnuis Dubh they called him – that's 'The Black Face' to you and I – had past form in this area. They say the big bugger still roams this land, this island, as the Headless Horseman. Helped me solve a crime or two for all I know. Although he's never come knocking at my door. But none of this was an excuse for my actions, the consequences of which were more easily brushed aside back then. Anyway, for my oversight, I apologise. I should of course be addressing you as Mr President. And fuck. I once wrote to the man at the helm of SodaStream, and if I can grant him the title of President, then I can do the same for you. I will not make the same mistake again.*

I will sleep, and I hope be untroubled by falling birds. I notice there is a plastic sheet on my bed tonight. It appears I am to be gift-wrapped in baby sheets for my delivery to St Peter, stinking of my own piss. Mummified for my maker and all courtesy of Miss McBeth. That is if I am not in fact intended for hell. And fuck.

Yours aye,
I.P.
(Formerly Sergeant, Northern Constabulary)

PS: The night I heard the plane had gone down I sat on a hill well out of anybody's eyeshot on the edge of our town in the forest leading to Bloody Bay where my friend Randy would later slay a horse. Well, we both did a bit of that, for the meat. That is our secret, by the way sir. Anyway, I tried to cry that night. Until then I had never cried. And fuck. It was not the done thing for a local man representing the law. What a terrible thing eh? To go through life without crying; I suppose whatever their failings some people just can't.

Dear Mr President,

You'll be confused about something I realise. Why 'The Clock'? Well, from birth I had one arm noticeably shorter than the other, and you'll be aware, for I'm sure it is the same the world over, children can be unkind. My father knew that and so he set them running with it. For a stubborn old shot he didn't miss much. The sad thing is I acquired his same gift for damaging with the tongue. Still, it could have been worse – my superior on the mainland was known as Sergeant Snickers. The bugger could have papered his office walls with the leftover wrappers.

Talking of childhood nicknames, Randy came around earlier. I saw him first pulling up the Mobile Bank van outside and then passing the side window, at which point he gave me that over the top thrusting arm-in-the-air wave of his that is textbook Nazi. He is even sporting a small moustache I see. I swear the bastard times his visits – he arrives always just after Miss McBeth has delivered my lunch. Still, I cranked up the SodaStream. I offered him a drop of Cola and he did that thing he has done all his life of replying 'No No No No No No,' which I know through many years of experience in fact means 'yes'. I swear I once counted fifty different versions of No, when one simple Yes would have done it. What a waste of my little life remaining, I told him. And fuck. When he got to the front of my house today he had his handkerchief tucked into his collar before he crossed my threshold. Next he'll bring a knife and fork. Edna can't be feeding him. His head seems to have grown in old age if that were possible. The bastard sat square in front of my TV and all I saw was the back of his dopey head framed in dark wood. Angela Lansbury might as well retire. A television set with ears; even Mr John Logie Baird never imagined that. Then he asked if he could drop a touch of vodka into my SodaStream. All he talks about is that show Who Wants To Be A Millionaire? Says it educates him. The bastard could pay for head reduction surgery if he ever won. Not that that is likely. He has a nephew, Oak Tree they call him, who is similarly endowed, at least in the skull department. Randy ate and then said he would stop by tomorrow. I told him I'd count the seconds.

Which makes me think now back to one of the anniversaries of the plane going down – when we took my nephew Jake on his first overnight Christmas tree hunt. Horrible thinking. And fuck. I am a better man now than I was then, at least on the surface, at least on the page.

And now for some reason I remember another time, when Randy went missing. While doing his bank rounds he had shoved his cock – one instalment too many you could say – in a woman who was not Edna and so needed to flee. I raised a team of men for the search, much as I suspect you do in times of emergency Mr President – for dealing with captive hostages and the like. Eventually we found the bank van, and then his shoe, which had been taken by the peat bogs, and that then led us to the rest of Randy, crouched behind a wall up within reach of Bloody Bay. The bugger was mumbling about the Clan warfare which took place there in centuries past, thought he was Randy the fucking Bruce or something. Still, on those occasions I was proud to wear the badge. But fuck. I look back now and ask: what was it really but an ounce or two of tin?

The plane. I understand a decision has been made about the man who carried the bomb. That was my reason for writing to you. I've tried my best to ignore the news coverage. But a man has eyes and ears, even in my crippled state; even with the sound down it is virtually impossible to shut out the world. And fuck. If I could walk better, I'd place my hands on my old handcuffs, and take off to our Parliament in Edinburgh myself. Your people will be disappointed in us, in our government's decision, Mr President. I believe we are to endure a dip in shortbread sales across the Atlantic. All that just to save the dignity of one unpronounceable man. A killer. I see now they call it terrorism. I sometimes wonder if it would ever exist without the media; without the volume or the TV. But then I look in the mirror . . .

Let's just leave it at that. I am tired.

Yours aye,
Ivor

PS: Come the time Mr President, if you need a Christmas tree, a real one, you'll let me know.

Sunday 16th August, 2009

Dear Mr President,

I woke this morning in a state of some confusion. I swear the older I get the more vivid are my dreams. And so I ask you now: when is an animal, or a country even, small enough, suitably insignificant not to be capable of threat, that we don't consider it worth harming?

There is a new chick in the coop to tell you about, but first I must consider your big towers. Last night I watched a programme that did not require sound. It was graceful in a way that I haven't seen since my brother's record long jump. One of these letters I really must tell you more about that. Anyway, I watched with my own eyes as a man on the TV walked on a tight rope between those tall buildings of yours. I wondered then, as I did all those years ago when crouched below my brother's leap, if it was possible for a man to fly. I watched as the bastard walked on a string no bigger than one of Miss McBeth's sewing threads. And he had the cheek to sit on his arse at the mid-point to look down to the streets of New York and fully admire his feat. At that moment the balance was in his body; he was balance. He had fuck all to do with the city or people or anything else he towered above. At that moment his poise had more in common with a bird or, dare I say, an angel. An angel with sideburns. Policemen like I was myself and all other sorts of clowns looked up at him and waited with their arms crossed. What a commotion the bastard caused! And going by the numbers of others with sideburns on view, I think it must have been the 1980s. Well, I thought earlier, as I do now, at least they – the 9-11 fallen – shared in this man's form of poetry which, we can only hope, provides them with an epitaph more beautiful, if that is the word, than the desperate images we more often see of their bodies plummeting. Those towers that became crumbling, if graceful, collapsing buildings, which at the time caused me more trouble with my chest. My heavy chest. And fuck. I hope my brother was allowed the same grace in his final moments as he demonstrated in his life.

And talking of things crumbling and decaying, just now I saw myself in the bathroom mirror, so I must be alive; it is months, maybe a full year or more, since I looked at myself with such detail. My face is not the one I was born with. There was a time in my middle life when I was still clearly an older version of that boy, and in uniform to boot, but fuck, not now. Maybe you will be luckier, Mr President. I'm not sure of the ways of your darker skin. And earlier the young girl from next door came round. The daughter of the Polish woman. I hope she doesn't catch

sight of Führer Randy. She was enquiring after the new chick.
I told her I ate it in a sandwich for lunch. I know, Mr President,
not kind of me. But she almost laughed. And fuck. She has the
pain of war in her face; any war. I recognise pain in features.
I see it looking back at me in the mirror. She won't know this
of course, but pain is like good looks – it can be passed down
through generations. She was here to collect empty Tupperware,
they call it; little containers her mother sometimes puts a cake
in. I give her an egg or two in return. And fuck. We talked a bit
about those two boys I see on a Saturday night on the TV. I have
never heard their voices but the screen has them as 'Ant & Dec'.
They are really a pair of fools but they make me laugh and so I
wrote to them care of London to tell them as much. And fuck.
We all need a laugh. I have no idea which of them is Ant and
which is Dec, but I'm sure their parents do, and really that is all
that matters.

Anyway, the Polish girl – Adrianna she calls herself –
pointed that phone of hers at me and then turned it around
and immediately showed me the film of this old man wagging
his arm while walking towards her along my hallway. The
impressiveness of the technology was overtaken by my sense of
anguish at what it captured. A stooped old man. But yet I stoop.
The ground must have something my eyes want. I was troubled
with old thoughts when the young girl was here; I had the desire
to harm her in some way. He still troubles me now: the earlier
Ivor. I wonder now if my impulse to cause pain was simply
because she is so young and full of life – so expectant of the
world that I resent it. What a cunning shit I can be. I have
been so troubled by death that I resent the living. And fuck.
What a disaster. I wanted to harm her. I hope I didn't because
now I don't remember much of what was said or done when

she joined me out in the chicken coop. Evidently, it would seem the capacity for inflicting cruelty is also passed down through generations. What a shame. Even the new chick, Gorbachev, is not out of danger, just as the doves of my youth suffered. So the answer to my question at the beginning of this letter is I think you can never be too small to escape harm. Your nation has proved as much with your foreign policy, sir.

Two thoughts for you now, from stories I read in the newspaper Miss McBeth brings me: I see we have many immigrants now in this country, as you have too. And fuck. We even have one in the local police force now I hear, a lad from the mainland. I read about a sorry lot who arrived illegally by way of a shipping container at Dover down in England. Surely if these buggers have the grace and ingenuity to make it over here then they are in possession of traits which would be of value to our country? Just a thought.

You know, in my role of Sergeant here on the island my responsibilities were many, some expanded quite beyond the jurisdiction of my badge. And fuck. You'll no doubt be troubled with similar extras in your job, warfare being one. Yes one time a local man we call John the Goat even asked me to go down and have a look at his tool, said it was hurting and that he preferred me looking at it rather than the local doctor, Muir the Cure. John the Goat trusted me. Even with his manhood. He laid it on the counter in my office, right in front of me. He asked if I needed a new truncheon, you know, so as to break the ice of the situation. The bastard could have played the chanter with it, holes all over the thing. Even that fucking squirrel of his couldn't bear to peek out at it. It wasn't a renegade dictator to be dealt with, I'll grant you, but still, it was a matter of extreme importance. And fuck. This was a man's foremost weapon.

Anyhow, the repair was successful and I've forgotten why I was telling you. Maybe it was something to do with the hope that you will not balls it up, so to speak, like your friend Mr Clinton.

And the second story is a tragic one: a young aid worker has been killed in Afghanistan. Your American soldiers attempted to blow her free. That could not have been an easy order for you to give. I cannot get what I imagine to be her final thoughts out of my mind. Did she want to be saved? Was she by then more one of them than she was one of us? After all, she had been in their country long before our military presence there. And fuck. She was doing good. I fear her final thoughts were the same as the doves when they heard my teenage footsteps approaching with rifle in hand to end their lives. If doves can think at all. Something is, and then it is not. Poor girl.

Myself, I maintained sideburns into the early 2000s, when they would grow no more. It's how we do things here.

> *Yours aye,*
> *Ivor Punch*

PS: You'll no doubt be wondering how I repaired the man's tool? Well I took a small container of bath salts with me, a drop of surgical spirits and a large bottle of the Famous Grouse. Do you know what John the Goat said after the work was done? He said, 'Tha ainglean nar measg.' The angels are among us. The bottle makes a poet of us all. I haven't seen the man in a while but he was more cordial in his relief. Like yourself, sir, he's a solid fellow. Well, he wasn't during the repair you understand, but you know what I mean ... Despite the success of my restoration, I doubt if he is still, you know, reporting for duty.

And fuck. It was the first time I realised there was no Gaelic translation for 'genital warts'.

7

The Headless Horseman

1864

A s the man carefully disembarked from the rowing boat and set foot on the island, his face, in particular the jut of his forehead and impressive growth of his bristly eyebrows, did not look unlike that of the local fishermen who were busy making repairs to their lobster creels further down the pier. However, despite being of the same species, the man's finely tailored clothes, shining boots and colourful waistcoat marked him out as being quite distinct from them. The fishermen knew who this man of world renown was of course; word had got around. They had been expecting him.

Isabella Bird moved quickly from her vantage point on the pier to greet her visitor. 'Charles, I can hardly believe you are here, on our little island! How kind of you. Please tell me your journey was not uncommonly haphazard?'

'No, on this fine day it was a special joy,' said the man in an English accent stronger than Miss Bird's. They shook hands. He rearranged his silk cravat. 'I would not think of complaining, given the extent of your explorations.' He paused and spun gracefully to take in the panorama. 'And well – these wondrous views – quite stunning.'

'Oh,' Isabella blushed, 'well you are more famed for boat journeys than my own self, dear Charles.'

'You are kind,' the man said, while looking back to check

that his bags had arrived safely on dry land. He fished for something in the pocket of his waistcoat to give to the two boatmen. 'Will a farthing suffice?'

'Oh please, Charles, do allow me,' Isabella said, rummaging in her purse, 'I will not hear another thing about it.'

She moved towards the boatmen who had brought her esteemed guest from the mainland. As she progressed her orange dress caught the sun.

'Fucking biggest *giomach* I've ever seen,' one of the fishermen whispered, comparing Miss Bird to a lobster.

'D'you think the famous man will be giving her cock?'

'I'm sorry gentlemen, I didn't quite hear?' Miss Bird said, stopping beside the men.

'I – I said . . . is he here for the clock? Ma'am?'

'Oh, yes! You've heard?'

'Aye. Right enough. A man like that is not an easily kept secret, Miss Bird.'

'Of course,' she smiled. 'Do you approve?' She turned to the new village clock, which stood resplendent at the point where the pier joined the main street.

'It's a fine erection . . . Miss Bird,' the first fisherman replied, smiling through his rotten teeth.

'Indeed it is.' Miss Bird meandered her small, rotund body out of earshot, towards the other men tying up the boat.

'She's bigger than Victoria herself, getting,' said the first fisherman as he watched Miss Bird's progress. 'Although I'm not sure even this man has the necessary biology to find her hole. Bugger would need one of his ordinance maps.'

'You think?'

'But she's a good one, I'll grant her that. We made them our own. Both the Miss Birds.'

'Is he a big man?'

'Who?'

'You know – *him*?'

'Have you not eyes, man? Look for yourself!'

'Shush! *He'll* hear us ... I'm not sure I should look at him.'

'Who?'

'*Him!* He'll be watching down on us more closely now, you know ... given the fuss over our visitor's book an' all ...'

'Well, I suppose you could consider this man the opposition ...'

'No. I'd better not look.'

'He's got a *bod* and two balls like the rest of us,' decided the first fisherman, who then looked over to Miss Bird. 'Fuck. Maybe even the lady Bird has one between her legs herself.'

'Well, it's also because of the man's fame. If I look then I'm not sure I'll be able to take my eyes off him again. Tell me, has he a *feusag*? They say he has a fine beard.'

The first fisherman looked to his friend with some exasperation, and then more studiously to the famous man. 'Aye, well, he has a *feusag*, right enough. With good length. In fact maybe he's giving her one, a length.' His eyes narrowed and he nodded towards the visitor's beard then more proudly to take in the village. 'And here he is ... standing here on our wee pier,' he whispered. 'But fuck, enough of this.' He returned to their job in hand. 'Take a bloody look at him for yourself will you!'

'No. I'd better not. I'm frightened. There's something else.'

'What? You're frightened of his *feusag*?' asked the first fisherman, running his fingers through his own; he wondered why his beard was not of similar interest. He continued his repair of the creel. '*I* have a fucking beard!'

'It's because they say he can turn a man into something else. A monkey or something. Evolu ... or some fucking thing they call it. Sounds like danger.'

'Well, if you won't look at him then try looking at your work,' the first fisherman ordered, spitting tobacco on the stones below. 'Sounds to me like you uncorked a bottle this morning ...'

'They call him a genius.'

'And they call this a creel.' But then the first man too stole another sly glance at their visitor; he felt something, but wasn't sure what it was. He had never seen a finer leather boot on a man.

'Will this be enough?' Miss Bird asked the boatmen as she handed over two farthings.

'Aye. Quite, ma'am,' the boatman replied; his straightened back confirming his authority as the island's Pier Master. 'We can always be trusted with important cargo, just as we can with bringing your letters to the island.' He took one coin and handed the other to his fellow crewman. He turned to Miss Bird and said: 'That payment should see your acquaintance halfway back to the mainland too, when he wishes to return. We're not a vessel of discovery, you know, like the HMS *Beagle*, like the kind he'll be more used to, but we are just as vital to this community.'

'Indeed,' Isabella said, turning back and shouting down the pier, 'and you have done a grand job. And I am quite rude, I really must return to our visitor, to see him *in*.'

'Nothing surer,' the first fisherman said under his breath, pulling a creel from Miss Bird's path.

Isabella returned to her visitor who was still staring in the direction of the new clock, and in particular, at the plaque.

'Well, there it is, Charles. My dear little sister Hennie would be so ...' her voice broke off and she retrieved a silk handkerchief from her basket. The man nodded and moved to comfort her, to touch her arm, but decided he had better not.

'Your letter did not do it justice, Miss Bird.'

'She was such a quiet, sweet pet, and, well – you know nothing of her end, but ...' Isabella stalled. 'I fear word got around.'

'Miss Bird,' nodded the man; he had no impulse to know more. 'Even as a child she was surely a treasure.'

'She was so proud of the work you have done, dear Charles. As am I.' She thought better of saying it aloud, in this place of all places, but Isabella could not deny that her bible had lost some of its significance due to her visitor's work.

'Despite her young age at the time, she was a good friend to me in Edinburgh, as were you, and of course your dear father, rest his soul. It is a very kind thing you have done, to honour your sister, the other Miss Bird.' The man glanced out to the boats then swivelled to the rest of the seafront, which curled away from this new clock.

'That is my fear, you know, and it pulls on my tail, so to speak, that she was always the "other" Miss Bird.' Isabella looked seriously to her visitor. At that moment the clock chimed twice. Isabella's face lit up and her visitor laughed. 'You know, I just cannot get used to it!' She clapped her hands.

And then she looked more solemnly up to the clock face. 'Of course, the time is quite wrong.'

The man pulled a gold watch from his waistcoat and looked to it then to the clock face. 'I'm sure it can be reset in time for the opening? It has a beautiful tone. The best I have heard. As a fellow Fellow, I can assure you even Sir Christopher Wren will be turning in his grave.'

'Oh Charles! Yes I have a man at the local ironmonger. You know, he climbs inside and, well, I had to plead with him to come back out. He was hiding from his wife the poor soul told me!'

'Quite the place to hide, Miss Bird, I'm sure.' They both looked back to the Pier Master who was now approaching with the luggage. 'Do you mind, Miss Bird, if I take a closer look?' asked the visitor. 'The stonemasonry looks quite exquisite.'

'I hope you approve of the words, Charles? We have issued an invitation to encourage all the island's folks to attend the unveiling.'

'Eh, it's a fine thing, Miss Bird,' said the Pier Master. 'Your sister was an angel, of sorts.' He coughed, bowing his cap then pulling at his breeches.

'Oh, thank you Alasdair,' said Miss Bird. She knew his 'of sorts' carried a reference to the man Punch, now departed. But she had to convince herself that nobody on the island knew the extent of the liaison.

'Tell me, who performed this fine work with stone?' the visitor asked, looking to the towering clock, which was some thirty feet high.

'Well . . .' Miss Bird gulped. She was reluctant to say more. 'It was—'

'We called him Punch, sir, Duncan Punch,' interrupted the Pier Master, saving the lady, '... he was a local man. Died last year when his horse turned the cart it was pulling. He was almost as tall as the clock itself. Had he lived to see it complete he could have placed the hour and minute hands on with his own, unaided, I'm sure of it.'

'Well not quite, Alasdair. Really!' Isabella turned incredulously to her visitor.

'How dreadfully sad,' the man removed his fine, tall hat, and tilted his balding head in tribute. The Pier Master had seen the man's bald head sketched in a national newspaper, and here it was now, just two feet from his own; if he wished to he could touch it.

'And he finished the work?' asked the visitor, reapplying his hat.

'Well the village men stepped in to complete the last of it,' answered the Pier Master. 'I can never be late for my shift again, I know that!'

'I see. Yes,' said the visitor.

'But you know, Miss Bird has been very generous with paying all the men. We made repairs to the pier, erecting pillars with the leftover stone while we were at it,' said the Pier Master. 'The men will not mind their sleep being interrupted by the hourly strokes as long as their pockets are full, and tumblers.'

The colour of Isabella's face matched her dress.

'I'm sure,' the visitor said, smiling to Isabella.

'He's a big loss to our community. The horse landed on his head,' confirmed the Pier Master, who caught an even closer glance of their visitor; he had never seen such a well-clothed man, and standing here, now, beneath his own name in stone.

'I'm sorry for your loss,' Mr Darwin turned his head again. He had known private loss of his own. He woke up with it every day. 'This Mr Punch sounds like a mighty figure. A truly *evolved* specimen, I might say.'

'It was actually the stone off the falling cart that finished him, the man would never be defeated by a horse. Not a chance!' the Pier Master laughed, and at the sides of his mouth froth appeared. '*An Gnuis Dubh* we called him. The big bugger was more peat than he was blood! Crushed his skull it did . . . they say it took his head clean off.'

'Awful,' said Mr Darwin.

'But we still have him in spirit at least, in the community – Punch,' confirmed the Pier Master. 'Yes in *spirit* no less.'

'Well we should really make some progress Alasdair . . .' tried Isabella, now embarrassed. She knew her visitor preferred pragmatism, and proof of events, the journey of the mind, rather than this propensity to myth making, to fabrication. It was this very tug towards philosophical realism that was causing her to privately question her own attachment to the bible's teachings.

'Oh aye,' the Pier Master dropped to a whisper, 'he has been spotted, on several occasions out around Bloody Bay on the back of his big horse, Seamus, and with nothing on top of those big lop-sided shoulders.' The Pier Master's eyes widened. 'The Headless Horseman we're calling him. Nothing surer.'

Isabella watched as Mr Darwin's eyes narrowed. To her surprise she could see he was quite taken with the story. 'Well, I'm sure Mr Darwin has heard enough Alasdair,' she interrupted.

'At least the island looked after her while you were away

on your travels, Miss Bird – aye we did that, right enough. The other Miss Bird.'

'Indeed Alasdair, and that was very kind I'm sure,' she said. 'Now let's—'

'Good sir,' Mr Darwin interrupted, 'might I ask have you caught sight of this, this headless *being*?'

The Pier Master now wished he had more to offer. 'Eh, no, sir. But half the island is spooked, I can tell you that. I have heard a hoof or two in the night. They say a man down the other end of the island even took a shot at it. Turned out to be a fence post, but still . . .'

'Oh,' Darwin smiled, 'you shoot here?'

'Yes Mr Darwin – are you a shot?' The Pier Master now rocked merrily on his heels; he had never before been called 'sir'. Now he wished he had shaved. 'We've been known to trouble a grouse here.'

'Well,' Mr Darwin looked to the ground in some discomfort, 'I have been known to trouble a tin can – I prefer to allow nature to live at its own will, of course.'

'Eh, aye of course.' The Pier Master shook his head in frustration; he knew he should have known better than to mention the bird, given the reason for the man's renown. He picked up the luggage once again as an offer of penance. 'Yes, we are not dissimilar men – mostly we only trouble the occasional rabbit here, you know . . . for the pot,' said the Pier Master, now blushing at the equal billing he had given himself.

'I am quite certain in Oxbridge they are just at this moment talking about you too, Alasdair,' Isabella smiled, her superior tone and composure restored, but not sufficiently to hide her affection for the local seafarer. 'Am I right Mr Darwin?'

'Yes, Miss Bird, in the mastery of a pier and all that involves, this man's effect is indeed far travelled.' Mr Darwin smiled, and nodded enthusiastically at his contribution. Isabella laughed out loud and then the Pier Master decided he should laugh too.

'Yes I remember hearing how Prince Albert himself would often trouble a grouse with his shotgun,' chuckled the Pier Master. 'Poor man. The wife is still in mourning.'

'Yes, poor Victoria,' nodded Darwin.

'No, I meant my own!' countered the Pier Master.

Isabella shifted impatiently; she had met the Monarch, but it was not becoming of her to diminish the boatman. 'Well now, Alasdair,' Isabella said impatiently, 'enough of your friends in high places! These bags will not walk themselves.'

'Quite, Miss Bird,' said the Pier Master. 'That is, unless Mr Darwin has brought us another miracle species which can walk this suitcase and save my back the lug?'

'No miracles, sir, just my books and some clothes for the week – oh and a gift for Miss Bird.'

Isabella looked bashfully to the earth. 'You are most kind, my dear Charles.'

'Right – I'll take them to your house Miss Bird. It's been a pleasure, Mr Darwin, sir. Or – if I might do you the honour – Teàrlach.' *Charles*. The Pier Master removed and then reapplied his cap ceremoniously. Isabella shifted uncomfortably. As the Pier Master walked away, and with a smile already evident in his voice, he said the thing he had been thinking all morning: 'May our God be with you ...'

'And mine,' replied Darwin over his shoulder, smiling to Miss Bird, as though he had been expecting such a challenge, 'and mine.'

'Well, Charles,' said Miss Bird, 'let me take you home to restore yourself. You must be tired.'

That evening Mr Darwin and Isabella dressed for dinner. After their meal they sat down in the front room to enjoy a glass or two of sherry wine.

'Those snails were delightful, Isabella,' said Darwin. 'A fine appetiser and quite a surprise. What did you call them?'

'Periwinkles, dear Charles. Sea snails. I am so glad you enjoyed them. They were hardly escargot, but a little butter brings them out ... those we can eat, but some we cannot.'

'You have a local supplier?'

'Yes, you met him today.'

'Oh! The Pier Master, how splendid, he was quite a character.' Darwin smiled and took another sip from his glass. 'And he has quite a knowledge of the seabirds.'

'Yes, he and so many of the community have been so kind to us both, well ... you know ...' Isabella reached for her handkerchief, and then turned to the blackness of the night framed in the front window.

'Indeed. That is pleasing to know, Isabella. And for Henrietta too.' Darwin felt the need to change the subject, to brighten the woman up. 'And tell me, I was quite taken with the local legend of this *headless horseman*? In fact, I have been hardly able to think of anything else.'

'Oh?' Isabella reached for the decanter. 'Well you see I have been off the island regularly, and am not so well versed in the mythology, so to speak ...'

'Well I am intrigued,' Darwin smiled. 'I recall on the *Beagle*, Captain Fitzroy would regularly recount stories of mythology, or legend, from his family's origins in Suffolk.

In five years you find out a lot about a man, as I did of those flat lands. A curious life for two men it was. And he was a curious man, was dear Robert. For example, do you know in those five years we voyaged together not once did he tell me he was engaged? Not an utterance! But he was married the minute he stepped off the boat. The folk at the Royal Geographic Society staged a party for him in neighbouring Hyde Park I recall. Every one of them was dumbfounded, but quite delighted for him.'

'What a beautiful tale,' said Isabella. She hoped to distract him from the Headless Horseman. She didn't want to believe a word of it, despite how even she missed the man Punch. It was better if Charles did not know more about Punch and dear Hennie.

'The Pier Master said it has roamed around a specific area of the island, was it *Bloody Bay* he said?'

'It was.'

'Such an evocative-sounding place,' Darwin marvelled. 'Is it nearby?'

'It is on the northern coast. You know, I haven't yet been.'

'And to think of all the places you *have* been!'

'Of course you are quite right Charles. It is on my doorstep. Sometimes we don't look right under our noses, so to speak.'

'Yes it sometimes pays to look further, for us as humans to delve more.' Darwin paused. 'You know I often think of you Isabella when I recall my time at the Galápagos,' he nodded, his cheeks rising as he smiled to his memories.

'You changed the world from there, dear Charles,' said Isabella. 'You did. You *have*. Eternity will remember you. I feel certain of that Charles. My goodness, if they were ever to put a man on the moon he will hardly be on a par.'

'You are kind Isabella,' said Darwin. 'Although, we must remember all species are equal. But unique. And,' he paused, 'like that fine Pier Master no less, perfectly adapted to their environs.'

'He is quite a unique species indeed.' Isabella smiled, and then grew more serious, 'You must be exhausted Charles. All that work, consolidating all your findings. None of us knew the scale of your work, let alone the impact it would have.'

As Darwin smiled, his grey beard jumped. 'I don't pretend. I am tired, my dear. But it all feels a little more worthwhile now; as you well know, and as I read even Dickens confirms, publication gives a sigh of relief to us all. I am truly grateful for the book's reception, if not the controversy.'

Isabella thought for a second. 'I am flattered that you think of me, in relation to the Galápagos.' She shifted uncomfortably. She had always admired this man, or was it more? Had only she been born earlier she felt sure her father would have wanted him as a son-in-law.

'Yes indeed, the Galápagos's biggest island, the "Isla Isabela" – your father immortalised it, in you!' Darwin smiled broadly.

'You see, that was the influence you had on him at Edinburgh,' said Isabella. 'He even named me after your explorations.'

'He was a great man, my dear. He must have known you would follow suit. He was my teacher.' Darwin leaned forwards, 'I can still see those finches above Isla Isabela before me now, how they swooped and glided over those aqua blue waters,' Darwin motioned his hand, and then laughed. 'I hardly do them justice.' He stifled a yawn.

'That is wonderful, Charles.' It was such a treat, thought

Isabella, to hear these accounts first hand from Mr Darwin, and in her very own front room; like Dickens, he was more used to filling grand halls with his tales.

'But tell me Isabella, have you heard these hooves, that the Pier Master spoke of?'

'They attach themselves to rocks I am told,' said Isabella. She missed Punch more and more each day but dared not acknowledge it. How strange that the big man had got so under her skin. With his untimely loss she had lost her sister all over again, she realised that now.

Darwin's brow furrowed. 'I'm sorry my friend, what do?'

'The periwinkles. Well, I'm sure you are tired Charles.' She looked to the clock.

'Oh, I see. Yes indeed. And very good they were too.'

The following morning Darwin awoke uncomfortably to a bright summer's day. He had endured a terrible night of sweats and unsettled sleep – he felt as though he had barely closed his eyes such was his continuous turning, which he put down to the sherry wine Miss Bird had served him before bed, combined with the effects of the seas the day before. It had felt like his bed was back in the *Beagle* and bobbing through a storm. At his home in Kent he was not much of a drinker, or, these days, a sailor.

'Did you sleep well, Charles?' Miss Bird asked, as they sat down to breakfast of kippers poached in milk.

'Truly fine, Miss Bird. You are most kind. Like a baby.' He gulped to compose himself; his clumsy choice of words made him think of his daughter's small coffin.

'Please call me Isabella, Charles. We are old friends are we not?'

'Indeed we are. That is what it shall be. The kippers,' he sniffed, 'freshly smoked are they?'

Isabella nodded proudly.

'Just like those wonderful sea snails. I tell you, we'll have to stop the French coming here in their droves!'

'Surely non, dear Charles ...'

Darwin rested his cutlery. 'Tell me, Isabella, something is troubling me ... You will think me quite strange.'

'Charles, then you must say – what is it?'

'Well, during the night, when I did awaken briefly, for it is a splendid bed Miss Bird, eh, Isabella, a fine bed – I heard an uncommon noise.'

'What would that be Charles?' Isabella put down her best silver cutlery. 'You simply must say.'

'Well, I know it was around 4 a.m. because I heard the chimes of the clock. But look I, I feel almost silly to be ...'

'Not you, Charles – you are the brightest of us all. Some of the fishermen do pass the house on their way down, they set off so early ...'

'Mmm. Might they go on horseback?' asked Darwin.

'That would be uncommon ...' said Isabella. 'But we have horses in a field, up the village a bit.'

'Well, it was nothing then. It was probably nothing. Wonderful kippers.'

The next morning Mr Darwin did not show at the breakfast table and Miss Bird pretended to be busy in the hallway; she waited for sounds of movement. She had forgotten to powder her face and made an attempt at fixing her bun using the mirror on the bureau, which below, housed galoshes. Perhaps, she thought, Mr Darwin would like to take a walk? A shoot, even? She had kept a gun, just in case, since the death of her sister. She had been taught to shoot by the cowboys of Colorado no less, in her travels across America.

She walked to the kitchen table and made sure her breakfast preparations were correct. Isabella thought back to the time two years earlier when she had received the telegram in early 1862, while in that very part of the wild west. The telegram, she remembered, had been sent many weeks earlier. The postmark was from the island in Scotland. By the time she journeyed back to the island her sister Henrietta's body had been cold for a month. Nobody but the undertaker saw the large, black peat hand stains on the back of her sister's dress. Nobody but her sister's live-in nurse, whom she appointed, and knew she could trust, heard the baby's cries. She had ensured that Henrietta, and her growing body, would be hidden from view, even from Punch himself, by pretending Henrietta had voyaged with her to the United States. But the end was a devastating shock. And she knew that Punch had got to her sister before the grave.

Isabella worked her way through some correspondence as she waited for Mr Darwin and fished into a drawer in the kitchen sideboard – she had a sudden desire to rest her hand upon her sister's bible, but instead discovered the unsealed envelope, and in it the letter from Henrietta which she had first read some months before that telegram, the contents of which had first sprung her into a deception of damage limitation on her younger sister's behalf. She placed her magnifying glass once again over the page and sobbed to the empty kitchen.

She collected herself with a deep sigh, now remembering the morning of her sister's memorial service two years earlier, when she had put on the new black dress, which had been transported from London by John Murray, the man who had published all her tales of worldly exploration and had come a mighty distance to offer his support. She was devastated to have missed her sister's last breath. On that morning she had put on her winter's fur coat, a gift from the Native American Indians of Colorado, picked out two of her own books and walked with them in hand down the hill then up the incline and through the upper village – she recalled she was slower on her feet, her joints stiffening as they often did on her return from a long trip. After several minutes' walking she had turned into the lane that ran alongside the rear of the Punch house, which stood in glorious white. She had then walked along the lane and turned into the workshop. The door was slightly ajar and the familiar cart was parked outside next to the horse, which was crunching an apple. She could see the beast even now. She didn't knock; her footsteps and Seamus's blow had been enough. She recalled how Punch stood with his back to the door and stopped what he was doing; his hands were black with peat. He was stacking a freshly cut load. As she entered he remained facing the other way with one slab still cradled in his arms.

'I believe you are owed my thanks, Mr Punch,' Isabella had said. She recalled now that the hair clasp inscribed with Henrietta's initials was on his shelf. Punch had said nothing. He had simply run his eyes along the workbench that Henrietta had told her defied the theories of her friend's life's work – the famous man Darwin, who was now asleep in her home. Isabella looked up to check the kitchen door but all was silent.

'... For my sister's coffin,' Isabella had explained. 'Fine work indeed Mr Punch. What recompense am I due you?'

She remembered the coffins stacked against the back wall of the workshop, and that memory now caused her to inhale deeply. She put her hand once again on Henrietta's letter. On that morning in Punch's workshop, she had quickly adjusted her gaze away from the coffins and towards the ceiling, to the orderly rows of hanging wooden swords, each identical and beautifully carved. She could see them even now. There was poetry in their presence, she recalled, as well as the possibilities of youth, of war. 'A terrible thing. I wish we knew more about the human body, I really do,' she believed she had said, to try to comfort the man. She had looked to the doorway. 'To think it was growing inside her all along. Well, I cannot …' she had begun, and then stopped. Now she wished she had not said that in front of the man.

At that, Punch had dropped the slab of earth. She was sure he had never dropped one before. He had mumbled something about 'his departed queen'. Then he had said he preferred to call the coffin '"the box", woman'. He had removed his cap, picked up the fallen cut of peat and thrown it as hard as he could against the others stacked along the side wall. The earth had dispersed like gunpowder across the workshop; Isabella flinched at the memory. She had turned sharply to the workshop door and left without saying another word. But she had lingered outside. She had watched Punch cough up sawdust, place the hair clasp in his nail bag and then grip it tightly. But he didn't attend Henrietta's memorial service later that day, she knew he wouldn't, and she knew why. Still, she hoped that he might have lingered close by, perhaps stealing a glance. The man deserved that at least. She had watched as he slumped to the bench; his forehead resting on the surface where a snail had apparently begun its voyage of discovery. He had then looked to the books, which she had placed for him at the other end of the bench, *Letters To Henrietta*, by Isabella Bird, and the other, her handwritten manuscript, *Coming to the Gates of Death*.

'Good morning, Isabella,' Darwin said from the door.

Isabella startled. She did her best to wipe her face and return from her reverie.

'Oh! Charles,' she said, patting her bun. 'I hope you slept better?' She looked to make sure the sideboard drawer was securely closed, and briefly expected to see Punch's discarded peat strewn across her kitchen floor.

'Well . . .' he started. 'In fact, I did not . . .' He sat down at the table and Isabella got up and brought over their plates.

'It was as though they were, ahem, they were in fact galloping in my head . . .' Darwin said, as if to nobody, as he shoved back his chair, causing the legs to squeal on the stone floor. 'All night, in my room.' He shook his head towards the kippers, standing his ground as it were.

'Oh Charles, perhaps you must lie down again? It was a long journey you endured.' Isabella brought up her eyeglass and stole a closer glance at her visitor. 'None of us are getting any younger.'

'You know I think I shall. I shall. I am sorry, dear friend,' said Darwin. And as he walked out of the door to the hallway, Darwin repeated, 'Sorry, dear friend.' He returned to the doorway. 'But I am interested, no, in awe, of this man, *Punch* was it, the Pier Master said? Who built the clock?'

As I was too, thought Isabella. 'Yes, that was his name. Please do get some rest Charles, take the weight off your mind.'

'I shall. Sorry for my burden.'

In the afternoon Darwin woke in Henrietta's room from a longer nap than he had anticipated.

'Dear Charles,' Isabella greeted him from the bottom of the stairs.

'I'm sorry Isabella. I am not as young as I once was, it is true. When I put my head down, well, it can stay down ...' He itched, and then reordered his beard.

'While you are there, please go through and look out of my bedroom window at the view; you simply must see the view.' Isabella lifted her dress several inches off the floor and moved her large frame up the stairs. She was eager to distract her visitor's anguish, to dispel the spirits at work.

'You know,' said Darwin, as though he were answering a question in his head, 'I have read of similar sightings in Iceland, "the Undead" they are known as; they are *hidden* people, not yet ready for the ground, distinguishable from ghouls only by their tangible nature. I should like to explore them more ... many of them are missing limbs, apparently ...'

'I'm sorry, Charles – what do you mean?'

'In fact, this reminds me, before I left Down House to begin my journey here I took some time to read a Royal Geographic report into those fascinating people of St Kilda. Their cliffmen are becoming really rather renowned due to their haphazard fishing techniques; they are scaling there on the island of Hirta the highest cliffs in all the British Isles ...'

'Yes Charles, they are indeed, and with some trepidation, I have heard. I have never been,' said Isabella. 'Not quite on my doorstep are they, but I would hazard a guess at fifty miles westwards from here ...'

'Well, I read that over the centuries, to enable their attempts at securing a food supply, which is almost limited to gannets, their feet have developed a kind of clawed toe, to help them get a hold of the rock on those fearful cliff-faces; and as a result they have fashioned much wider feet than a normal foot, yes markedly broader than the foot of you or I.' Darwin demonstrated with a splayed hairy hand on the bureau. 'And so it has got me thinking of this Headless Horseman ... and if he is some sort of relative species of these St Kildan people?'

'I...I...' Isabella stalled. The delivery of her visitor's words was speeding up.

'And then of course religion comes into it,' said Darwin, 'because the other thing I discovered is that they worship every day, every day. And on Sundays for six hours! It has become a problem because these long hours of worship have evolved, as it were, at the expense of their survival, of their time fishing gannets, of their very quest for food. God is starving them so to speak.'

'Please will you come in Charles, to take in the view?'

'Ahem.' Darwin paused. 'Oh I'm sorry. I am not accustomed to entering a lady's bedroom Miss Bird, but, if you insist.' The man's face brightened a little.

'I do insist,' said Isabella. It was a joy for her to see her esteemed guest almost smile. 'Are we not old friends?' He had looked so dour ever since yesterday's breakfast; even at supper he had not touched his food. She followed behind him as quickly as her bulk would allow and pulled the curtains open. 'You know,' she went on, 'we cannot see the gannets diving on St Kilda but looking out from this window to the busy sea, sometimes I feel there is too much of us, and not enough of this.' She opened her arms wide and then cupped them as if to applaud the landscape. 'Despite my travels, I am quite honestly at my happiest when at this window, looking at this world. I simply adore it.'

'I wonder – is it the view, or where you receive it, that gives you the most pleasure?' Darwin asked. He looked around the bedroom, at the various artefacts, which gathered as evidence of the lady's travels. On the wall there was a Native American carving. He noticed one of his letters was framed and resting behind the door, which Isabella had all but closed. He sighed at his mention of the impending birth.

'I'm sorry Charles. What did you say?'

'You will not be going back to America so soon I presume, given the problems?' he asked.

'No. I was there in recent years. It is simply too dangerous right now, and mightily disturbing to witness a nation such as that turn on itself.'

'Yes. We are still evolving, it would appear,' said Darwin, pushing his tongue to his cheek. He looked to the postcard attached to Isabella's mirror and the illustration of the monarch on its front. 'Victoria herself, I see?'

'Oh, yes. She has written to me from Balmoral. Poor lady is in a bad state.'

'As I understand . . .'

'I have wondered – will she knight you Charles?'

'No. That is not likely, or warranted, or . . . actually *desired*. Remember she is also the head of the Church of England. They are not exactly my . . . bedfellows.'

'Well, it is our State's loss if that is the case. Tell me, can you see what I mean about this view? Oh come, please feast your eyes on it my dearest Charles. See it as Hennie did.'

Darwin moved in small steps towards the window. He was

138

not interested in the view if he could not see St Kilda; instead he looked down to the dirt track that served as a road in this godforsaken village, for any signs of last night's commotion. He daren't tell her he had heard the hooves again. He wondered was this really happening or was it madness? An uncle of his had gone a similar way. How could he begin to reasonably explain the ghostly and vulgar sight he had seen? But in his recollections it was already becoming a memory of some beauty – a most frightening, alarming beauty.

Isabella noticed her powder on the bureau, but thought this not the time for application. She looked to her possessions – these items that confirmed her status as a traveller of the world. Here in her bedroom, she thought, was none other than Charles Darwin and she appreciated her place in the world anew. What would Henrietta think? She looked to her bedside table at one of her travel books: *Letters to Henrietta*. She wondered if he had noticed, but was then embarrassed to see the framed letter was partly in view. She had taken it down because of the mention of his daughter, and had meant to turn the words to the wall.

'I do love this view, dear Charles. And not the slightest whiff of the smelly Thames!'

Darwin forced a smile, and nodded quickly. He could not see a single hoof-print on the ground below, and it had not rained since he had arrived. Quite the opposite, it was uncomfortably and unexpectedly hot.

'Miss Bird ...'

'Oh please, dearest Charles. Please do call me Isabella.'

'Pardon me – is it at all likely, Isabella, that an animal capable of a deep groaning sound would have passed by my window last night?'

Her heart sank. 'No, I do not believe so Charles, I cannot. Why do you insist on this?' She moved quickly for the powder.

'I am a man of science,' said Darwin, 'who quite contentedly lives as a hostage to logic. What is happening here on this island is not even connected to logic.' He collapsed on the bed then sat up and shook his head. 'You have to understand, I have no clue as to the grotesque being's *origins*. I cannot categorise it. What can it possibly have evolved from?' He noticed his own book on her bedside table, a first edition. He shook his head at the sight – did one single word of it mean anything any more? He feared that the previous night was quite possibly the biggest rebuke to his theories he had yet encountered.

Is it the church? Is it that book I have offended – to warrant this, this uncommon curse?

Isabella looked to her bible. She picked it up and rubbed it, deep in thought. She looked in the mirror, at the reflected view of the fishing vessels behind her, at the wind making white horses of the waves.

'Isabella, do you actually believe in the words of these, these prophets and evangelists? These mere storytellers?'

'I – I only keep the book as an academic exercise, and to honour Hennie; it is a comfort, you know she was more of a believer than I. You do know that Charles. Why else do you think I feature your own book so prominently?'

'Well, it too is now open to question.'

Isabella put down the bible and began to briskly powder her nose. Her visitor was in the poorest form and the unveiling of the clock was tomorrow.

'I am truly sorry,' Darwin whispered.

'We should eat. And it was good of you to bring my supplies and books from John Murray, dear Charles. That awful man our publisher even has me a new blouse.'

'My pleasure, Isabella.' The blouse was in fact a gift of his own but Darwin thought it too late now to say. He stole one last glance down at the road. He had heard a cart in the night too, and voices, some outside his window and some inside the room – and he was certain a man had appeared who seemed to be torso only, who had penetrated his ears with a hissing sound. But this fearful figure was gone before Darwin could muster another glimpse. How could he tell Isabella that? How could he tell anyone? Now he wished he were back in Kent, in the tranquillity of his study in Down House, on his reliable chair, with dearest Emma pottering by his side, and his remaining children running free, and he too free, released from these poorest of nightly sleeps, to instead view the green and pleasant land.

The following morning Isabella put on her new blouse and a brooch, which the good people of the Sandwich Islands had given to her. Yes, she acknowledged, this man in her house was indeed held in the highest of esteem, but was she not the first woman ever to cross the American mid-Western plain? And it was not she who was behaving so strangely. The brooch reminded her of that dreadful cowboy Nugent who pursued her through the Rocky Mountains, and whom she had quite failed to understand in his curious, but somehow memorable ways. The man was not unlike Punch in fact. She had been charmed, she was afraid to admit it to herself. This was the morning Henrietta's clock, the work of Punch, was to be officially unveiled. Isabella was feeling more confident when she descended the stairs, careful not to wake her visitor, and pushed the door to the kitchen.

'Oh, Charles – my dearest. Tell me, how long have you been awake?'

Mr Darwin said nothing. He was sitting at the breakfast table and she saw that he was quite pale and unkempt. Isabella tried once again. 'Did the clock blight your sleep? We are all still getting used to its chimes ...'

Mr Darwin inhaled and exhaled loudly through his hairy nostrils.

'I do feel like the worst of hosts,' Isabella went on, 'and you haven't even had tea? Let me trouble the pot with water and the table with a cloth. Oh ...' As she passed behind him Isabella noticed how dreadful her guest looked, it was as though he hadn't slept for a month. What little hair he had was bunched in untidy greying clumps. He was not even wearing his boots.

'Miss Bird ...'

'Oh did the clock keep you awake? I assure you, you do get used to it ...'

'Miss Bird ...'

'... to such an extent that you do not hear it all. Oh, on second thoughts, I hope that is not what will happen when people look at it, that they might forget dear Hennie altogether ...'

'Isabella.'

'Yes?' she said, moving to the sink to fill the pot and in her haste splashing water on her new blouse. She looked around but the man remained silent. Now she noticed the soot marks making an empty rectangle on the white wall above the sink where the framed letter had hung; she should never have moved it, and she feared that in so doing she had awakened some fearful island curse. The water splashed to the floor.

'I have decided,' said Darwin, 'I will cut the ribbon on the clock and then I must leave for the mainland, back to *sense*, back to a common order, and away from this Presbyterian charade. Why, to think the good Fellows of the Royal Society of Carlton House Terrace, London, even postponed a meeting for me to attend this, this … I am sorry.' He shook his head and wagged his hairy hand upwards, not to God; that, Isabella still knew.

'Oh Charles.' She pulled her hand from her mouth and moved quickly to stoke the coals. 'Perhaps it is best not to trouble the spirits of the past,' she said, and frowned towards the window, 'they say they still burn out there on the peat-bogs. Best to leave them be.' She knew it; it was the revenge of the island; it was Punch.

'Oh yes, I will still do that for dear Henrietta,' Darwin continued, 'but please, I would be gratified if you would notify the boatmen of my revised intentions.' He thought about his office back in Down House, the place where he was respected. 'I need to see my dear Emma, you see, this sleeplessness has brought back some quite appalling memories of my saddest time – the death of my darling daughter. Oh my …' he stopped himself from saying one more three-letter word which he was alarmed to discover sat surprisingly readily on his tongue. 'It was her going, which, well, shall we say, radically altered my beliefs. Now I don't know what to believe.'

Isabella turned around fully and now noticed the worst – Mr Darwin's waistcoat was not buttoned and his fly was gaping. He had not even applied his cravat.

'All night it was, again, a heavy nasal blowing sound. But how could it be in my room?' reasoned Darwin. 'And how so close?' He sat back at the empty table. 'A man-horse. I feel like I can hear many crazy men shouting at once, and then they turn out to be one voice. But it is not my own voice.'

'Why Charles?' Isabella sat down beside her guest. 'You are next in my affections only to my dearly departed ownest.' Isabella cupped her hand around the ring on her finger, which had come from the hand of Henrietta.

'No, that is it quite settled. I must be off, I have important work to undertake.'

'You are an esteemed man, Charles. But, I must confess I never heard a thing all night. Either night.'

Darwin walked in a considered fashion from the kitchen to the front door. He unbolted it and Isabella was blinded by the light. She feared the villagers would now be witness to her guest's unfathomable decline. The great man, reduced to a state of confusion she had only witnessed in the dying. Perhaps they would welcome such a sight? She moved as quickly as she could up the stairs and entered Darwin's bedroom. She saw the pitiful stains of his sweat, his entire frame now fossilised in her fine bed linen from Farmer & Rogers of Regent Street.

She moved to her own room and to the window. There he was below, inspecting the fabric of the land as he had once done in such fine detail in the Galápagos, that almost mythical destination, to which the world would forever wed him and which had given her her name. For even in her farthest travels Isabella had noted how the natives would always have heard of one man as renowned as God himself – it was 'Darwin' they said. But was it really *An Gnuis Dubh* he had seen? And if so, why had he not visited her? She rushed back downstairs and stopped in the doorway.

'I will have to reassess my life's work. There is nothing more to it,' Darwin was on his knees and running his fingernails through the dirt. 'I must obey these messages – this sign.' He rose to his feet, walked inside and sat at the bottom of the stairs.

'What? Charles, your work is done. Why – all the world knows your name?' Isabella touched his shoulder, which flinched.

'Isabella,' he said through tears, 'she was so small, so kind. And the coffin – it was the size of a suitcase.'

Isabella removed her handkerchief from inside the sleeve of her blouse and offered it. 'I am so sorry Charles.' She thought of the other baby now.

'No,' Darwin said, 'I must not sob. I simply mustn't allow the wells to flow. Emma will think me weak.'

'Oh Charles. You are not weak.' Isabella heard people passing and so she rushed to close the front door. The ceremony at the clock was due to begin in half an hour.

'I have seen something on this island that the world and his brother has not yet offered. Even those clawed-footed folk of St Kilda are no rival. I saw it last night in this house, Isabella, I saw it. And I touched my own skin to make sure I was awake. And now I fear the worst, that my work is nothing. I realise I have been blind until now.'

'What did you see?' Isabella had seen many a man confused by tiredness, worry and disease – the world over. 'Oh please, who can help?' she asked of the hallway. Perhaps the local veterinarian would have a pill? She knew she could not ask a favour of the almighty. Not now she had housed this man so opposed, this man who had rendered him redundant in certain quarters.

'It had no head,' Darwin whispered.

'What?'

'The Headless Horseman, my lady...'

'Oh Punch,' sighed Isabella.

'I saw it,' Darwin waved his arms uncontrollably, 'at the end of my bed. I must leave this island. I am worthless on it. But – but I am further confused, Miss Bird...'

'Why, dear Charles?' Isabella was struggling to keep up with these developments over which she had no control. She liked to be in control of every situation, every eventuality – had she not proved as much in her handling of her sister's predicament? They would soon be gathering at the clock. The entire village was expected. It was said even the *Cailleach Taigh Geal*, the mother of Punch himself, would be leaving her knitting perch, which, apart from on the occasion of receiving news of her son's death, she had not done since the Queen had lost Albert three years earlier.

Darwin scratched at his beard and hunched where he sat. He slowly nodded. 'Or is it indeed proof of a new species?' he asked of the carpet. 'Is it, in fact, something as yet *undiscovered* that I saw?'

'But nobody has ever seen a being of this kind, Mr Darwin. It is local myth, nothing more.'

'No, Miss Bird. But no man had seen very much before I showed him where to look.' Darwin rose quickly to his feet. 'Perhaps this is the greatest gift I am to receive. Tonight I must follow it. I will wait for it and go where it goes. I am to turn the heads of the Fellows once again! This beast Punch, I shall bring him with me. I realise I have been looking for him my entire life.'

'As you wish, Charles. But might we prepare ourselves for the opening?' Isabella looked worriedly into the mirror above the bureau. 'We mustn't be late.'

'Of course, Miss Bird. Let me make better with my appearance and I shall be at your service forthwith. Yes, that is what I shall do. I am a man of my word.' Darwin smiled and touched her arm. 'Or should I say, I am at the service of dear Hennie – it will be my honour.'

With that, Isabella tried to smile.

After the clock had been officially inaugurated by Charles Darwin, and Isabella had said a few words, the crowd of some two hundred people gradually disbanded. She had avoided asking Mr Darwin to say anything for fear he was still not himself. Isabella had noticed that the Minister was absent and some of the local congregation had worn their church clothes in protest.

At the end of the pier the fishermen continued their work, making best use of the good weather to repair their creels.

'So – did you look at him this time?' asked the first fisherman. The clock chimed, catching him unawares. 'For fuck's sake ...!' He shook his head at it.

'*Tha beagan*,' confirmed the second. *A little*. Neither had left their position to attend the event.

'And are you changed, or the same poor bugger you always were?' asked the first. 'We can't make unreasonable demands, even on the man Darwin ...'

'I'm only different on the *inside*. You wouldn't notice. He even *looks* like a monkey. Seeing the man,' continued the second, 'and knowing that he is made of the same common flesh and blood as you and me, well it has restored my faith in the man upstairs. Because something higher, greater, must have put him here. And us too.'

'Speak for yourself.'

'I will.'

'Good. See if you can shine some light on a creel or two then,' said the first. He looked to the quiet sky and then to the shimmering sea. 'God or whoever has certainly done us proud with this weather.'

'Aye. The man Darwin saw to it.'

That evening Darwin sat at the end of his bed and waited. Thus far nothing had appeared other than the wind coming through his open window. He had decided he would give the beast the best chance to write his next book for him. The world would once again be astounded by his discovery, this half-man-half-horse. He didn't know what to do about the absent head but then he considered, his health willing, he had another twenty years to ponder this missing intelligence. He had done so before. It was all about origins. He knew that. It was about finding them, being informed by them, led by them – towards the prize that was the discovery of new species. He got up from the bed, still in his day clothes, and took a fancy to walk. To go where it might be. And so he took off in the direction of Bloody Bay. In the direction of Punch.

When the morning arrived it came with bright flickers of light spilling over the long grass and through the trees. The heather had been Darwin's mattress and his head hurt. The daybreak felt heavy on his chest – desolate, leaden, like part of him he couldn't shake off. As he received the colours of the morning he noticed the silence, and then the cold. He sat bolt upright but the horse-man had gone. There wasn't a mark where it had been. He had sat with it. Nothing surer. He turned to the sky and there was a body hanging from a tree. Darwin screamed and pushed himself back, sliding on the dew. The body was hanging from its feet and the head was missing, but he recognised the torso as that of Henrietta Bird. He vomited where his body had lain. He ran in the direction of the village. He heard his voice echo like several of him as he ran. Then further through the woods he saw another body hanging. He stopped. All he could do was watch this body, so still, hang like a decoration. It was his daughter, Annie.

There was a galloping sound; or was it the pulse in his ear? He was running as fast as he could through the trees. No matter how quickly he ran the shape of his breath stayed out in front of him in the early morning air. He must leave, but then what? No matter. He must leave this place. He repeated the name of his daughter over and over and then he glanced up and saw Miss Isabella Bird looking down at him. 'Here, here,' she said softly, while removing his sodden bed sheets, 'you are in a bed, in a room, in my house, dear Charles, that is all.' She reassured him he had been visited by an uncommon ghoul which was only in his mind. But as he came to full consciousness, Darwin knew better; he had proved it once already to the world and he would do so again. From an island.

∞ 8 ∞

The Wrong End of a Pig

1957

As Eliza approached the croft her seventeen-year-old heart was racing and her feet moulded the bog. She had heard the sound of her father's bagpipes carried in the wind and dug her nails into her palms; she knew what they signified. It was the sound of death. Her pig was gone.

Fingal McMillan played so rarely; the last time had been when his most productive heifer died ten years earlier. Eliza could hear that his lungs now took the strain of his heart, as they had in battle.

It had been such a slow death that Eliza had become used to the idea of this day; it had been almost impossible for her to bear her pig's gradual decline. She and her mother had tended its brow but now her mother was on the mainland, called for the weekend because her aunt was dying. She had taken Napoleon their puppy with her for comfort, so the pig was now entirely Eliza's project. Eliza reached her house and stood outside the back door trying to catch her breath. She was bent over double, shaking, but would not allow the tears to flow. Despite her desire to cry it was a perverse form of excitement that she was feeling most; her skin tingled.

Eliza took a deep breath and entered the house. The sound of bagpipes was deafening. They broke their hum momentarily and then picked up another lament. Her father had his back to her; below his deerstalker his neck was inflated like the sack she once witnessed him drown cats in. He stopped playing to reposition the windbag under his arm.

'Dress her; your mother said that's what you want,' he said to the wall, his voice weak, some of it left in the bag. Eliza realised he was going to play through this grief. It had been his final pig and it meant as much to him, she knew, even if he didn't know how to show it.

'Yes, Father,' Eliza said.

'Corporal,' he said sternly. 'Call me corporal when I'm playing these pipes.'

'Yes, Corporal.'

Fingal McMillan had found it hard to slaughter this one remaining animal – its existence kept at bay the demise of his family's croft.

Eliza stood to attention behind her father, who remained facing the wall; he turned a little to her and flattened his moustache, wet his lips and once again faced the wall as he blew on the pipe. Eliza had briefly forgotten what his face looked like, and wondered if now, at this new dawn of death, at the death of his croft, it had changed and he must hide it.

Through the gap beneath her bedroom door Eliza could see the pig's trotters at the bottom of the bed. She dug her nails into her palms again but felt something more than lightness in her head, as though she were becoming somebody else, as though she too had a new face. The pig's demise had been so slow, the preparation for its end so exact, the croft's demise so incremental, that Eliza could hardly believe the point had been reached. She had a strange sense of feeling more alive, her adrenaline stirred. She crouched to her knees and didn't know whether to push the door or cry. But she didn't really feel like crying any more. Even when she had been down at the beach – it was from there she had come, fearing the final moment – she did not know whether it was right to blame her tears on the force of the wind. Even the water in her eyes was behaving in a new way.

The pipes were relentless, taking on thrusts and murmurs of life beyond the lungs of the player. Eliza took the book in her hand, the one she had been loaned by her school teacher: *Coming to the Gates of Death*, it was called; it was dated 1862. It was from the school library and had a silhouette of a dead body lying across the cover. It told what to expect of this other state, which it said brought the living with it; so death involved her too, she was discovering. It was the section on the work of undertakers to which she was mostly drawn. She enjoyed reading of their efficiency, the pride they took in the job, the contrast between their polished shoes and the upturned earth. Her teacher had believed that Eliza's understanding of this role, which the book termed 'a duty', and its particular codes of practice, would help her understand where her pig was going to next. The beautiful text on the front of the book read, 'By Isabella Bird'. Eliza had never heard of somebody called a bird before. She had also never previously held an original, handwritten book. The artefact was especially precious to her because it carried not only the author's signature but also an inscription on its inside page, two letters that had been written more haphazardly in another's hand – they read 'D,P,'. How odd the use of commas, Eliza thought.

She looked again at the trotters she had tended so religiously for the past week. She dry retched several times but was drowned out by the pipes. She had never seen death before and her grief was becoming intrigue. She rose to her feet and pushed open the door. At first she was struck by the foul compost smell in her room. She held her nose and ran through the dense air to the window and opened it. Bodies 'need to be aired', Isabella Bird had written, to allow the spirit to release, like bed sheets blowing in the wind. Eliza faced the window and saw the beach in the distance. She looked to the mainland, to where her mother had escaped on the new ferry. Eliza held her stomach once again, preparing to turn around.

Her pig looked somehow more naked on a bed. The sight of it caused an almighty shiver to run up Eliza's back to the crown of her head. It was a very different house to the one she had left only two hours earlier, when her pig had offered a grunt. Eliza would never know which particular wave had rushed to the shoreline at the precise moment when her pig finally went; which gull's cry had marked its collapse. She expected her pig's eyes to slowly open and engage her, as they had done only yesterday.

Eliza gulped for air and felt her heart drumming to the rhythm of the pipes. She breathed deeply and tried to be composed, as Isabella had said to do in the book. She quickly did her best with the available garments of her mother's that were folded on the chair, trying not to look too closely. She was more used to seeing her pig in the trough, but dressing her in a skirt and red cardigan was the correct thing to do, she was sure of that. She had recently finished a book called *Animal Farm* by George Orwell, which, along with Isabella Bird's book, had mostly inspired this response to her pig's end. In the book the animals had talked and seemed human to her. And so she had now cast her pig in the role of Mr Orwell's Minimus, to her father's Mr Jones. She fantasised that her pig was going to a ceilidh and not a grave. She held her pig's leg and at that moment her body collapsed onto the lump of death, dressed so prettily, as though it had taken to wearing Mrs Jones's clothes. She lay down beside it. The sight of the body clothed on the bed made Eliza think of the time she walked in on her mother bathing in the tub by the fire in their front room; it was the most beautiful sight she had ever seen. Now she heard the water as it fell gently down her mother's back on that day, each drop confirming that her mother was not only a farmhand in overalls, but also a woman. But her pig was only a shell. Something had left, flown out of the window, but Eliza felt sure that part of it was still here with her too.

The pipes stopped playing and Eliza stared at the door. How she wished she had an undertaker present to finish preparing her pig, to make her look beautiful, as she had read they could. She feared now that she was not up to the job. The only man who performed this duty was away on the mainland, where her mother was, and so it would be her father who would see to the transportation, if not the dressing. The book by Isabella Bird had told of clothing being applied, but it didn't mention this had ever been done to a pig. So this was her very own creation. It was easier for her to imagine that her pig was soon to attend a great farm-animal ball in the sky, where her skirt would turn. Eliza's heart raced once again as she heard the last ugly murmur of the pipes leave the bag. Her mother had told her that her father had been taught to play the pipes indoors, by his father, but that it was more common for men to learn in the open air, and by the tuning of their ear, which lent itself well to the fields of battle. Her mother had said her father had taken his pipes to Flanders, but he 'returned without the bag, and his puff spent'; she had also said that war was something that happened to those left behind at home.

She heard her father preparing for the journey; he had said he was going to go off and bury the pig. Then came the sound of him relieving himself in the outhouse. While he was there she quickly wrapped a shawl around the pig's shoulders, but screwed up her face at the lifelessness of the half-woman-half-pig. She moved to the door, but then returned to the pig, bent down and kissed its head. The pig was sticky on her lips. She closed her eyes as she did it and was overcome by the foul smell again. She got up and ran through the kitchen and out the front door, then stopped in her tracks. The plough had been taken off the back of the cart and now sat as a redundant lump, its teeth still holding bites of the land. Dead earth. Eliza knew what the plough had made room for and felt a hole inside her opening up.

She ran back through the bog towards the beach. She regretted not taking a final look, one for her absent mother too. There was release in the air, which she acknowledged and enjoyed with a sense of shame. No longer would she have to watch her pig suffer. The sky was white but for occasional lumps of grey. She had read they were called *stratus*, and it looked to her like the great expanse could never hold a sun or a moon again. Hawks darted and swooped. She slowed to a walk and tried to breathe as though it were any other day, until her tears came, in spite of the wind. She cried above the swoosh of busy wavelets. The pig was gone and all that was left was this hole. Had she made a mistake by dressing her up? The sand felt heavier underfoot.

*

Eliza's father was rougher than usual with the horses and had already made some progress. The cart swayed from side to side as he travelled along the coast where The Looming was believed to lie – that island of mystery which had never been seen by his generation. He would normally steal an enquiring glance in its direction but not today. The horses were doing their best to run away from this heavier form of death they were not used to carrying. He had laid down the shell of the pig in the cart that he used for transporting cattle to the market or the slaughterhouse in Fort William, on the mainland. Well, he knew now, there would be no more of that. He was going to dump the remains in the sea, and with it, his croft. It was the girl's wish to clothe the rotten lump. He had heard of folk burying their dead on their land, but he did not wish to be reminded of this pig with human pretensions. His lips stung from his lack of practice; despite puffing on a roll-up he could feel his lungs slowly becoming replenished. He enjoyed going towards the ocean, the sea was more a friend to him than the land had ever been. One day he would have his own vessel, something more than the pathetic remnants of a wooden rowing boat, which was his current craft. He had dragged it from the shore to dry land, where he would sit in it outside his croft, wishing for tide. That was his dream: to sail away in the direction of The Looming, to get away from this rotten version of himself and the things he had done.

Eliza kicked at the white sand more aggressively. She heard the cart rattle by as though it were part of another story, but stole a look. Her father's deerstalker, she noticed, was standing to attention as he passed in plumes of smoke. The pig was horizontal. She was relieved her father hadn't sat it up in the passenger seat. Briefly she thought she could see not the outline of the pig but the body of her mother. Then she caught a glimpse of herself in the water's reflection: this stretching, bobbing image of – what was the thing Isabella Bird spoke of? – grief. She felt it coming in waves, from the soft sand below, the skies above, and in the wind that bounced off her on the beach. Her knees gave way and she sank to the water's edge. She didn't notice as the blood from her palms stained the sand. Eliza looked to her friend, the Atlantic Ocean. Somewhere out there was another continent, sophistication, and other people – one of them her uncle who had emigrated to Canada – moving through their daily lives. Would she ever board the ferry and leave the island? She knew what the feeling was: she would never be free.

Her father returned late that evening and Eliza heard the horses blowing out. Her father opened the front door then move clumsily through the front room. A glass hit the stone floor and startled her. When she was very young she used to enjoy hearing him move around the house, when he was more sober and before he started touching her. She could hear the uncork of another bottle.

She lit her reading candle and pulled a book of American verse from the shelf beside her bed. She was fond of the American poetry books that her uncle had sent her. In his letter he had written of following the ripples of the families uprooted during the Clearances. It was to North America that she too longed to escape. Distant cries came from the livestock on the neighbouring croft; she imagined Mr Orwell's Old Major among them, and their sounds made her feel snug between the bed sheets; but she knew her impression was false. Still she was numb. She hoped her father would not step on the shards of glass but she knew better than to go into the front room. She would never do that at this hour, especially with her mother away. If only her mother and Napoleon the pup could have stayed. Eliza would see to the mess in the morning. Her mother had once said the war ruined her father. The War: it always surprised Eliza how such a thing could be summed up in two short words, as though it had been an event, a destination. It was even the subject of films, she had heard on the wireless. The War.

Eliza longed to leave but could not grow old enough or leave her mother. Her mother had told her not to let life pass her by, as though she suspected Eliza would remain a spectator for too long. She was too distracted to read and blew out the flickering candle. A mighty wind was building outside and finding cracks in the walls. There was further commotion in the other room. She heard her father stumbling to his feet. Often he wouldn't even make it to the outhouse and she would hear her mother crying, 'No Fingal!' And soon after, the sounds of her mother cleaning up his mess. Eliza could hear her father's footsteps getting louder. He turned the knob of her bedroom door. It released from the latch and Eliza trembled quietly. She faced the wall, pretending to sleep, and heard the whisky go down the back of his throat. She turned slowly and, peeking above the covers, could see him in outline. He groaned and she heard him say her mother's name. He stumbled from the door and landed at the bottom of her bed. The bottle hit the floor. He threw his deerstalker on the bed.

'Father!' she cried, trying to sit up. But she had the weight of his big frame on her now. 'Father!' Despite his broken state and the ruination of his body he was strong as an ox. Fingal rolled on top of his daughter. He wheezed and Eliza smelled the full effects of his drink-sodden state. She heard the buckle of his belt rattling and then felt the hardness of that thing below. She struggled her legs free of the bedclothes but he was stronger. She felt the hard thing on her skin and the tearing of her nightdress.

'No!' She fought to remove him, to lift him to the ceiling, to make him float to the sky. Her father fumbled with his free hand. The other he used to pin Eliza's flat chest down. 'Fingal!' she yelled. She felt the whiskers on her face. She couldn't stop what was happening so she tried in vain to avert her consciousness, to think once again of her pig, of the beautiful, desolate beach nearby, but the images disappeared giving way to blackness as she felt the pain of him entering her.

Her father rolled to the floor with a glump of his boots. His hand searched for the bottle, and then his hat.

'*There*,' she heard him mumble.

In the morning Eliza was awake before the cockerel's call. She cleaned up the mess, bathed thoroughly, and scrubbed and washed at her skin until it felt like somebody else's. She used one of the cattle brushes and worked so hard to remove him that she bled.

She often escaped to the lighthouse near the big village on the island, and it was to there that she would soon go. To the lighthouse. But first she lay numb on the bare mattress. She fished under her bed for what she liked to think of as the Book of the Dead, by Isabella Bird. Her hand alighted on her father's discarded whisky bottle and she flinched. Then she found a book but it was her copy of *Animal Farm*. She put it aside and eventually found the Bird book. As she brought it up onto her bed she noticed two loose leaves of yellowing paper. She quickly retrieved them from the floor. One was a short entry in a diary, written in a familiar handwriting. Eliza read to herself:

December 21st, 1862. Diary of Isabella Bird

(To whom it may concern: strictly not for publication.)

I feel I simply must document these events, if for no other reason than to explain to myself my actions, and to reacquaint my own self with reason. It was a terrible time, from which I will never recover. I received the telegram while in the Rocky Mountains. It had been sent weeks earlier. The familiar postmark was an immediate worry. My dear Hennie was dead. When I made it back home to the island the undertaker reassured me that only he saw the large, black peat hand stains on the back of my sister's dress. Well, it was the man he used for transporting his bodies who had done the deed. Still, despite his recklessness, the mess, as we shall call it, was tidied, and so I presented Punch with an original, handwritten work, my book on death, for it was helpful for me to share my grief. I had no desire to send it to John Murray in London for typesetting and publication. It was not meant for that. I was hopeful the man Punch could in fact read, as opposed to simply recognising the names of the recipients of letters on his round – if that would not have been an impressive enough feat in itself. I have no wish to travel any more. I fear that this island has seeped under my skin. He arrived, Mr Punch, back at my door one morning after she was gone with a delivery of more peat, his black eyes were lost in his face with grief, burdened, as if God the Father had sent him himself. And so I taught the man: I taught him properly, how to read and write. And, inadvertently, I realise in his own way he in fact taught me how to grieve.

But God was not the father, he was – Punch. It was a wonder I managed to conceal my dear sister from the island's gaze, but it was for her own good. But then, the poor thing, my dear Hennie, oh she tragically died, in childbirth. She lasted until the child's cry and then she went, wrapped in Punch's wretched jacket. I do fear now that my arrangement, as it were, that the nurse should take the baby as her own, was evidence of my Playing God. I do hope my secret is safe here on the island, if not from the maker. But it is done, and the lady was more than willing. And I take some comfort in that, as I do of the fact Mr Punch can now read. And he can now tell the time, for I bought him a watch for the end of his chain. Which then got me thinking of a project on this theme, on a much bigger scale . . .

As I return to the page on this coldest of mornings oh dear bliss I have seen six swans on the seafront, near where Henrietta used to sit, what beauty! They came to me – a mother, father and their swanlings, like a line of white light in the winter's sky. And I considered whether I shall stay to watch the child grow up. 'Fingal', the nurse and her people have called him. He is a McMillan. They are croft people, so at least I do not need to suffer the baby in the village, if that is the correct way of seeing things. Punch gave a nod of satisfaction. I think it was at the choice to wrap the baby in a woollen shawl knitted by his mother, the white house woman. But the trouble is, for all my travels around the world, I had never seen anything like this, like the situation I found myself in, and had to deal with. And so all I can do now, as I write, is be enchanted by these *swans – the symphony of the swans; this high-pitched refrain, which rises and tends to remind one of an infant crying. Oh father. Oh dear sister!*

Here the entry stopped, but Eliza was briefly thrilled to see this document from the same author as the book about death. And then confusion set in. Why was her father mentioned? Or, given the date of the letters, and the distinctiveness of the name, was it in fact her *father*'s father? For he too had been Fingal. She wrapped herself more tightly in her mother's dressing gown and began to unfold the accompanying piece of paper, which was written in another's hand.

1861, Letter To Isabella:

'What on earth is the matter with you, sister?' I know you, my dearest Isabella, will say. But it was only once. By now you will be shaking your head in confusion. I must come right out with it and you my dear should prepare yourself for an almighty shock: I am with child, I know it. It is such a relief to tell another. But folk will think me a shameful thing. Mr Punch's it is. You will have your hands to your mouth, my ownest, but you must not return from your trip. That would only add weight to my already heightened sense of guilt. Your readers in this modern age do so need you to share your pioneering story of travels through America's wild west. The first time I saw his dark eyes, it took me by such surprise. I already knew him. It is love, it must be.

I hope you my dearest can forgive me. I have been so fortunate to receive your wonderful letters, but I have never been anywhere, never where I wanted to be, and then suddenly, I was there. I am here. I fear movement in dear father's grave for this act out

of wedlock. But I never want to wash my skin again. All I am
left with is this want, this need, to the disregard of common
sense. And it will never be any different. I should get back to the
house, I am writing this by the pier, where you know I like to sit
nearby the fishermen's creels. If these terrible vomiting fits which
have befallen me will subside then I will surely add more to this
account so that you can try to understand. But for now, you can
know that I have found it, that thing you wished me to believe in:
Duncan Punch.

Your own pet,
Hennie

Eliza replaced the pieces of paper inside the handwritten book. She realised now that she had heard of these sisters at school, but had no idea to what they were referring or who she could ask. She felt a throb of pain between her legs and knew she must leave the croft. She had heard of livestock being 'pulled out' for prevention, but was sure her father hadn't. Could he have filled her up with babies, as had been done to this woman Hennie? She knew then that even after the bruising faded, wherever she went, she would always feel her father's weight on her. She would forever be burdened by this violation, given to a belief that it had been her fault, her dead pig, her door off the latch, her elusiveness, and her stupid desire to give the pig a human ending – all of which had made possible his pitiful desire.

She *did* say no. Surely she had screamed it aloud. Eliza was certain she had. But she also feared that maybe she had encouraged the union by simply being female. She envied these Bird sisters for being dead, as she had the filthy water as it escaped down the plug, on its journey to the earth; but worse

– she envied her dead pig for having exited this story and, like Mr Orwell's Old Major, for having been more human than she would ever feel again.

9

The Writer

2009

W*hat tense, the sea?* I am a man of fifty staring at the Atlantic Ocean, looking northeastwards at something I used to be. I glimpse an outcrop of rock in the sea and, becoming disorientated, my hopes rise then fall again. I realise it is not The Looming, that mythical island of my youth which was said to lie to the west of my own, but simply the base of an American lighthouse, the full disclosure of which has been obscured by the sun. This catches me unawares. I have not considered the direction of The Looming for some time; instead I have preferred the incontestable, the irrefutable – yes, for a long time now my constant has been this more conclusive shore of the Atlantic. I look once more for The Looming. Just as a stopped clock tells the right time twice a day, the community in which I grew up believed a sighting of the island could validate their existence twice a century, as though it were some form of periodical astronomical wonder.

You never can know what you will end up doing with your life, how you will seek that validation, but I could never have predicted my half-century's journey to this place, and to what I do for a dollar. Not that it ever really feels like work. On any given day I can be pulling up weeds, or answering fan mail, fielding emails from publishers around the world, or driving him into the city for a meeting. Or, on special days, swinging in a hammock listening to one of the finest writers of our time reading his famed work aloud to me, just me.

I feel my left hip vibrate, a sensation that, in its own small way, complements the roar of the ocean, and look down to retrieve the pager – he still prefers to use a pager, the Writer – and the message reads:

Alexander – can you pick me up some relish and slices of that smoked turkey from that nice lady at the deli? Make her thinly sliced – the turkey.

He doesn't know I am some forty miles away, having on my day off decided to follow a desire, a once-familiar tick. But I am happy to oblige the Writer – I am quite peckish myself. I should make it back in time for a late lunch and, I hope, some time in the hammock. He will only read his old work to me now, saying it will help him with new ideas, but I fear he might never have those again. He is old but still youthful in his demeanour, teenage even, as the very tall can be. Occasionally he asks me about the Hebridean island of my birth; my Scottish roots, he calls them.

He is particularly interested in The Looming, the mysterious island 'that never was', as he puts it. And so I will talk a little about the people and way of life which are lost to me now. Sometimes, to make this separation feel less melancholy, perhaps even to bridge the disconnect, I like to think of the mass of land on which this country sits as a large island. But when I explained that to the Writer, he couldn't help dryly reasoning that someone, most likely of Spanish origin, must have decided it would be better described as a continent.

But he knew what I meant. He finds very simple things funny, the Writer. He is comfortable in his own skin in the way a man with a lifetime of global success might expect to be. He has the confidence to smile broadly in recognition of his way with a joke, with a humorous turn of phrase, of mouth. Perhaps I hope some of that will rub off on me.

He is at ease with, even proud of, being known in this patch of Connecticut woodland simply as 'the Writer'. The term could just as readily identify him throughout the US; no mean feat given the thousands of other very good writers who reside here. Is he ready to die? Is he nearing the final bookend of his life? It's true that he seems to appreciate the tall, knotted, groping trees that surround him more and more each day. And he hums a lot.

I get in the Writer's car, or rather one of them, which he has bequeathed to me. I put on my sunglasses and begin to drive away from the lighthouse, the sea, my past. I think I will need to come back here again. I have missed the ocean. On my return journey, even when I have already travelled more than twenty miles, I can still hear its roar in my ears. Maybe it is always there in my eardrums, lying dormant for undetermined periods, only to re-emerge as a raging, rollicking presence, and remind me of a young woman's tragic fall, of another lighthouse, another landscape, a folklore I cannot refuse. However much I might wish to. Maybe it is a part of me I cannot deny. It was angry today, the ocean, and very possibly at me.

What tense, the sea?

And so off I go in search of thinly sliced turkey ham. As I drive in the direction of the nice lady with the surgeon's headgear and the lethal meat-slicing machine, I notice red neon dots along the highway. They advertise the upcoming programme at the local amphitheatre, which I know to be there but which is hidden from view by tall trees. Collectively the dots spell out: 'Santana – September 13th 2009'. Here is another man who can be recognised globally by his surname alone.

In spite of these humdrum tasks, there are perks of the job. Despite growing up on an island which, to this day – I suspect, I no longer have family there – still functions without a cinema, I am a genuine friend, by way of my association with the Writer, of our neighbour, the actress Mia Farrow. And despite her general air of discretion I am privy to delicious stories, little gems such as the extraordinarily large feet of Woody Allen's mother.

I have a pleasant enough conversation with the lady at the deli. I know how the Writer likes it, she tells me, as though he and his taste buds belong to her and her alone. I drive back to the secluded, roaming expanse of acres on which I live in a small stone cottage, or 'bothy' as he likes to call it – this, he tells me, to remind me of my crofting upbringing. I have suggested a cockerel would complete the effect. As a renowned heterosexual he is comfortable to share his pile with a wholly unrenowned homosexual. I did try to write myself, but instead my life has wandered off course, possibly due to that instinct of mine to side with life's incontestables. As a result, I am filling the role of personal assistant to a writer. But what a writer.

I prepare lunch and take it through to his sitting room at the front of the house. There he is, with a thick brick of historical biography on his lap, framed by squares of white-surround windowpanes. He tells me fiction becomes less interesting the older you get, you know too much truth – and so he has been flirting with Stalin, Hitler, and more recently, Joseph Kennedy (there is crossover, he tells me). He is still in his dressing gown, but there are denims underneath. We are halfway there. We eat and his sparrow-like face occasionally smiles and nods, chewing enthusiastically into what remains of the turkey sandwich that he waves at me from his lean, lined, relish-stained hands. I'm unclear if this sign of approval is for me or the lady at the deli. He always eats a sandwich with both hands, his long fingers clutching either end as though it might fly away on him. He looms over the long wooden table that perpetually houses books, newspapers and an assortment of spectacles. We are both almost finished lunch when I ask him:

'What tense, the sea?'

'Mmm?' He lets his reading glasses drop, and twists the string. He takes a few final bites and rubs his eyes enthusiastically.

'What tense does the sea *inhabit*?'

'I get it already,' he says, reapplying his glasses, his expanse of forehead creasing below the familiar hair. He looks mock sternly at me over the rims. I'm increasingly getting to know that look, it means, *We're not quite ready for tearing the black ribbons yet, dear boy*. He lets the glasses fall again. 'Because I get *you*, Alexander.' He delivers that line eyes wide open, with an incredulous smile.

'It depends,' he says lazily, flipping his armchair and reclining to what he calls first-class position; I study the trademark brackets which frame his moustache. Like a clown, he gives the impression of perpetual sadness. I realise I have seen the expression before, on Fingal, my grandfather.

'It depends on . . . on the sea? The ocean?' I ask.

He tilts his head further back and bobs it skywards,

expectantly, as though he is looking for the appropriate words to fall into his mouth.

'It depends on you,' he says finally, scratching his nose and pulling his green blanket over him. 'Or whoever *is* this voyeur.' He hums a short melody and tucks the blanket up to his prominent Adam's apple, which I realise was also a distinguishing feature of my grandfather. 'The sea has many possibilities, so we mustn't be too hasty in ruling out the future – the future is a cunning carrot, it opens up many potential storylines. We always need the right "wrong" topic to kickstart any narrative.' He scrunches his eyes more tightly, as if to peer further into this potential future, as though if he screwed them tightly enough he might see something of significance through the dark void, or perhaps what lies beyond C. S. Lewis's wardrobe. 'Go on, admit it,' he jibes, 'you expected me to say something awful like, "Your answer becomes apparent as each wave crashes, and with them the arc of the story will develop, piece by . . . *wave*?"'

'Guilty as charged, your honour,' I deadpan.

'No. I feel the matter warrants further consideration, Alexander . . .'

Soon I hear the Writer snoring. I swing to the sound of perhaps the world's most famous novelist belting out a parting gesture which would make a sea liner proud, from his long, rugged, Jewish nose.

The next day the ocean is still troubling me; I can still hear its roar. We sit over breakfast discussing an approach that has come in overnight from a director in Hollywood.

'Send it to the agency,' he instructs, in that alluringly singsong voice, while holding a piece of half-eaten toast above the front page of the *New York Times*.

'I have already.'

'Thank you Alexander, you do a good job – always *thinking*, so I don't have to. I won't start on the Oscars acceptance speech quite yet ...' He blows the text free of crumbs.

'No.'

'He's not in my good books anyway – the director,' he says, stifling a yawn. 'He needs a twat.'

'The same has been said of me ...'

'Ha!' He smiles broadly. I can almost see the streets of Newark lined on his face.

'I haven't heard that word in a while,' I say.

'Well you have just made a very common mistake – if a funny one. No. It is seldom that people use *twat* now in its strictest, most powerful, sense.'

'Which is?'

He waits until he swallows. 'As a verb. To punch a guy's lights out.'

'Ah.'

'I mean, to punch *his* or *her* lights out. I'm forever upsetting feminists in this way.'

I move onto the other unopened letters piled on the linen tablecloth; the Writer's mother always had her own mother's linen on the kitchen table, and now so do we. It has travelled with him to London, to New York, through marriages, and now to here. *Don't harm mother's linen!* he is wont to exclaim, in overly dramatic fashion. I don't know for sure but I guess he is resurrecting the delivery of his long departed father. The kitchen table in the croft on which I was raised had no cloth at all, linen or otherwise. Instead it sat naked below my grandfather's vacant stares, an occasional landing station for his deerstalker.

From that kitchen I went to Edinburgh University, and then to London – where I spent ten years accumulating a taste for red wine and urban bicycling, floating on the edges of the burgeoning literary scene that followed, yes Amis, Barnes, McEwan and Rushdie, without ever really breaking through; instead I worked at a bunch of publishers in various roles and from there I emigrated to Canada. I always knew I had family in Canada, my mother's uncle having taken the same course as me some sixty years earlier, but I never sought them out. Somehow my mother's death, or the nature of my mother's death, has always followed me as an embarrassment of sorts, one which keeps me distant. Despite being on the surface an amiable enough presence, something inside me always closes down the prospect of pursuing autobiographical conversation. It is probably the reason most of my relationships have never lasted long – the fall, *her* fall, is always there, casting a shadow.

The Writer has gotten closer than most. I'm not sure how much of that intimacy we share, of his ability to prise me apart, is down to the simple fact he is heterosexual and therefore not a genuine threat, or is it due to the fine-tuning of his enquiring mind. From Canada I moved again, this time to a literary agency in New York City, and it was there that, thrillingly, over time, I came into daily contact with the Writer. When I received a surprising invitation to come and work for him full-time, well, I jumped at it. I have been with him now for five years. But really, I wonder now if all my trans-Atlantic journeying has simply led me back to where I began, to the sea, and to the island; I am part of the sheep's coat left on the barbed wire fence. The ocean has followed me; I just can't escape its grey, rolling mass – its truth. I seem still to be searching for the light my grandfather once spoke of.

'This one looks interesting,' I say, applying the letter opener.

'Mmm?' he looks up.

'It has the White House seal on it ...'

'My deportation, finally ... or, actually,' his bushy eyebrows jump mischievously (they are not unlike those cultivated by the fishermen around whom I grew up) – 'maybe yours ...' He grasps another piece of toast and troubles his mouth. His eyebrows now wilfully realign themselves, reordered like two caterpillars waiting in line above his stop-sign eyes.

I read the letter and then, after blinking a few times in recognition, I pass it to him. He places it on top of the article he was reading and then, after he has fully digested its contents he erupts – *Ha!* – and slaps the table with the palm of his hand. I almost jump. This is something he often does when he is surprised or amused. It is something my grandmother used to do. She would bring her hand down on the croft's kitchen table on the rare occasions when she laughed, and with it I would startle. But I consider the gesture differently now, as a dying art that translates freely between the Celts and the Jews.

My gaze is taken by his 1998 Pulitzer Prize, which stands on guard next to his bread bin, a reminder of what it must keep bringing into the house. And I recall that I read the news – that he was to receive this prize – while on my journey back to the island; my last time home. My grandmother was already dead by then. I had returned for a memorial service, which was to mark the tenth anniversary of that terrible Lockerbie disaster. I can still recall the young lad, Jake, playing his violin to the crowd at the service. He would have been about fourteen. It seemed that most of the island had come out. I can still recall the beauty of the lone violin, piercing through grief, filling each grain of the wooden acoustics in the old town hall as the crowd gathered in silence. There they stood in rain-soaked clothes, each considering, no, accepting, a note for themselves, as the music fell from Jake's strings in tribute to one of the island's lost sons. It is almost too painful to think about.

'Will you accept?' I ask, attempting to silence the violin playing in my head, the notes rising still.

He removes his glasses and puts his toast down on the letter. I recognise his expression; he has the open, confused face of a child still searching for the burst balloon. 'I fear my dear mother would never cease turning in her grave if I didn't; she'd end up on the other side of New Jersey. Let me work on a reply. The man is a man of letters after all, not just a President. Actually,' he places both his hands to support his lower back, 'given the hereditary shape of my family's spines, it is unlikely we can turn in our graves at all. Instead we would have to burrow our dissatisfaction.'

The letter is an invitation to the White House to accept the National Humanities Medal.

He rises from the breakfast table and I see he has sneakers on below the hem of his dressing gown. 'I was thinking *this* might work, for the ceremony?' He stretches out his arms to fully reveal his attire, playing the part of the Central Park flasher.

'Perfect. Maybe just wipe off the crumbs.'

'*Crrumbs* . . .' he mimics me, 'you Celts get so much more out of a word. 'I'm reminded of my favourite line of all fiction, which is James Joyce's in *Ulysses*, when Bloom sees Gerty MacDowell on the beach, his hand is fiddling in his pocket somewhat mischievously, '"At it again," he says!' He crumples with laughter. '"At it ... *again*,"' he repeats incredulously, laughing into his chest and then it seems the laughter is penetrating his soul. He is faced with a joke he cannot get enough of, get rid of, alone with it – as I have seen before in the old – frozen in his own private history, which we cannot understand. He fully savours its repeated joy but really it is pain, a form of crying, which must remind him of another time, or an earlier version of himself.

I recall my uncles had the same stamina for a joke. I think of the characters which populated my youth on the island, men who were blessed with a similar succinctness, a resignation to laughter, and – what else was it? I have never been able to capture nor fully comprehend what it was that made them so funny, and also, I realise now, so universal. Often the Writer will say my full name, *Alexander McMillan*, just to satisfy his desire for a rhotic syllable; but I tease him, he sounds more like Mel Gibson's *Braveheart* than the real deal.

'"At it again" ...' I chuckle.

'Huh?' he straightens up and looks confused. Then, just when I fear I have briefly lost him to the oncoming years, to the fog of his future closing in, to the ghost of Mailer, he turns and asks, 'Alexander – do you need to go back to the sea today?'

I nod.

'Go. And listen,' he says. 'You can't get an apple by just looking at the tree. And consider Eliza. You know, we do also throw ourselves away, off the cliff if you will, to become an artist.' I am left wondering why he says this last bit, and why now. He leaves the room, already off to his study, to face up to the President (whom he has supported from afar) with a pen on a page – this, the only way he knows how to duel. But then he returns, standing with one foot in the kitchen, and a thick pencil behind his ear, as though he is a joiner returned for measurements he has forgotten to take. I have never seen him look more serious. 'Was it her, Alexander; on that stormy evening? And could she have come from The Looming?'

A strange thing happens on the drive to the ocean. Whether by the Writer's prescription, or because it is the work of the ether, I do start to think about my mother. She has been lurking, I fear. And then my thoughts are taken up by my grandfather too, Fingal McMillan, and his boat *Eliza*. I pull over into a parking lot, still some twenty minutes from the ocean. The Writer will say, *But Alexander, you took your love of the word from Eliza, from her very own* Animal Farm *– that, surely, is why you are here?* He will say that as if he knew her, as if he knows more than I do; and I wonder now if that is the work of the novelist – to know more than I do. Because that is the only detail of significance he does know of my past (the name of my mother, and that she died tragically) other than my stories of the island's myths, and the beauty of its landscape. But in my weaker, and more arrogant moments, I come to think that I guess these details are enough, a carrot of potential plotline dangled to keep me here, to keep him interested in me. And, knowing my mother's love of literature, I hope she would not have minded being cast in the form of such a vegetable, so to speak, and to such a writer.

But still, I am confident enough of the work I do here, of the experience I have gained, to more often keep the chitchat to bookish relevance. I suspect he knows there is more. Occasionally he will say, *Tell me more about your grandfather's boat*. (He has a penchant for the terminology, the mythology, of boats; the rigging, the masts. But has never owned a boat – he tells me there wasn't much of a tide flowing through the streets of Newark.)

In those moments I really have to pinch myself – that I am here, with the man who wrote the great American novels of the late twentieth century, and still – he wishes to hear *my* stories. It leaves me in a strange state. There really is nobody left from that other, past, world, whom I can tell this to, with whom I can share my incredulity. There is no one else who can provide context for the divide between what I was, *where* I was, and where I am now, to gasp at the ridiculousness of the situation; to make it a shared, albeit absurd experience, and to realign the tenses of the sea. There is nobody to tell me, 'You're a lucky bastard McMillan,' as indeed my childhood (or is he lifelong?) blood-brother Charlie would have done. And if you can't share such a thing then it just resonates above your head, out of reach, floating like the string notes of grief or the ghost of a burst balloon.

I am now inclined to tell the Writer more about *Eliza*, the old rowing boat, in the knowledge it will lead on to Eliza, the woman, the mother, the potential protagonist; in the hope it will lead on to the tale he will spin of that evening when – or so he believes – she appeared as if dried by the sea, as a mermaid ghost to the sound of the Bay City Rollers. I don't know whether I should suspend my disbelief in the hope it might spark the Writer's curiosity enough that he might then return his focus to filling up a page, and to a girl's life cut short, the lifeblood of fiction. I get to fearing that if the Writer does not fill up any more pages then my work here will die out, or he will, and I will be returned to the banal, to the sea, to the island, to face my past. Maybe only by becoming a character in one of his stories, can I keep him alive.

And so I sit, twenty miles away from the ocean's familiar, sweet smell (it too must be stored in my body without my knowing). On the passenger seat, where sometimes he reclines to the sounds of his favourite Shostakovich, *String Quartet No. 15*, sits my mother's copy of *Animal Farm*. It means everything to me that her hands once touched these pages. It is the only part of her that was saved from the croft. Well, apart from me. The croft went into terminal decline after my grandfather rowed off.

I sit here in the lot of a shopping strip, facing the dark wood-panelled interior of an old-fashioned barber's shop. The Writer's protagonist, Herman Cotton, in his masterpiece, *The Blemish of Man*, might himself frequent this shop to get a short back and sides. I think of that generation of America's men who maintain the haircut as a reminder of their youth, their strength, their time in the service of their great nation, before Elvis, before the sixties, before that decade's sense of freedom ruined everything for them. I wonder whether those men, those God-fearing architects of the suburban dream, would have appreciated my grandfather's paintwork: GOD IS LOVE.

I realise I can hear it already and need not go any further. It is the sound of the cycle of waves that constitutes the ocean. I put my hand on *Animal Farm*; the book and the ocean are all I have left of my mother. Thinking of my grandfather, the way in which he left us, makes me realise it is he who has made the sea such a puzzle. I can hear his voice now; *Call me skipper.* It is because he went to the sea without telling me, never to return, that I cannot fathom my relationship to it – past, present or future. *I will go to the sea. I am at the sea. I have been to the sea.*

To Eliza.

I realise I have not travelled at all; my life has been bookended by the Atlantic Ocean. Now, over thirty years on, the pragmatist in me wants to believe that the Writer is wrong, that it wasn't her. I never saw her, Eliza. I couldn't have. Maybe only Charlie did? Maybe the Writer wrote it?

But I wonder now, with more maturity and the undeniable advancement of years, that if it *was* her then, during those few seconds that Eliza and Charlie spent alone in front of his brother's Vauxhall Victor, did they form a pact to protect me? Perhaps just with a few words, or a knowing look, or her hand on his forearm. Maybe that is all it would take for two people who love you to cast such a spell. But I'll never know. And I recall that just a year later, in 1977, Elvis died, the king of the haircut, and the very land on which I now stand, a man who in three or four thrusts of his hips made the world an island.

I start up the car. I want to believe. I look again to the urban landmass before me, towards what I know to be the direction of the ocean, The Looming. I realise that island of rock is like the tide: you never truly see it, only its effects, what it washes in. I hear the engine ticking over as Charlie's once did, and I feel something new. I am open to all possibilities, both fiction and fact. And it hits me: the Writer is correct – even though I have never seen a photograph, because one was never taken, I believe now that she *was* in fact Eliza. She had to be, because she has stayed with me ever since. And until I met the Writer I had not told another living soul about her. As far as

179

I'm aware, neither did Charlie. Now I realise I chose never to mention her appearance and the events of that night again because I feared that if I did, then my mother might never reappear. And to this day she hasn't. But I'll keep looking, and waiting, knowing one day that smell will return.

❧ 10 ❧

The Government of Nouns

2009

IN MEMORY OF MY OWNEST AND DEAREST PET,
HENRIETTA BIRD, FROM HER SISTER ISABELLA BIRD,
THIS CLOCK WAS OFFICIALLY UNVEILED BY
CHARLES DARWIN, FRS.
JULY 1864

From her seated position below the plaque on the town clock Adrianna peeled open the scrunched-up piece of paper she had recently found on her neighbour's floor, the old man Mr Ivor, who kept the chickens she liked to visit. She tried to read his handwriting:

What I am feeling now could well be something to do with a lightness, or perhaps weightlessness is a better way of putting it. All this putting pen to paper has left me empty. And fuck. I wonder if you have reached inside my chest and plucked my heartstrings, Mr President? Something has changed since I have been writing to you. I have been silenced. And fuck. As I sit, I watch with no control as the sun takes ownership of my garden. I see the girl from next door, sitting alone the way she does, with the sun her backdrop. Her features are lost to me. And fuck. How reliably the sun turns things into outlines of what they once were. Just a shape remains; and then, long after, only a memory of that shape.

And one such memory rushes shockingly to me now, of my father as he was at his end, in a darkened room with the island's early morning light streaming through an open curtain behind him, and you see, his body's outline was convulsing violently as he sat in his chair with his lungs fading as now mine do.

I hope I have ended my life a better man than him. But that morning I watched him a long time in his chair before attempting to do anything to help his pathetic situation. And then he died, right in front of me. Just as he forced me to murder innocent doves. And fuck. Now these are all I have – memories. I can tear off a page and scrunch it into a ball but I cannot discard these words and feelings as much as I would like to. It is the memory of the brightness of that sun that clouds me now. And fuck. I am waiting to see my brother again. Little miracles must come with death; because this did happen, a plane did fall, and he is not here.

I've decided I won't send you any of these silly letters that gather here. No. Maybe the pen has done its job and there is no need. You're not doing so badly without me. Megrahi too has a chance to be a better man. He is freed from my handcuffs. Now I must sleep. I am tired. Every person has a time. Even you, Mr Barack Obama, the miracle maker . . .

Adrianna stopped reading at the unfinished line. The writing looked very old to her and almost like the written Polish of her mother. She wondered why was he writing to President Obama. She was flattered to have been mentioned, noticed even. On the few occasions she had been in his house she had seen piles of paper on his living room table, where he liked to sit, sometimes dressed in a police uniform and slippers. He always had a mug full of pens and pencils next to him, and the mug had a picture of the two smiling little men from the TV on it. She had listened one time to the old man as he sat in his chicken coop talking about the plane and all the people that died; on that night he had fallen asleep holding a can of beer.

Adrianna didn't want to spend her summer holidays cleaning rental homes on the island; she wanted to be a miracle maker. She watched the seagulls sitting on the strip of sand on the seafront below the main street; they had arranged themselves near the water's edge in orderly lines as though in worship of the sun, each facing the light like barrel-chested little emperors. She knew she was alone in noticing how perfectly the gulls positioned themselves. The other children sometimes threw stones at them, which disrupted this beautiful order, but Adrianna always liked to sit patiently until the gulls returned to their places. Even her mother, when Adrianna dragged her down to the seafront to witness this phenomenon, had questioned what beauty her daughter could see. But Adrianna was sure she could control this display.

The sun had retreated so she walked from the clock over to the white railings that ran the length of the seafront. Down below, the gulls were beginning to disband, in so doing ending their ritual as the evening tide crept in. As they took off, some became silhouettes just as Adrianna had in Ivor's letter. She had no clue he could even write. Somehow reading his description made her feel more alive. She could be the miracle maker. She needed to do something special for the old man but she had no idea what.

Adrianna walked up through the town and stopped at the island's War Memorial. Above a list of names were the larger words: *Our Dead.* She looked to the names. They meant nothing to her but for a moment she saw lives, imagined parts of their anatomy, what their dead bodies would look like now buried underground or scattered in fields. In school they had been told about the world wars and how Poland had suffered more than most countries. That had embarrassed her and given more power to the class bullies. The memorial had a beauty too: she was discovering everything had if you looked closely enough – even Ivor. If she looked really closely she could see it in the way the names were aligned. She walked further up to the beginning of Transmitter Road and soon arrived at the gate of old Ivor's house. She wanted to see the injured chick. Adrianna was surprised to see Mr Ivor sitting in the chicken coop.

'Oh, hullo lass, you're a quiet foot right enough. We could have done with you in the service. And fuck.'

'Hello, Mr Punch. A quiet what?'

'Oh, never mind,' croaked Ivor, 'you'd have been handy on the Christmas tree run too. Never mind though.'

'How is she?' Adrianna asked, ducking her head fully in through the doorway.

'The chick? *Gorbachev?* He's recovering fine. We'll have him working that phone of yours soon.'

Adrianna smiled. 'Why you say Gorba ...?'

Ivor motioned behind him. 'You've not seen the stain on his head?'

She shook her head.

'Oh never mind.' Ivor turned in frustration to the West. 'Is nobody old any more?' He looked directly to the chick in

184

question. 'On better days I've seen the little bastard start a revolution in here right enough though. And fuck.'

'What is *the service*?'

'Oh. I was in the police force lass – that's what we called it. You won't know but I was the local bobby. That's why I have so few visitors.'

'Is that why you wear a badge all the time?'

'Aye.' Ivor touched his sergeant's badge, which was fastened to his blue cardigan.

'And the police hat too?'

'We call it a helmet; it's a helmet.' Ivor touched the rim. 'Aye well. Even in retirement you never know when you might be called upon, especially the way this world is heading. And fuck.'

'But the old man visits you though. I see him?'

'Randy? Oh aye. The irony is I locked him up more than most.' Ivor patted down his cardigan. 'It's a wonder he leaves this house a free man, even now. Do you know the idiot once tried to revive a dead goldfish in his, what do you call it, his microwave? There's the intelligence ... The bugger's got fancy – I've seen the day when a hot breath on a horse would have been cooking enough. He's forever getting the wrong end of the stick. It's in the blood. It is repeated even now that when Randy's father first heard the news of Kennedy's assassination he was devastated, believing it was Fergus Kennedy, a local folk singer, who had perished.' Ivor shook his helmet. 'And to think he is trusted with driving the Mobile Bank. I came to his rescue a few times there too. Anyway, he is soon to retire from the bank van. Sir Tom Whatshisname and the rest of the world's money men can rest easy.'

'My mum ...' Adrianna began, but then stopped; instead

she leaned back to look into the straw behind her in the coop. She knew she had better not mention she had taken Ivor's discarded letter from his house.

'He's still sleeping,' offered Ivor, 'and his wing is improving. These buggers have five-star treatment here. And fuck. It's cosier than a cell back there.'

'A cell?'

'Oh never mind. What about your mum?'

'She says that you ... are a sad old man.'

'Well ...' Ivor's Adam's apple moved quickly up and down like a ballcock.

'She says you are sad about the plane?' Adrianna looked into Ivor's black eyes for the first time. Usually she avoided people's eyes.

'Yes. And fuck. I am sad. But it's better than being angry. For many years I was an angry shit. Excuse the French, it might even be Polish ...' Ivor's mouth curled at the ends and he coughed into his hands.

As Adrianna giggled, she noticed for the first time how one of his arms was shorter than the other. She asked: 'What makes you so sad?'

'My girl, you can't know everything.' He wiped the phlegm from his hands on the ground. Adrianna noticed it was almost black like treacle.

'I don't know everything. I know *that*,' Adrianna said.

'That's a good place to start.'

'Are you, like ... okay?' Adrianna leaned closer to him.

'I have never spoken about it. And fuck.' Ivor shuffled his backside along the ground, closer to the injured chick. He peeked his head into the straw. 'No. Never. Only four people ever knew. Not even Randy – *especially* not Randy.' Ivor

186

forced a smile through his brown teeth. His face reminded Adrianna of a Halloween mask.

'But then I sometimes think I know too much already,' Adrianna said. She noticed a bit of straw had stuck to Ivor's stubble as he brought his head back up. She moved her hand gently to his face and removed it.

'Well, hardly a surprise, what with your personal phones and everything!' Ivor let out a sound like an explosion. 'Sit down close to me lass. Aye, your generation knows plenty right enough!' He coughed again into his cupped hands and wiped it on the ground.

'We do?' Adrianna asked.

'Knowledge is power, that's what they say, right enough,' said Ivor. 'I never knew anything. I was stupid. Don't be a stupid bastard.'

'No,' said Adrianna. 'But I know about a lot of things that happen in the world, Mr Ivor. In other places.'

'Oh really? Well, that's grand. Too many on the island think this is the world.' Ivor choked. 'I was one of them. But . . .'

'I watch the TV. I have a friend in the Middle East.' Adrianna realised she had never told another living soul about this. 'I look for her on the TV. We are friends on Facebook.'

'Well that's no surprise. And fuck. You should let that young brain of yours rest once in a while, mind, you might find it liberating. Like taking a shit in the woods.'

Adrianna watched another strand of straw fall from Ivor's cheek, floating to join the others below. 'Could I bring my seagull to this coop, to get better?' she asked.

'What? A gull?' Ivor straightened his helmet.

'It's just . . .' Adrianna looked at the old man again, to his still head, 'you're so good at fixing things. It has only one leg.'

'Fixing things? Like what?' Ivor gradually sat upright; he was warming to this new status. He kicked the door closed with his boot.

'Like the chick, Gorbachev.' Adrianna nodded back to the straw; she heard her own voice and the way she said chick sounded like 'cheek'. She could almost hear the local girls' voices mimicking her.

'Well, that is just a wing. Really, I've mostly broken things in my life. And fuck. No – I can't grow back legs I'm afraid; I can barely grow an arm by fuck.' Ivor stopped. Adrianna could see his eyes were wet. 'Yes I've broken a few whales, a human heart, the hopes of doves, fuck – even the law!'

'Doves?' asked Adrianna.

Ivor went on: 'I smashed it down right enough, with my own teenage hands. I did that at least.'

'What?'

'The dovecote; I tore the fucking thing down. My father thought it was the wind that did it.' Ivor looked straight at Adrianna but she could tell he was glazing over; really he was looking at these doves he spoke of, she knew that. The coop was made even more intimate, dead sounding, by the hay bales and now the closed door. 'I thought if I healed Gorbachev then, well,' Ivor shifted embarrassedly, 'a few less doves I slaughtered with a rifle will turn in their graves, or in the sky, or wherever the fuck they are.' He flinched at the mention of the sky and looked back down to the chick. 'It will not heal the past though. And fuck. Really it's just a feather in the dove.'

There was a moment of silence between them.

'And fuck. I never broke one thing though,' Ivor erupted, shaking his head to the grassy ground; then he punched it.

'What?' Adrianna kept still and tried not to look alarmed; despite his frailty she had felt the force of his fist on the ground in her backside. It was more alarming because he then removed his cardigan to reveal the rest of his uniform. She saw now that his name was stitched into his chest – 'I. Punch'.

'I never broke a promise. And fuck, lass. You don't know everything! This is one thing anyway you'll not see on that intelligent phone of yours ... you see, the plane fell and I could never tell. Not then. Not before then either, really ...'

'You like to stop talking now?' Adrianna asked; her mother had told her how the old people in the care home where she worked liked to talk about the past but it could make them very tired and sad. But Mr Ivor went on talking more quickly as if she weren't there:

'No. I never broke that. You see, I was already a young police officer – a man of authority requiring of respect, what a joke! – and so it would have been a scandal. But I am an old twat – I should have spoken up when he was older. The boy should have known.'

'What? What boy?' asked Adrianna; she sat closer and touched the old man's shorter arm. Ivor nearly went for the girl but then grasped his badge. He looked to the earth and imagined her dead body lying there and the satisfaction of it.

'Help me!' he shouted.

'What?' Adrianna startled and shifted away.

'I ... I was his *father*, not his fucking brother!' He looked in desperation at Adrianna. She could tell this old man had never said these words aloud to anyone else. Was this the miracle, she wondered, *her* miracle?

189

'My brother …' Ivor explained, his voice now sinking lower to a matter-of-fact tone, 'was in fact my son. There.'

'The one who was on the plane?' asked Adrianna.

'The jump. The record. The boy was my son, and instead I treated him like a brother. And not a very good one,' Ivor said.

'Was he on the plane?'

'Eh? Aye, he was. I lost a son who never really knew me. Instead I was an angry cunt and a fairly useless brother. He couldn't know. It would have been a scandal because of who his mother was. She was too young, my Mary. My mother made the baby *her* son. My father was confused to his dying day, especially given the age gap between the boy and me, but said nothing. They didn't back then.' Ivor got onto his knees, then slowly up to his feet. 'Bastard hadn't been inside her for ten years. You'd think he'd have known. Well, they say miracles happen. And fuck. You know the nicest thing he ever said to her?'

'Who?' asked Adrianna, shaking her blonde head.

'My father to my mother. He said: "I know your bowels." That was it! He could time her toilet visits to his watch and somehow took pride in that.' Ivor screwed his eyes up at this memory. 'They fought like a pair of cockerels. Their guts lying on the floor, ripped out by each other because of a lack of love. And so I was incapable too. Except deep down I knew I was not. But I could never show it, to anyone.'

'But miracles can happen. I believe that,' said Adrianna, trying to unsee the image of guts on the floor.

'I know now the thing that has always escaped me, the thing I couldn't grasp. It was the completeness of the event. The dead are curious creatures, you'll discover – he looked down at the chick – they're so suddenly not here. They make fools or bastard wrecks of the living. They just leave us behind. It's as if they mean to do that.' Ivor's back was stooped, his helmet rubbing against the corrugated iron roof of the coop. Adrianna could see his fist was clenched.

'I am sorry you lost your son, Mr Punch.' Adrianna couldn't imagine losing her mother.

'You know I never got a chance to get used to it. There was no warning of thunder like we get out in the woods. I've lived in a cell of sorts ever since. But I've made better of it since I retired. Since my illness, really. And fuck. I know that much. Until the talk of that bastard bomber getting released started ... It's all the talk of him I hate, and what it resurrects, more than he himself. I even hate that.'

'Did your son ever wonder?'

'No. He knew nothing. My ... *son* ... ha!' Ivor coughed again, and shook his head into his hands. His helmet toppled off and rolled to the ground. 'It's the first time I ever said that.' Then he looked at the girl. 'He was part of a world event but the world doesn't even know his name. His young woman died too. I never really knew her, an American. She didn't seem to come from much family, the girl. Her past seemed to vanish along with, well, her ... And you know, I don't even know the name of the person he was sitting next to when he died – can you believe that? I should show you the legal jargon printed in one of the bastard official reports – do you know how they actually referred to the names of the dead?'

Adrianna shook her head. She was cradling the helmet. Now she could see the red line imprinted in Mr Ivor's flesh under his chin, his scarring from the strap; the line seemed like it marked a cut-off point between his head and his heart, or maybe between the man and the sergeant.

'Nouns!' Ivor yelled. 'And fuck. My son: a *noun*. I should have stuck in at school more. I had to check a dictionary to know what the hell they were talking about. There was some legal reasoning for it. I didn't need a dictionary to know my life was in a jam jar, to know I'd left it too late to bring out the truth, and to tell my brother how much I loved him, admired him. I've never seen his grave, because there isn't one. I've never been able to visit the field, *either* one.'

Adrianna looked away. She wished she could help him.

'Mr Punch. Can I ask you—'

'You should have seen him climb to the sky,' Ivor interrupted, 'his arms outstretched in the way only his could. Fuck, girl. You should have seen it.' Ivor shook his head. 'What?' he turned to her.

'Do you ever fear for the future?' asked Adrianna.

'No,' said Ivor.

'I do.'

'The worst of it is I have a grandson out there somewhere. Jake. He left as a teenager, some time after after my mother died – she raised him. He probably wouldn't know me now from Adam. Anyway, enough,' Ivor said, 'I have to go and pee. I don't have much control over the waterworks these days.' He turned to the seated girl. 'Keep this to yourself. And no. No gull. It's a fucking *chicken* coop. The clue's in the name. A seagull, even minus a leg, would turn it into a fucking bloodbath.'

'Yes, sir.'

'Call me Sergeant when I'm in uniform.' Ivor booted the door ajar.

'Yes, Sergeant.' Adrianna handed Sergeant Punch his helmet and he fastened the tie under his chin.

Adrianna watched the old man walk back through his small garden to his house. She noticed how his feet seemed to kick imaginary goals as he walked. Beyond him she could see her mother's washing line. She hadn't taken any under-wear from there – how could she dare? She opened her bag and pulled out all the other ladies' knickers and stuffed them deep into the straw. She wanted to know what they might smell like but it was better that she hid them here for now. Nobody would suspect a former sergeant. She wanted them away from her, before she was caught or arrested. Then she had an idea.

'Mr Punch – I mean Sergeant!'

Ivor turned back. Adrianna caught up with him. 'Would you like to know?' She waved her phone in the air. 'We can Google the flight records! We can find out who your son was sitting next to.' Adrianna punched excitedly into her phone.

'Eh?' Ivor looked around. 'Keep your voice down lass. No, leave it. I don't know what you're talking about. And fuck. I need to piss.' Ivor turned into the back door of his house but then turned around. 'You're right to though, I think,' he said.

'What?' Adrianna stopped.

'Fear for the future. Anyway, you'll soon have the coop to yourself. Make hay. I'll not be around to stop you.' He took one last look at the girl as she walked away; he studied her as though she were withdrawing to the regiment of the living. He closed the door.

Adrianna didn't know what he meant but looked at the page on her phone, at the list of names she had summoned into being – this list of nouns. It was time to wave her wand. Adrianna walked out of the garden and turned to take one last look back. She was embarrassed just thinking about the knickers she had hidden in the coop.

The next evening Adrianna went down to the seafront. It was becoming colder and the sun was disappearing below the trees on the other side of the bay. The seafront was empty of people and so she took her chance to climb inside the clock, entering by way of the door that the clock master used when servicing it. It was dark inside the clock and she placed the bag which held her paints, brushes and torch on the stone floor. She had better save the batteries. Her mother had seen her taking the bag out earlier so Adrianna told her she was going to paint the seafront; that it was a school summer project. She was discovering that, like Mr Ivor, she was good at concealing the truth. She waited for five hours inside the clock; all she had to eat was a Lion Bar. At one point she heard voices outside and a dog barking, but then they were gone. She counted the chimes each hour and when the clock sounded ten she took out her torch. It was time. She opened the door and got to work on her miracle.

At 6 a.m. the fishermen were gathering as usual for their own form of village parliament on the pier. Slowly, one by one, as the dawn light came up over the bay and the sound of the sixth chime faded, they surrounded the town clock. It wasn't until they saw the name – the name of the local man they all recognised – that they understood what this act of vandalism was. For this name, this *noun*, was famous locally on the island for one thing – for being the young man who had jumped an unbeaten record on the Games field, who had hung in the sky they said for an eternity, like a cloud refusing to disperse. He was noteworthy internationally for another reason – for having taken a seat on the plane that was blown up over a mainland border town called Lockerbie, killing 270 people. And here he was, listed among the other casualties to whom he was infamously bound; the names covering the town clock, save for the plaque in honour of Henrietta Bird, the lady for whom it was built, which was untouched. 'A tribute', the fishermen agreed, created on the day the body of the bomb victim's relative, Ivor Punch, would later be found on his kitchen floor with a bloodied knife and an opened letter by his side, which had within it a picture of the decorated clock, and the figures '6B' written on the back.

The young man was returned to his island, the fishermen agreed. At last he was home. His seat number they recognised as his Final Position of sorts.

II

Man Who Walks the Earth – I

2009

. . . and so Jake lad, I hope you won't think the worst of me. I
went along with lies that were spun without me having a say. I
was young, too young. And a mainlander to boot. Please make
sure you are sitting down dear. What I have to let you know is
that I am afraid Ivor has died. He has gone. And now you should
know something more, well there is a lot more. Ivor wasn't
your uncle, as you were led to believe, he was your grandfather.
Because, I'm sorry about this dear, because he was your dad's
father, not his brother. Yes. That was a lie that lived with him,
and all of us. A lie that we all had to follow.

You will have a lot of questions. I'll try to explain more,
and the whys, when we speak. I hope we can talk. There was
such a big age difference between them I often wondered if you
suspected something was amiss. The truth is that all this means
I am your grandmother, Jake. And so very proud to be. Because
I was, I am, your dad's mother. But he never knew me. There
you are, that's the way of it. I am sorry. But finally now you
know, and I am free of it, to a point. But I always loved you, as
I did your dad. Even from a distance. Please think about coming
home, Jake. Ivor is to be buried next week. Despite how he was,
he loved you. And then we can talk. I think you must have
known something, that I was more than a housekeeper. I think
you knew that, lad. Those nights we spent together in front of

the TV. Your violin. You're all I have left, dear. I hope this reaches
you at the orchestra. I really hope it does. Please let me know that
you get this.

    My love,
    Mary
    Mary McBeth

As he lifted his eyes from the page, Jake gulped for air. He was standing perfectly still in a pocket of greenery within the city. It was the second time he had read the letter. He didn't feel stricken; he felt struck. As he looked around and as his breaths slowed so at last he could swallow, he took comfort in the familiarity of the fluorescent cyclists, the symmetry of the mothers with buggies, the gargle of passing red buses, and the beginnings of a casual football game beside him in the park. He looked more closely at the grassland, the turf. Despite the fact that he had built a successful life away from the island, he now found himself hoping that somewhere in him was the air from that place, and the grains of sand from the Games field. It was the land and the oxygen of his homeland he craved, rather than its people. Six years had passed since he had last been home. It was late summer and he was standing in London's Hyde Park, in front of the Albert Memorial, directly opposite the Royal Albert Hall.

He clasped Mary McBeth's letter. She was the woman who the rest of the island, the rest of the world even, had they cared, believed was simply Ivor's housekeeper. And now he questioned all that had gone before, every moment he had been Jake. He looked to the familiar beauty of the Victorian building. When he was a child, it had only been accessible through his TV screen, and now here he was, performing in it. It was a reliable, steadying influence, this iconic round of red brick. He had read that it was Queen Victoria's tribute to her departed husband, Prince Albert. And here it stood; except all Jake could think about was not Victoria and Albert but another love story, the story of Ivor and Mary.

Now it was clear to him, and strangely, it made sense. He thought about Ivor, his grandfather, who in life had been his uncle and despite all of this was already dead and – what was it the Americans said? – unimpeachable.

Jake wondered whether the world in which he stood was different now, without Ivor. Was it a different Royal Albert Hall? He considered Ivor's duplicity, and realised it had always been there. In life, Ivor was forever threatening to be two things at once: kind and mean, intelligent and ignorant, lawmaker and lawbreaker, forthcoming and secretive – and now, he realised: brother and father, uncle and grandfather. As Jake stared at the posters of world-renowned conductors, he knew he must decide whether to return for Ivor's funeral, whether to acknowledge the death, and the deceit. And, as he kicked the football back to the laughing, carefree, Europeans, among whom he did not look out of place, he wondered was it the Jake he had been who he now craved, the Jake who hadn't opened Mary's letter?

Several days passed and the Proms numbered 32, 33, and 34. Jake told nobody of the interruption he had received from his old world and did his best to focus on the orchestra. In any spare time between rehearsals, he had taken to searching on his phone for the obituaries of 9-11 victims. He imagined it must have been something to do with the plane his father had been on. He then started reading other obituaries, which he cut from newspapers and kept on top of the piano in his flat. Sophie, his girlfriend, had even started cutting them out for him. He still had not been able to open up to her about the bomb, let alone about Ivor and the lies he had been spun all his life. Sophie wouldn't even know who Ivor was. But nowhere in him did Jake feel anger. He felt suspended between worlds.

He appreciated now that the bomb had strengthened Ivor's bond with the island while loosening his own. Beyond the shattered remains and dispersing smoke, Jake had discovered another world. The memory came clouded with pain, and then guilt, for having made another life away from the island, away from Mary, and Ivor, for having chosen Victoria and Albert instead. But he couldn't quite escape the images of the fallen plane. If people ever did get close enough to discover his connection with Lockerbie, then he became a ghoul by association, and one that had to field unwanted questions. And so, like the conductor of an orchestra, he tried to ensure that he was always one step ahead of such a mention, so to take the lead, to deflect, to protect himself. It was better if nobody in the classical music circles of London knew; it was better if he didn't know either.

Five days had passed since he had received Mary's letter and Jake found himself on a rest between Proms. This was a dangerous time; he was concerned that the absence of duty, this silencing of the neatly arranged notes, might present an opportunity for his old world to finally breach his new one. That morning he was browsing through the local Camden newspaper over breakfast. Usually he would throw it straight in the recycling bin but on this day he decided to check if it had an obituaries section. He focused in on the face of a man about the same age as Ivor had been. Here was a life condensed to four column inches. He scanned to the bottom of the entry and saw that the funeral was today. Jake shaved and dressed – the black suit he wore for performances was as good a choice as any. Then he set off with the newspaper clipping for Highgate Cemetery, to see off George Swan, a man he had never met.

When Jake arrived at the cemetery he walked up the hill and noticed two busy undertakers. He didn't recognise either, then wondered why he should have. He was early. There were several men standing dutifully in council overalls with spades. One of the undertakers nodded towards him and Jake returned the acknowledgement. He could tell the man thought he was a son or even grandson of George Swan. One of the Swans. He looked to the gravestones erected like large dominos pointed to the sky. And he was here, part of it. The gravediggers began making final preparations for the adding of George Swan to the earth. Soon more people gathered, slowly decorating the hill. They stood so solemnly that Jake felt guilty. The wind gathered and made tears in his eyes as he walked towards them, past the climbing maze of gravestones.

After the graveside service Jake watched the Swans disperse; they patted each other's black-suited backs as they progressed. He heard the cluck of their London accents; saw fleshy, heavily lined faces, like human accordions. They were sporting the sort of formal wear which might have been modelled by the Kray Twins. As they shuffled away, their faces wore nothing more than vacant stares; the London Eye was their backdrop, and beside it, the big clock; but those landmarks had become inconsequential to Jake. This scene, he now imagined, happened countless times around London every hour, carrying with it the prosaic light of day – but he could sense something different was within his grasp, it was the sharpness of the here and now, and with it came the realisation that when there is death, some must remain to deal with it; some must remain on the island. But at least the present was more forgiving than the past, than being blown out of the sky. Jake knew that in his own life, whatever happened after today, he would appreciate that thought more than ever. He caught another gulp in his throat before it became anything else, something bigger – something that could give way to Ivor, to the blue livery of the Pan-American Airlines plane, to the memory of his father.

In the distance Jake now heard the murmur of the city – out there clocks still ticked and roads were clogged, and politicians shook their papers in the air. And orchestral players still drank too much while dutifully preparing for another night of the Proms. He walked past the hole in the ground. This was the closest he had come – would ever come – to George Swan. Jake stopped and spoke softly into the hole:

'*Aingeal.*'

He looked into the pit and imagined the miracle taking place inside the coffin: those incremental acts of ageing would now be speedily reversing – each wrinkle, each crow's foot around George Swan's eyes, would be airbrushed out – but by whom? He didn't know the answer but he had called George Swan an angel, this man without wings whom he never even knew, and never would. But really he did not see George Swan, he saw his father, he saw Ivor.

'We're sorry for your loss,' said one of the gravediggers, standing at a respectful distance from Jake. The thought that this unfamiliar urban spot could one day be his final resting place sent chills up Jake's spine. He had never considered such a thing. He looked at the slabs of stone and saw them now as the doors to what comes next, through which Ivor had now travelled. But who would attend his own burial – surely Sophie?

A small grey creature poked up from behind a tree stump. Jake watched the squirrel extend its paw and pull on a bud as though it were the last piece of food on earth. Jake looked to the city and thought again of Ivor, and of that night in the woods when he had forced a knife into a horse then watched as Ivor ate it. He remembered Ivor's rough, lumpy hand in his own. Jake now took that hand in his other. He was re-adjusting to this new version of Ivor in death. And it was going to take some time for him to get used to thinking of Ivor in this way. He realised his grandfather had finally pulled it off, he had achieved definition, a kind of oneness in death. Ivor was everywhere: he was the emerging city and the receding coastline, all at once.

'It's not much, is it?' said a voice. Jake turned to his side. An old lady with a solid frame was sitting on a bench under the trees with a clear bag full of crumbs on her lap. She could not have been a day younger than eighty. Jake looked at this lady, a seated testament to the accumulation of years, who had the stone face of a child. To him, her presence signified a prick in the passage of time.

Now he could hear Ivor's coarse voice, his bullet-like delivery on that evening fifteen years earlier near Bloody Bay, when Ivor had been the unlikely one to introduce him to Pavarotti. Ivor's voice was now frozen in eternity. *And fuck.* Jake remembered how Ivor was forever in awe of the island's fishermen and how easily they could be taken by the sea, by death, their Final Positions so theatrically documented. He found it almost impossible to arrest any of them.

In one of his rare, softer moments, after documenting the wellbeing or otherwise of his chicks, Ivor had written to Jake that *confusion arose when something was gone because nothing earthly remained*. But Ivor too was now just a memory. Ivor was as distant to him, as far out of reach, as the ego-driven celebrity conductors Jake played for. He could not decide whether to go home. Here, he was needed. Bach, Mozart, Sibelius, Beethoven – they were all relying on him. There, he was just a boy.

'The dead,' began the old lady. 'How much attention can we reasonably grant to a rectangle of grass and an upright, weathered slab of stone? But here I'll come every day. I like to do the feeding too.' She raised the bag. Her face was flushed, and Jake noticed how her skin, a dollop of which hung from below her chin like on Ivor's chickens, tightened and loosened as she spoke.

Her voice sounded like the accents Jake had heard in black-and-white films made during the war – cockney, but at the same time refined. Her teeth were yellow.

'But then, I suppose we could say the same of the living,' said the old lady. 'I keep waiting for this new century to teach us something new.'

Jake smiled at her.

'You know,' the old lady went on, now looking to the city, 'you hear a lot about London during the war, but to us children it was really a playground. All the upturned earth and empty buildings to explore. And sleeping in the Underground, my golly, I'm ashamed now to say it was fun.'

'It always felt a bit mysterious to us outsiders ... London,' managed Jake. He looked out at it: tall, rising, questing to be New York.

'Oh? Well of course a lot of us Londoners never leave it; we're not so full of experience or half as worldly as some of us would like to think.' She paused. 'We used to call these "stop and think moments".'

'Yes?'

'We don't seem to do that any more.' She paused, and rubbed her foot over the dirt. 'To think we used to pour salt on slugs, back during the war. I remember that now for some reason. I feel bad about that. But we were all looking for each other's weak spots back then.' She looked to the metropolis. 'Can't you hear it?'

'What?' asked Jake.

She was silent for a moment. 'This is what I hear,' she said, 'a faint noise like a lone owl. But who knows if there are owls in the city.'

Jake watched her smile. He turned away to a small family of trees which he must have passed before, but hadn't noticed. 'It's beautiful in a way isn't it?' he said. 'For a city.'

'Oh, you're far from home?' she asked. 'Scottish?'

'Yes.' Jake smiled.

'Are we treating you well?'

'Very, thanks.'

'Do you like us?'

'I do. Like. I'm living with one of you.'

'Oh well, that's nice. I hope you are happy. My husband's bones are down there and that is where I will be buried also. But his soul is in the air, in this city – with the grime on the walls and in the song of the birds. It's a kind of symphony. At least that's how I like to see it – on good days. These wrinkles can be a burden you know.'

'Your husband has a tremendous view,' Jake said. He realised they were now talking about the things too elusive for a conductor's baton or a violinist's bow.

'It's a mystery in a way, you know – where we all go,' she said.

'Right now I'm pretty much shrouded in it,' said Jake. He thought of the decision he had to make.

'I realise more and more ...' The old lady paused and Jake turned to her, 'that there is beauty and significance exactly *because* of that mystery.' She threw some crumbs to the ground.

'I have lost somebody recently,' said Jake.

The woman looked probingly at the city, as though it were now a fabrication, 'Well I am sorry for your loss. Truly sorry.'

Jake couldn't speak. All it had taken was this utterance; now the world knew.

'Anyway, I won't ask how you knew my younger brother,' she continued, 'but thank you for taking the time. He liked life. I'll miss him, but at least he's free from pain, and he made the most of it – life. Every minute that goes by does not come back to you, you know. We're just blips in the universe. I didn't know that when I was a teenager.'

'Are we?' asked Jake, turning to the lady.

'Yes. Was it not T.S. Eliot who said, "The dead hold no shares"?'

Jake gulped and looked up to a plane passing high overhead. To its passengers, London would be the size of an allotment. He heard the old lady inhaling heavily through her nose. In the way of people who have been so closely affected by death, she was now, however briefly, elevated from the ordinary to a place removed from him. She had achieved top billing; she was a celebrity clad in black, and Jake, like the rest of those gathered below, mere acquaintances, wanted a part of her. They wanted to be near her, to be cast right at the epicentre of life and death. And she had chosen in her moment of grief to be closest to him. He wished to be closer to Mary. He realised he had felt this way all his life. 'The plane,' he said, *it fell from the sky. My father fell from the sky. He feels like more than a blip though.*

The old lady shuffled to the edge of the bench. 'Okay, would you mind taking my arm? They'll be waiting for me . . . I've been hiding but now they will make a terrible fuss of my absence. When you get to my age you are permitted this egotism.'

'Of course,' said Jake. As they started to walk together he noticed how tall she was. They emerged from the protection of the trees and at that point Jake passed the lady on to one of the Swan men who was waiting for her at the end of the path. She moved away without looking back, and now her support was restored, Jake watched her take the hill's decline. Instantly he missed her, and then Mary.

It was colder, Jake noticed, as he nodded to the busy grave-diggers and walked past the hole in the ground.

There were things about today Jake could not explain. He didn't take the tube home – instead he walked. And along the way, as Holloway Road gave way to Camden Road, he looked more closely at passing strangers on buses, in cars, on streets, and to those robustly trying to give away free newspapers – he even paid more attention to walls. This was Jake Punch, the former boy, now a man, walking freely – with a slightly pronounced overstep, going completely unnoticed in the metropolis among the living – towards Sophie, his island. As he progressed he waved his hands through the air, conducting the movements of the crowds around him as though he were Sibelius with his majestically lilting *The Swan of Tuonela*, that exquisite mix of the hopeful as musical bedfellow of the mournful, the sound of which forced Jake to dip his fingers into the city, straight into the old lady's husband's heart. It was warmer than he imagined.

He was not yet ready to take the train north, for that would involve an unavoidable stop at an unwanted train station sign. But he would hire a car. The music had reminded him. As had the Swans. He needed to return to the island. To the memory of the doves. To the dead.

It was just over a week since he had received Mary's letter, and Jake stood sufficiently out of view, feeling ill at ease. He could see there were now fifty people gathered on the highest gravel path in the town's graveyard; they were standing next to the hole. These were the sum total, an amalgam of flesh and blood, of Ivor's life. Jake had come straight from the ferry terminal, and was now here as one of them, one of Ivor's people, looking in from the outside. He crouched nervously behind a tall gravestone that was shaped like a cross. The Minister spoke out to bring those gathered closer. Jake fought his conflicting impulses, one to join them, and the other to flee. They were becoming something, together. But even from this distance he felt something was lacking. They were like a concertina without wind, without its lifeblood. At that moment an old man wearing a flat cap came walking slowly up the hill, as if emerging like an hour, a minute even, from the past warmed up. And on the man's arm was Mary.

The coffin was now carried over to the grave. There were six pallbearers – men whom Jake watched closely, most of whom he recognised, several of whom Ivor had at one time arrested. He could see that despite his accumulated years, Randy, with his unmistakably shaped head, was one of them. Jake felt a desire to take the weight. But in such company he was once again *the boy*. He was worried about being caught; he felt as though he shouldn't be here, spying creepily like a funeral-junkie, a pervert of the macabre. He could now see that one of the pallbearers was a young police officer, dressed in uniform, who was taking his share of the load next to a fisherman in bright waders, whose pink skin caught the emerging sunlight like a salmon dowsed in silver. Jake knew Ivor would have appreciated the presence of both of the men, and especially their attire. There was another person in the crowd that Jake recognised, and then realised it was a woman from the local school. Jake's desire was now to know these people.

Jake could hear the Minister speaking the consigning words; some of his eulogy was taken by the rising wind. The coffin that held the decaying flesh and bone of Ivor Punch was lowered into the pit. Jake watched the straps hold firm, as they were intended to, as did the men's backs. The clouds dispersed over the hill and cast horizontal flashes of triumphant light into Jake's eyes and onto the undertaker's bald head. A blonde teenage girl was standing near the front of the gathering alongside a lady Jake assumed was her mother; he didn't recognise her but then why would he? Jake now understood that if he had changed during his time of absence, then the island had altered too. The girl had her head down, her hands cupped considerately as though in prayer.

'Our power comes from God, and from his love of Ivor Punch,' the Minister spoke theatrically, 'take the blessing of the Lord. Go now, Ivor, on your journey to the safe keeping of the Lord, of the land.' The Minister closed his eyes and looked to the ground and then to the sky. 'And we recall the teachings of 1 John 4:8: "Whoever does not love does not know God, because God is love." Amen.'

The Minister stepped away and it was then that something occurred, which Jake thought could not have been unplanned. Then again, in a place such as this, he knew that things happened of their own accord. He could see that his face was not the only one registering surprise. The old man with the flat cap stepped forwards in his waders like a clockwork figurine, a battery-powered Hebridean sea-god. Jake watched as the man lowered his big, skinny frame. He assumed the man must have flowers concealed in his coat, but then recognised him as John the Goat. As if on cue the wind let up. John the Goat had a roll-up in his mouth, which he puffed with a lifetime's experience from the side of his mouth without the aid of hands. His eyes narrowed and his nose looked more pointed. He was gaunt and braced to the starkness of the task in hand. These were signs of deep concentration, thought Jake – his fellow players in the orchestra looked exactly like this when at their most intense, when their powers of coordination were at their most stretched by the genius of Beethoven or Bach. It looked as though a sparrow could fly out from John the Goat's face. The old man then picked up a handful of earth with his bony hands and threw it into the hole.

Jake peeked further above the stone and watched as John the Goat stood up once again; he was remarkably sprightly.

John the Goat then reached into his pocket and from a pink handkerchief he produced ... not the red squirrel Jake and his friends would marvel at as children, but a piece of paper. This hill, in this town, on this island, had become John the Goat's stage. Jake felt as nervous for the old man as he did when he would première a piece. John the Goat unfolded the paper fully and it shook in his hand as though it were a part of him, escaping. He cleared his throat, spat out the roll-up and put his flat cap under his free arm. Jake watched as each of those gathered moved forwards a step to capture the anticipated words. Jake stepped closer. John the Goat wiped his silver beard and cleared his throat above the earthly remains. He leaned over and looked down at the coffin for the first and last time. He bowed his head to the gaping hole and looked to the piece of paper, his lumpy tongue popped out to line his lips with saliva as he declaimed:

'God bless, *Sergeant*.' John the Goat folded up the piece of paper again, replaced his flat cap, and stepped back from the dark hole cut into the hill. The young policeman saluted. John the Goat turned his back to the grave as though he had forgotten a word, but instead unfastened his coat. From within it he produced a white dove. He cupped the dove in his bony hands; as though preparing a launch pad for it, and swooshed it into the air.

Jake stood perfectly still. It was as though in just several seconds he had experienced an entire symphony. He grabbed the gravestone for balance.

He watched as Randy, in his banking uniform, moved to hand John the Goat the roll-up that he had retrieved from the ground and revived with a puff or two. Jake looked on as John the Goat walked off the hill in the opposite direction, and he was in no doubt it was on Ivor's earth, Ivor's world, that he now stood. Jake watched John the Goat's cap disappear from view and was reassured to discover that nobody can really know from where such strength comes when it is needed.

And then he saw Mary McBeth, her neck still craned skywards, this lady who had been Ivor's housekeeper and the love of his life. Jake stepped out from the protective cover of the dead and strolled upwards, to the hole in the ground, to the living, towards Mary, to his grandmother.

12

Island Historical &
Archaeological Society

The man known on the island as Pluto flicked on the outside light and opened his front door. He already knew from the familiar knock that it was his fellow board member Dave. Despite the newness of the man's appointment, Dave had very deliberate and impressive ways, thought Pluto. They were to be expected in a man of such obvious efficiency.

'Chairman, we have a serious problem,' said Dave, looking down. Pluto took a moment to appreciate the fine construction of Dave's perfectly domed skull; he was always on the look out for good design. Dave's use of his official title was enough for Pluto to know the matter was serious, if the lateness of the hour had not already.

'It's that bastard MacIntyre – he's at it again,' said Dave.

Pluto imagined his colleague's head without its body, floating in this dark night sky like a planetary discovery of perfect dimensions and form. Pluto appreciated how lucky he was that Dave had moved to the island. He didn't regard any of his fellow islanders as being suitably qualified to join his society, and now to see the beauty of the man's skull – to really see it – was a wondrous accompaniment to their shared passion for the island's past and the good administration of exclusive societies.

'Please tell me you own – we own – the domain?' Dave asked, still on the outside. Pluto was sure he owned the domain – almost certain. But this moment was worth drawing out. The droplets on Dave's head had discovered a pathway and were now gathering above his top lip. Pluto was of course aware of the problem that his friend was so keen to share on this stormy black night, which had made his muddy driveway thick like treacle. It was nothing to him to allow his colleague, his Treasurer no less, to take hold of this moment of high drama.

'Eh, I'm getting wet . . .' said Dave.

'Oh, of course, Dave. I'm sorry!' Pluto stepped sideways, allowing his glasses to fall on their string from his nose to his chest. 'Come away in yourself. I'll prepare the Situation Room.'

'Call me Treasurer, man, on nights such as these, please,' instructed Dave, not looking at his Chairman.

'Aye, Treasurer, of course. In you come anyway. Mind the new water feature.'

'Eh? Aye, well . . .' said Dave, stamping his impatient wet feet on the doormat, which bore the embroidered letters 'IAHS'. The 'A' had been more recently added with paint, clumsily, Dave thought, as he embraced the warmth and glanced at the tacky, Thai fountain, its centrepiece a dragon's tongue.

Pluto found the ripple of water therapeutic as he watched his friend progress down the hallway towards the kitchen, which at this late hour was deemed the 'Situation Room'. In the dim light, the planetary skull moving ahead of him was even more impressive. After all, he had an interest in the discovery of skulls to promote. He turned into the kitchen as Dave took his seat at the bottom of the table.

'Will you have a small one – to settle the grey matter?' asked Pluto, his forefinger on the open whisky bottle. He remembered how the oilmen in re-runs of *Dallas* often decanted a measure in similar times of strategic importance. He enjoyed daytime TV; that was, when his time was not taken up with the island's historical and archaeological concerns.

'First,' said Dave, 'I'd appreciate it if you would update me on the status of the domain, Chairman?'

'I can and will,' replied Pluto, although he preferred to be the one asking the questions. 'We do own the domain. And the fine people at GoDaddy recently added two more years. Have you not got the receipt of payment?'

'Well that's one thing, I suppose.' Dave sighed with relief. 'No I don't have any such receipt. I'd appreciate being kept up to date with all treasury matters.'

'You're right, Treasurer. I apologise. I'm still used to working solo – you know, like the North Star. But with you on board I am confident it is worth the extra expenditure.'

'Aye. Good. Well that's something,' said Dave. 'Yes, please pour me three fingers' worth – Henry VIII ones. There's more to discuss.' Dave wondered what extra cost he could possibly have been to the organisation, other than the extra measures of whisky, which he had mostly provided; in fact, joining the society had actually cost *him* money, given he now made a regular standing order to Pluto. But still, tonight was not the time for such deliberation, even if the sight of the payee 'Pluto' on his bank statements always appeared a tad crude.

Pluto poured whisky into two mugs; each emblazoned with 'IHAS' (the 'A' on each drawn on in marker just above the 'H' with an arrow below it, somewhat carelessly, thought

Dave) and slid one up the table to his Treasurer. Pluto put on his glasses and, on the flipchart above the table, he slowly but deliberately wrote 'E.G.M.'. Dave nodded approvingly towards the flipchart, although he would have preferred a typed memo. But then this *was* an emergency. Pluto took the Chair's seat at the other end of the table. 'I welcome you to the Situation Room.'

Dave looked to the table in disapproval. 'The salt and pepper?' He cleared his throat and gestured, 'Should we not...'

'Oh!' Pluto moved swiftly to his feet. 'Of course, Treasurer, I'll remove them right away.' Pluto placed the condiments on the seat next to his. 'Clutter in view clutters the mind,' said Pluto. 'My mother used to say that. She applied it to my father.'

'So, yes...' Dave began, keen to move proceedings along, 'I read in the local paper he has decided to call himself "Island Historical Society" again. And he is coming home to perform here soon... if performing is what you can call that racket. I think we need to explore the implications of this musician's name change back to IHS.'

Pluto nodded to the tablecloth. 'I'm just glad I – we – decided on the *Archaeological* arm.'

'Indeed,' agreed Dave, 'it was a fine distinction, Chairman. Good crisis management. Even though in my time we haven't so much as troubled a blade of grass with a spade...' Dave looked back to the Thai fountain with some disregard.

'Yet...' Pluto shuffled uncomfortably and played with his glasses. As his nickname suggested, he preferred the skies to the ground. He wished now he had made a different call on the name change; *Astronomical* pursuits would have suited him much better.

'And, while we're on this subject, should we not at the very least be introducing historical tours of the island? For the tourists?' enquired Dave.

'Eh,' Pluto shifted uncomfortably, 'no. Not yet, Treasurer. First I have more research work to do on the official *route*.' Dave was not best pleased with Pluto's decision to pronounce 'route' in the American way, rhyming it with Brussels sprout.

'And,' Pluto continued, 'you know how unreliable the roads are on the coasts of the island. We need more infrastructure . . .'

'Really? Well, anyway,' said Dave, 'tonight we find ourselves in crisis once more. And there are two of us now. I'm here to support.'

Pluto nodded approvingly. This was his Treasurer, thought Pluto, slurping from his mug. Pluto watched in fascination as Dave wiped the last drops of rain off his smooth bald head.

Dave was an undertaker by day and on this night he was still dressed in the customary black mac. It enhanced his objective not to be noticed; especially given the motion he wished to pass. Soon it would be time to reveal his plan. He looked to Pluto, a man whose origins nobody knew, who could, apparently, skim a stone the length of the Atlantic, who spent much of his day with his head in the skies, or so the locals said.

'Is there any news of him adopting an Archaeological arm?' Pluto asked.

'I'd like to *break* his fucking arm.' Dave thumped his fist on the table. 'See if he can play his rotten fucking tunes then. A pain between the ears it is.'

'Dave – I mean *Treasurer* – this is not a time for foolhardiness.' Pluto looked to his fellow member; in his mind he thought of Dave as a modern day Uncle Fester, possibly with the best bits of Harold Shipman thrown in. He was known locally as 'Dave the Grave'.

'No. You're right, of course. I'm sorry Chairman, and for my cursing,' said Dave. 'But that is exactly my worry: that MacIntyre has *archaeological* aspirations. I wouldn't put it past him. So we must devise a campaign.'

'I'm sick of the cunt too. Excuse my Gaelic.' Pluto was pleased to have displayed this measure of maturity; he was still disappointed and mildly embarrassed about the salt and pepper incident. 'What sort of campaign?' he asked.

'Marketing. We must reclaim our identity,' echoed Dave through his mug.

Pluto realised he must retain his authority. 'After all,' he started, 'it was me who first formed the Island Historical Society, and on my own. Since then this, eh, shall we say, *musician*, whose origins are indeed on the island, has come along and stolen our name as his own.'

'Yes,' confirmed Dave impatiently, 'we both know all this...'

'And,' Pluto went on, even more seriously, 'we have already had to, at some considerable cost, establish an Archaeological section of our organisation just to reclaim our ground and distinguish us from him...'

'... As the island's *foremost* historical society,' Dave finished authoritatively. 'We know this. But it's solutions we need. Marketing.'

'So, how are our funds looking?' asked Pluto. 'I need detail.'

'I knew you'd ask, Chairman,' said Dave, opening his wet coat and reaching inside. Pluto crossed his legs and shook his head.

'I have a copy in the file already. So this, for you, is the original statement, Chairman.' He slid the piece of paper towards Pluto. Pluto put his glasses to his nose and inhaled heavily through what little room was left through his nasal hair. He rose and with a black marker wrote '£128.42' on the flipchart. 'We haven't much.'

'That's enough for adverts in all the papers to cover the entire west coast. We'll wage marketing warfare,' said Dave. 'We'll make ourselves more known, at least locally. And that could start a ripple internationally, Christ, virally even. Did you not say we had an email from the Far East recently?'

'Eh, aye. A sweet little lass. We exchanged some pleasantries as you do and then she asked me to marry her, by reply.' Pluto flashed his bloodshot eyes. 'And does this account carry contingency measures to ensure your regular monthly payments are always met?'

'It does,' Dave confirmed. Then his eyebrows jumped; 'She has asked you to do *what*?'

'Yes. We could well be setting up our first international partner!'

'And *will* you marry her?' Dave frowned.

'I don't know. I'm not sure I could afford her airfare; she's asking for first class,' Pluto choked. 'In fact, maybe you can help me.' As if from behind his ear, Pluto produced a laptop with an external mouse and placed it on the Situation Room table. 'Her international membership form is attached to the email but I'll be damned if I can open the bastard.'

Dave frowned at the gleaming, expensive-looking device, which now sat between them.

'No matter how hard I try,' Pluto reasoned, 'the cunt doesn't want to open. I hope she'll be more obliging in person.'

Dave flinched at Pluto's uncouthness, quite unbecoming

of a man in his elevated position. It was no wonder overseas membership had stalled.

'I know you are a man who has shaken the hands of technology, Treasurer – so can you help?' asked Pluto, furrowing his brow.

Dave sighed deeply. This interlude was an irritation, especially on a night when he had intended to act, but still, international funds were on offer.

'Aye, well,' began Dave, 'have you at least hovered the mouse over the file?'

'That is exactly what I have done, but it refuses to acknowledge it is even there. Maybe it's the time difference or something?'

'Not likely,' insisted Dave. 'So wave the mouse slowly over the screen, back and forwards, to refresh the thing.'

'Are you sure, Dave?'

'*Treasurer.*'

'Treasurer.'

'I am, Chairman. Try it now. It'll find it, and then you click on the file. Wave it over the screen.' Dave took another slurp. Then, out of the corner of his eye, he saw his Chairman's arm waving, actually waving the mouse in the air in front of the screen.

'Christ, not like that, man!' shouted Dave, lowering his mug and turning to make sure they were not being watched through the windows. Such behaviour could cause an organisation to fold. 'You think it'll fucking wave back?'

'Let's get back to the adverts – and MacIntyre,' said Dave. 'We must make a decision tonight; time is of the essence.' This news was a worry to him, this proposal from the Far East. Dave had not the mindset to be bothered with the opposite sex – he was too busy caring for the dead. He considered himself, therefore, too close to the afterlife, to the answers, to the cold reality of dead flesh – to possibly believe in philosophical questions, or to bother with life's intangibles – such as the pursuit of romance.

'We will do what the majority rule,' answered Pluto, with more authority, having put away the offending laptop. 'And if that does not provide a definitive outcome then I, as Chairman and Founder, have the final word.' He ran his fingers through his wispy red hair; it was something he did when deep in thought, carried over from his days trying to read the clouds above fishing boats. It was the fishing that brought him to the island. He looked to Dave's shiny shoes. Pluto wasn't best pleased being caught by Dave in his pyjamas, but then good crisis management was about dealing with events as they unfolded, not being dressed by Savile Row.

'Yes Chairman. Excuse me,' said Dave. 'But if you'll allow me we do have the funds to start some marketing at least – perhaps we can encourage MacIntyre to revert to using his own name? We were just about to reclaim our identity, our land …' Dave was keen not to allow the society to flounder; he had already tried out the island's branch of the Masons but had found them unfriendly and too opposed to change. It was not uncommon, he knew, for the living to find a man like him, a man so trusted by the dead, ghoulish. 'Macabre,' his uncle had once said.

'But we need the funds for the metal detector. How can we justifiably call ourselves the "Island Historical – and *Archaeological* – Society" with no tools for the task?' asked Pluto. 'As it is I had to downsize on the choice of Thai fountain.

Aesthetics are important to our organisation, as are first impressions for potential visitors. Our HQ must look the part!'

'Mmm. Well, dragons aside, I advise an advertising campaign. A warfare of propaganda.'

'I advise caution.' Pluto looked to the window, which was now taking the full brunt of the evening's rain. 'Bloody storm brewing. My creels will be doing cartwheels.' He raised his gangly frame and reached quickly to close the curtains. Then he took a quick glance at his Treasurer and was relieved to see he hadn't noticed the security oversight. 'I could smell it earlier, the rain. You can take a man off the sea but try t'other way around and you're in pig shit.'

Dave looked down at the bankbook on the table, which he always carried together with the statements. A serious thought was brewing on this wild night, in his whisky-stimulated mind. He thought it best to let it fester; it was important to allow his Chairman this time to think his best thoughts too. His plan had been to make a challenge for the top job. But this night, with the wind blowing the arse out of flies and the seas reaching for clouds, was not one for a coup. He watched as Pluto put the laptop in its case, and vacated the Situation Room. Dave looked around the kitchen – it was in this same space that he had experienced his Initiation Ceremony just two years previously. He looked to the jar on the shelf above the sink with the heart inside it, which he had taken from a corpse around the northern coast of the island before closing the lid; he remembered how the face had looked up from his preparation table with a shine as though a light from heaven was already on it. Pluto had appreciated this gift; the finest Christmas present he had ever received.

He knew that Dave also kept a hand or two in his freezer, in case they were ever needed.

Next to the jar was a picture of an Asian woman who looked not much more than a teenage girl. There was an 'x' with four exclamation marks written on the photo. Clumsy punctuation, Dave thought. He heard rustling in the other room and Pluto reappeared, this time not with the laptop but with a small case. It was not much bigger than the dreadful coffins in which he had put children into the ground. No man, he thought, was ever ready for the first time he did that. Dave watched as Pluto rested the case at the other end of the table and then produced from it a banjo. The Chairman, still in orange pyjamas, put his roll-up to his lips and played some of the most awful noise that Dave had ever heard. Had he been told his friend had stamped on a cat's throat, the racket would have made more sense.

'Beautiful,' said Dave, through a warm gulp. 'Chairman, you are gifted in many ways. The sea's gain was the musical world's loss.'

Pluto smiled knowingly, his round face beaming at the cheeks.

Pluto reminded Dave of a proud, pyjama-ed sea lion. He watched with relief as his Chairman put down the instrument.

'Well, that is exactly my plan,' said Pluto. 'Maybe we can beat the bastard at his own game? I'm sure you have a lyric in you, Treasurer?'

Dave's serious eyes darted for more room in their sockets. This foolhardiness, he was not expecting. Whatever they thought of the man MacIntyre's music, and the musician's cheek to even consider stealing their organisation's name,

Dave knew the bastard could fathom a word and a melody more readily than he or his tone-deaf Chairman. No, surely there was a better way of raising some cash.

'I'm not sure, Chairman, that I could match your talent on that thing if my words of accompaniment were crafted by St Peter himself.' Dave was employing the best tactic he could to put his leader off this hideous idea. He felt his eyelid twitching the way it could when he lied. 'If you'll allow, I would motion that we need a plan that plays more – how can I put this – to our strengths? Leave the other stuff to the man McCartney and the like.'

Pluto noticed the movement above his Treasurer's eye, which gave the impression his bushy eyebrow was taking voyage, caterpillar-like, up that perfectly domed skull. He knew it was not a good sign. 'Well, Dave,' said Pluto, flashing his whiskers, 'I am not the best with the word. So that's it – we might well be stumped before we even take the world stage!' Both men laughed. Dave loved the man, pure and simple. He peered closer at Pluto's face, at the crow's feet making a reach for his temples, his eyes swollen behind Boots reading glasses, which Dave had bought for him on the mainland without Pluto even having left the island for an eye test. *A small miracle*, Pluto had said. Dave peered at his colleague's collapsed face, at the landslide of skin and bone gathering at the mouth, giving the impression he was perpetually sucking on life. Despite the expense of the Society's Thai fountain, and lack of historical records (they had yet to make one expedition since Dave had joined, despite his suggestion that the town's clock was of historical merit – or even deliver a single subterranean discovery, since the addition of their archaeological arm) Dave understood Pluto to be a man who appreciated that men must be aware of their own consequences, and he had started this society all of his own accord. He was in fullest admiration of his Chairman. But, despite their kinship, Dave knew he must say what was on his mind, and that a Treasurer must find a solution to a monetary problem; he was the Chancellor of the Exchequer to Pluto's Prime Minister.

'What I am about to say is not something of which I am proud, but it is a solution, and one I feel certain we could pull off.' Dave now poured himself a forefinger of whisky. 'Yes, it could work.' He nodded.

Pluto watched his friend's perfect head become perfectly still. Inside was a mind he admired. 'Then what is it, Treasurer?' he asked.

'Well,' began Dave, 'the bank van, which serves us here on the island ...'

'Yes, what about it? It delivered my new teeth recently from the mainland ...' interrupted Pluto, flashing his new set with some pride. Dave could see they were already showing signs of a golden hue.

'Yes. Well, when I was paying in some funds,' continued Dave, 'you know for my most recent burial, the man Ivor Punch—'

'The Clock. A fine sergeant he was.'

'So I'm told.'

'I bet you cleaned him up good and proper, Treasurer.'

'I'll admit, I did a number on him, his reputation deserved it.'

'Amen to that.'

'You could have eaten Cocoa Pops off his undercarriage by the time I finished with him.' Dave could barely contain his sense of professional pride. 'Of course he kept a clean one anyway – undercarriage.'

'Of course he would,' said Pluto.

'And he had the biggest prick on the island.'

'*Really?*' Pluto fizzed, leaning closer. 'And ...' he cupped his hands and rocked them reverentially, 'it was *you*, my friend, who put it to rest. What an honour.'

'Aye, well. I spotted that they are not the most, eh, secure with their arrangements ...'

'What? With the man's fly?'

'No – no. The Mobile Bank,' sighed Dave, more agitated.

'You mean because there is teeth where the twenty-pound notes should be!' Pluto exploded, and then quickly settled himself; it was not becoming of his role to be so flippant, especially as he was still better dressed for the land of Nod than the Situation Room.

'What I mean to say is I think ...' Dave took a larger gulp, 'it would be possible to, let me say, well, relieve them of some of their cash and put it to our good use. No bastard on this island likes us anyway.'

Pluto slowly nodded. 'I see. I'll not speak the words in here but I know what you're saying.' He watched his Treasurer's mouth – the way it turned down in perpetual sadness. His friend was not helped by the cod's jowls and the boxer's nose that arrived too soon to the space above his lips, which all gave the impression he would be happier in more aquatic conditions. 'I won't say the word "crime", but it sits close to the brain's surface tonight, nothing surer,' said the Chairman. 'Fuck – just as well Sergeant Punch is in the ground or, even in retirement, he'd arrest us for this conversation alone.'

'He is in the ground. I put him there,' said Dave. 'The man

is not capable of handcuffing an ant.' He reached for the bottle again. 'And we'd be doing this island and its people a service, even if they don't know it. An island needs an organisation such as ours, to remember its past. There is another reason – the timing is perfect.'

'Why?' asked Pluto.

'The man Tom Bywater, *Sir* Tom Bywater is apparently on the island,' announced Dave. 'So they say anyway. He's been spotted.'

'Sir Tom *who*?' Pluto shook his head; he knew of course he could not mention the botched historical tour.

'Sir Tom bloody Thumb,' sighed Dave. 'Anyway, let's just say he is somebody who could take the heat off us.'

'Well, such funds would pay for the domain for the next twenty years – protecting at least something of our legacy. Christ, we'll both be in the ground ourselves by then.' Pluto looked through the IHAS file on the table – his only file – for some historical records to spread between him and his Treasurer in case of a sudden interruption from the outside world. The papers amounted to some census information from the 1900s, which he had printed off the internet. Then he looked up to the photo of Mae-Li, his fiancée. It was best if Dave didn't know the level of his relations with the girl. These funds could come in handy with getting her to the island, or him to her.

'And how would we accomplish such a deed?' asked Pluto; he would be quick to pounce on what came next, so as to make it appear as though he had thought of it himself. 'Wait – I'll put on a dressing gown for this.'

'Aye, well ...' said Dave, as he watched his leader quickly leave the room and return in a robe that looked like it had once been modelled by Robert the Bruce. He at least was pleased with the less fluorescent attire.

'Go on Treasurer,' said Pluto, 'what is the plan?'

'I propose we work as a team to distract the van driver.'

'The man Randy? With the big head?'

'Granted. His skull could put an asteroid to shame. And, well, I hear he is not the most observant spoke in the wheel. I'm sure we wouldn't be detected.'

'I like it, Treasurer,' decided Pluto, rising to his feet. He could just about hear the water rippling off the dragon's tongue. And do you think we could use some funds to expand in the Far East?'

'Sit down – I think we would have to look carefully at the accounts as we progress.' It was important to Dave that he stamp his ground when it came to Treasury matters.

'Well, some time soon?' asked Pluto.

'Perhaps,' said Dave. 'But Chairman – I advise caution. You won't be plucking that banjo in Bangkok any time this week.'

Two weeks passed and the two men were once again signed in to the Situation Room; the robbery of the bank van had been successfully accomplished. They sat with a wad of banknotes between them where the salt and pepper had been. The robbery had gone like a dream; in fact, to the recollections of the two men it was less a robbery than a simple conversation to distract the man Randy. However, they had expected Randy to be sacked by now, suspected of an inside job, and they were alarmed that he had not been. To make matters worse, the local newspaper carried the headline that the robbery was most likely an outside operation. Pluto's leg twitched; to Dave it was a sign of fear, which was descending on his Chairman the way fog was crawling from the sea, making a menace of the island.

'You have made a serious strategic mistake,' Dave said angrily, looking to the photograph of Mae-Li. 'I knew I should have ripped that bloody photo up the last time I was here, before the, well, before we flagged down that bank van. Half the island seems to know you bought your fancy lady a plane ticket, and that you're about to upgrade the fountain. Could you not have kept that quiet at least?'

Pluto reclined in his chair. He knew his decision to wear his only suit was doing nothing to appease Dave's mood. Still, it gave him a sense of gravitas, despite the Wellington boots. 'I'm sorry, Treasurer,' he sighed, 'I told one soul – that fucker in the bar. You might as well put my heart in a jam jar. I'll make room on the shelf.'

'You might as well have bloody pinned it to the ironmonger's notice board. Well, eyes are on us now. On you. And so on me. I do not intend on going to bed with failure. The community respects me. I put their dead to rest. I'd sooner be in a coffin myself. And you really had to order more teeth?'

Pluto rubbed his hands through his ginger strands of hair. 'Dave. I feel bad enough about it already. I'm trying to fathom a plan, to remove our organisation from suspicion.'

'You could start with taking off that awful suit. I wouldn't bury the dead in it. Did nobody ever tell you man that a tie with a T-shirt is a mockery?'

'Fuck. Does this mean we're going to hell?'

'In a hand-cart.'

Pluto rocked back and forth in his chair. 'I need to leave the island for a spell, don't I? I need to get out.'

'You do.'

'We can't both go.'

'We can't.'

'But how?'

'Let me think on it,' said Dave. 'I'm sorry, my friend, but you're not taking me down with you. I'll help you leave the island, but after that, you're on your own.'

'I understand,' said Pluto, feeling his authority slipping away. 'And speaking for both Mae-Li and myself, and her parents, we appreciate your compassion, Treasurer.' Pluto cleared his throat. 'Kob kun,' he added. And then more sheepishly – 'I've been brushing up a little on the foreign tongue ...'

'Eh? Well, you can change that to *Chairman*,' said Dave. Now he questioned even the authenticity of Pluto's world-champion stone-skimming credentials. It was sad to witness this decline in a man but needs must. Dave then straightened his back and put both palms down on the table.

Pluto watched – he had seen the confident, Stetson-ed J.R. Ewing do similar.

'Then it is so,' said Pluto, loosening the tie around his freckle-infested neck. He knew it was the end for him. 'Can we keep the fountain?'

'You have fallen with honour, my friend,' said Dave. 'So let the record show, at ...' Dave looked to the fish-head clock above Pluto's sink which sat above the dead heart in a jar, '... at 8:57 p.m. on the 3rd of September, 2009, I am bestowed the honour of leading this organisation, the Island Historical and Archaeological Society. All those in favour say aye. *Aye!*'

'Aye,' seconded Pluto, reluctantly. He reached for the banjo and took the plectrum from his teeth. 'Will you want a tune to see you in?'

'That bastard MacIntyre,' Dave said into his mug, ignoring

the offer. 'He had better have something up his sleeve worthy of Beethoven himself, because I'm going for him. With or without you.'

'Or Mae-Li?'

'Or Mae-Li.'

13

The Letters of Ivor Punch

Wednesday 19th August, 2009

Dear Mr President,

Tonight I feel that way a man can feel about himself when he is nothing, or perhaps, everything. I feel it all slipping away but yet I never had it; it was never mine: my father, the doves, Mary, Randy, the whales, my nephew, my brother – even the grains of sand in the pit. Do you ever feel that way, or are you too young? And fuck. It leaves me, this feeling, with the notion that I can start again, that nothing has scared me: not any of the above. What a fragile existence I crave for myself at this dark hour, here on this dark island that houses ghouls. Mary. You know I left the engagement ring on the fencepost at the beginning of the track to Bloody Bay. She was not best pleased with that arrangement. I could go up there now, to the same fencepost along the same lane just off Transmitter Road, but the ring will not be there, and Mary will not be there. And fuck. If she were there waiting, it would be my blood doing the spilling in the bay. Anyway, I'd be left standing like a prick. And knowing my luck, Randy would pass by on his way to munch on another horse. I should have locked that bastard up for good and thrown away the key. I gave Mary another thing, a hair clasp that has been in my family since the nineteenth century. 'H.B.' is inscribed on it. Despite my powers of deduction I have no clue to the significance.

Adrianna, the Polish girl, came over earlier to check on the chick. Gorbachev is showing signs of recovery but I'll not be asking it for eggs any time soon. There's more chance of Randy in that stupid banking uniform laying one on my sofa. The idiot always arrives in his slippers. How far can a man reasonably walk from his front door in slippers? The bastard's father was the same; fought the war in them for all I know. I shake my head now thinking how many times I arrested and released Randy. If there had been electronic tagging back then, well there would have been only one place to apply it. If he uses it too often I believe a man can spoil his knob. I feel another rage coming on, but I'm fighting it, Mr President, I'm fighting it.

Yours aye,
I.P.

PS: I see I had deer in again last night – saves on the gardening bills I suppose. I wouldn't have said that when I was younger, I'd have shot at them, as I did the doves at my father's order. Still, it's good to keep the gun loaded.

Thursday 20th August, 2009
Dear Mr MacAskill,

Secretary for Justice, let me tell you a story. I am sure my words will not match those of yours, which I just watched you spouting on the TV. I even turned the sound up to hear your voice. And fuck. In a way your delivery reminded me of the soap opera characters' mouths I've watched for years without hearing their words, who will now in my mind forever more be given your voice. But that will not be long for me. For you see I am afraid of the word – of hearing it. And so I usually silence the world.

In much the same way a survivor of Auschwitz cannot get beyond the 'A', I cannot get beyond the 'L'. I am even fearful of hearing myself say it. A town that will never reclaim its name. But you spoke it with such perfect diction. Crisp as the earliest bird's call. I should think come the famous Oscar ceremony you will be up for a gong. Congratulations: you have achieved on the world stage. You seem a man incapable of critical thinking. I am not so blessed. I feared your decision and I was right to.

As I sit here in my old sergeant's uniform and slippers I am thinking about something that has always puzzled me. How much do we really know of those we love? I want to tell you about a man's leap; well, he was not much more than a boy. Just twenty he was. I have watched birds – doves even, the most attractive of birds; I have seen whales – the largest of mammals – and witnessed the way their big graceful tails take your breath away. And fuck. I have slain both. Maybe that is why I understand what you have done to me. Because I am no better. I can still see the big tails spanking the ocean. But of all these marvels of the natural world, not one ever matched the sight I witnessed in the summer of 1978, on the village Games field here on my island. It was a grey day, but the sort of mild, heavy day that the Gulf Stream often allows us. And fuck. I could hear the sound of pipes before I even left my house on that morning and the goose bumps stood to attention. You see, all my family ran and jumped. I was not a good jumper, nor the best runner – I was too eager to land; I have never been one who was happy to leave this island. What I lacked in talent, I made up for in determination. But it was never enough. At that time my father's record for the long jump was still standing, which dated back to the 1920s. Breaking it seemed about as achievable to all-comers

233

as did eternal life. But my young brother broke it. Fuck did he break it.

One of the other uncles – my father's brother – was a man whose words were taken by the Great War, if not his nerve-ends too. Well, this man who I never saw display an emotion beyond a curl of his lip on Christmas Day, who folk believed to be broken in some way deeper even than his soul, well, this man had tears in his eyes on his deathbed some five years later at the memory of having held the far end of the measuring tape. And fuck. I can still see his hand shaking, hovering just above the upturned sand. And, Mr MacAskill, I can still hear the sounds of the lad's feet pounding the turf, the same turf that I had laboured over, the same turf that my father graced, breaking a record which dated back to the times of men who still heard the bombs of WWI in their heads. And then I see my brother leaping. How high he is. He is leaping right over my head as I sit in this chair. Soaring over me. He is edging closer to immortality; and then he is gone, taken from my view, before landing. How were we to know then that his legacy would be his presence on a passenger list bound for New York? And as I think back to that final stage of the jump, well, the men around the pit . . . And fuck. I can see their faces even now. My stupid friend Randy never closed his mouth for a week. It seemed like the lad was in the air forever. They believed he was going to come down with stories from heaven – wet from the clouds – with angel's wings – for he jumped with such grace and swooped with such deliberation that the rest of us became a different ilk entirely. Simply knowing that his human body could do that, in such basic conditions, made me believe that higher powers were at play. I remember I looked up to the colourful crowd peppered on the hillside like a tube of Smarties tossed in the air; and they were

234

silent – or maybe it is just my recollection muting the world. My brother's record remains unbeaten. But, Secretary for Justice, I did not expect my brother's descent to last so long. Twenty years, it was last year, since the bomb. And still he falls. To think that in my dreams I used to see him rise. And fuck. His name is still printed each year in the Games programme of record holders. And now the long jump cup is in his name. I was there in my uniform on the end of the tape, with my old uncle, and our union was our disbelief. I cried with laughter later that night, for I had seen it, and I even felt my old father in his grave acknowledge it. And fuck. I realise now something we didn't know at the time, that it was a line far greater than the one here in our sandpit that the lad's leap defined, one that marked the before and the after in the fortunes of our family.

I believed during that briefest of moments in 1978 that my father and perhaps myself were redeemed; that even my distant relation, the first man Punch, An Gnuis Dubh they called him, would also be redeemed. But fuck, from that peak when my brother hung in the air, it has been only down, downhill for us. And now I have reached my lowest, Mr MacAskill. My days are now divided into life as it was before the plane fell, and life after it.

And fuck. Maybe now you will fall. You are an unpopular man, they say, in the United States of America for releasing the bomber on grounds of compassion. It looks like our shortbread tins will be floating back on the first waves of the Atlantic. I pity you. You are now the rabbit in the headlights as I was here in the local shop on those first raw days after the plane came down. When I knew my eyes were scared and blood stained in the way only those of an animal facing death can be; when I could barely face the people in a community I have known and protected for most of my life. But had to. Had to keep face, do justice to the badge, if not the family name. Justice. I am glad I stayed – we have things here on this island that other places do not have.

I am not ashamed to say I admire any man who has the backbone to make, and then defend, the decision you have taken. I made a few myself. But we must draw lines in the sand. A life lived teaches you that. I am not a legal man – and fuck, most of my working life I turned a blind eye to men's mistakes – but when it was said that blood would rain down in revenge, I did not expect it to be my brother's blood; those fine limbs crumpled beyond use.

I have one question for you – and fuck, it should be chiselled into your stone: how does a man grant compassion to the guilty without harming the innocent?

I Punch

Saturday 22nd August, 2009

Dear Mr Megrahi,

First, I apologise for not addressing you with your full given name. I'm not sure I have sufficient lead in this pencil.

You'll be busy living it up with Gaddafi back home in Libya, so I'll get straight to the point: there is a word I haven't used in a while. The reason for this is not because I am pious, or in any way closer to perfection than the next man, or the next sergeant, for that matter, because I am not, but it is due to the fact that my father once said it of my mother, in front of her no less. He called her a cunt. It was said for no other reason than the fact that she was a better human being than he. I cannot say I am any higher up the ladder to heaven than you, but I have heard you called *a cunt many times. And fuck. I have thought it myself. But I must resist; tonight, I must resist, because I can feel my own end approaching, my lungs failing.*

And fuck. I saw you board your plane like an ageing pop star, or an international ice cream salesperson, in your white tracksuit, your head down, your soul sunk to your heavy feet as you made slow progress on those steps to the plane bound not for your next concert but for your death. Another plane. I have never been on one. And fuck. I can't. But I felt no desire to say cunt to my TV set. Instead I felt shame, my own shame, at my feelings of empathy. And that is why I am writing to you. As I watched I thought to myself: what is it the world is trying to tell me? For as long as I have doubts, fears even, as to the possibility of injustice in your conviction, then I can build the illusion that the bomb was not placed, the plane did not fall, and forge a dream that the line in the sand might be surpassed once more. By my son. And fuck. Again. Again. Please do it again dear son. For me. But you cannot!

I saw your older self, Mr Megrahi; you looked quite different from the prison mugshot they have shown all these years. And then your private jet took flight. A vapour-trail to freedom that became cloud and then – nothing. I have seen that happen before. And fuck. I did not need volume to hear the swoosh of the thing as it reached a ceiling in the sky, and went further, through cloud, to cloud. And maybe that is where you should have stayed. Not to be judged by a higher power in the form that Mr MacAskill has intimated you will be, but by another force, something that floats above us, not a God, not a flock of angels, but instead by the souls and minds and spirits and dreams and bodies of those who were forced out of their seats just days before that Christmas

237

*in 1988. And fuck. My son's new American wife was among
them. Leaving behind their little lad without a mother – young
Jake. A tot. And I read there was a puppeteer among them, a
stamp expert, a dog handler, a seaman no less, and even a peace
activist. Imagine that. And some of them not older than their
seat number. And fuck.*

*Yes some of them were children. What a mess. And fuck.
Surely they were deserving of an epitaph more than the
scattered remains of books or newspapers they were reading
in the festive moments before their deaths. And to those on the
ground, surely they were worth more than the rubble of their
own homes collapsing on them and their Christmas trees?
And fuck. That is my hope. That when such an outrageous
event occurs in the life of a man or a woman or a child they are
quickly spared of their troubles, and pain, and that something
remains of them in the sky, something that reaches beyond
simple life and forevermore falls, like a dust, on us, the ones
who need and miss them most. After the plane came down I
even climbed our island's highest peak to see if I could feel some
minor recognition, some kinship with the dead, some small
experience, just sufficient, for me to stop believing in ghouls. As
indeed I try to climb mountains in my mind now, to reach a place
where I do not think of you as a cunt. If that is what the world is
telling me I must do.*

*But I have failed to listen. I have failed to turn the volume
up. I have failed myself, my mother; I have failed the screaming
world; I have even failed you. I hear my father's voice in my own
as I say this:*

'You cunt, you cunt.'

I am rage itself.

But there is something worse – I am not even convinced of

238

your guilt. I am sure I locked up innocent men – so am I any better? And fuck. Some of the bodies were found in a sheep meadow a mile away; a long way from home. And that is dreadful enough that somebody must pay. And it is me. It has been me all along. I am the cunt.

Sergeant Ivor Punch

Sunday August 23rd, 2009

Dear Mr President,

I am tired tonight. I coughed blood all day. And my body is sore. I cannot even trouble what little supper Miss McBeth has made for me. I fear she saw that I have a tattoo of a woman's pussy on my upper right arm – this from my time killing whales off Greenland. And fuck. I've tried my best to conceal it all these years but I think I have been unsuccessful. Well, she'll have seen one before.

There are some things of this world that cannot be reversed. He never got to really know about that. These things they cannot be undone, unsaid or unlived. Remember that, sir.

The wind still howls, invisible, like I myself am becoming. But the wind is not so bad because it is noise in itself, bouncing off my house – proof that I am here. Housed.

I had the young girl from next door over today. She was concerned about the failing wing on Gorbachev. I had to go back out to the coop after she had gone to collect an egg and found a pile of knickers stashed in the straw. You'll be wondering why this is of any interest, but I suppose I am simply putting my innocence in print. The most powerful man on this earth might as well know. Because with this pile of ladies' underwear I am

239

able to solve my final case. Randy has been telling me about the knickers disappearing off the clothes lines. It is the highlight of his conversation to be honest. The Knicker-Knocker, they're calling whoever has been doing it. So I left the knickers there. Let them think it was me, although I'm certain it must be Randy. He still has it in him after all. Miss McBeth is untouchable of course. My reputation was shot a long time ago anyway so no harm is done. I take other more pressing secrets with me to my maker . . . one concerns young Jake, my grandson, now living and playing that violin of his in London, and fuck, off the island. Can you hear me Jake? My blood? We had a tenth anniversary memorial of, what was it, my, my brother's death. And Jake played that violin of his. He was just a teenager. And I did not tell him how beautiful it was. I never even removed my sergeant's hat. Well, the music took him off the island. It got him away.

And fuck. I wonder this, as I drift off – it was a notion I first had after Jake moved away – what if Jake is an angel and I never knew? And his father is up there now, divulging the secrets of the living, and I, down here, know nothing of the dead – is that fair, Mr President? And what if, when my, yes he was my son, when he was a young boy holding my adult hand, I was only aware of mine when in his, and my heart beating only because it was next to his, and my eyes seeing only through his? And now I am old and tired beyond tired, I must make do with touching only using my hands, and looking only with my old eyes, and speaking with my inadequate mouth. And fuck. In my dreams I make it out of this chair and beyond this window, up to the Games field at the end of Transmitter Road. And he is there. Flying above the sandpit. He is so close in my mind I can reach for his shorts and touch. I want now to touch him again. He was Mo curaidh. My hero.

*And so there is a knife in the kitchen and it is time. It is time
to silence the rage. Time to put my body to rest. I pity the sight
Miss McBeth would discover, so well . . . I will try to time it
to just before one of Randy's visits. And fuck. I got him out of
enough scrapes, so he can return the compliment. Maybe he'll
prop me next to him in that fucking bank van. My Goebbels to
his Hitler. And better not to trouble the chicks or startle the lass
next door with the sound of gunshot. You see, Mr President,
it is twenty years on and I miss my lad more and more. And
these pangs to the past are not simply for the adult he was, it is
the child I miss. I remember when I was whaling during those
summer months in the Arctic and being bitten by insects that
left a mark the size of a small country on my body. And fuck,
they would itch. I'll never forget that. And what a tan I took on
the sea. The others on the boat couldn't see me at night, kept
bumping into me, the fuckers. I was darker than yourself. But
I wonder now was it the sun or its reflection off the sea that
coloured me? Was it the sky or the ocean? But anyway they
would sit, these bugs, hiding on our bodies with the expectation
to strike again, and so we discovered that if we poured alcohol
on the area of the offending itch then our bodies would pinpoint
the exact position where they were hiding and, we believed, tell
us where they were to attack next. The alcohol was a warning
bell of sorts. And fuck. We thought we were in control, and as
a result I was left with no specific pain but instead a collective
of discomfort – a oneness of pain. And in a way that is no pain.
And maybe that is what I am doing now, getting it all out before
the world bites me again. I have had enough. My lungs have
given up and I have just enough pride left in me so as not to turn
the stomach of the current undertaker on the island, Dave the
Grave, with such a pitiful demise as to present him with a sack*

of potatoes for a body to dress. I'll get the job done myself. Aye,
I'll return to the house of my forebear, Duncan Punch, to be
readied for the ground. And fuck. The only doubt is that I don't
know how deeply into the earth I'm headed.

I didn't realise he was the person I lived for until after he died.
I am to go now. To join him. Mo curaidh.

Keep yourself alive, sir. And thank you for your efforts
in blocking the bomber, but it seems something bigger than
revenge, or the rightness of things, has beaten us, as it has the
bombed. Maybe that is called life. I suppose we all have to kiss a
few frogs.

My best to your fine family. And remember: our love gets all
that it deserves. Never hurt anything sir, not even a fly.

Yours aye,
Sergeant Ivor Punch
(by the time you get this) 'Deceased.'

∾ 14 ∾

The Box

Zoe sat at the bottom of the stairs. She had come down from the bedroom where she had wept along with her two girls as they fought their need for sleep. She knew it was really the new day they were opposing, their fear of waking to find that it was true: that their father had indeed fallen to his death from the island's headland near the lighthouse; that it was not a bad dream or island myth. It was cold reality; it was grief. It broke her heart to have overheard the girls wondering whether this was one of their father's tricks, like the phone game he played with apple juice cartons, and that he would soon return, tracksuited and alive. She had discovered, talking to the local undertaker, that Tom was not the first to have fallen from that headland. A young lady had fallen, where now giant letters on the rockface marked the spot. And even now, after all these years, the island people did not know the reason for her fall, *if* in fact she fell. Zoe had found it all quite distressing.

She sighed loudly and got up to open a bottle of wine, but then thought better of it. What if the girls were to wake and she was drunk again? *Oh Tom*, she thought. She felt surrounded by death: first there was Henrietta, and then – she had discovered online – her older sister Isabella. And now Tom. Why did it shock her that no one lives forever? Despite the strangeness of her predicament, and of this as the backdrop to Tom's final exit, she had been pleasantly surprised by the undertaker's professionalism. Even if the man Dave had gone into unnecessary detail about the procedures he would undertake on her husband's body. It was there, at the undertaker's, that Tom lay tonight. She hoped by now he would be suited again.

The Victorian bureau caught her eye. A picture frame was slotted behind it. She lifted one side of the bureau away from the wall and slid out the frame. She was surprised, and then enchanted, to see that it held what looked like an original letter from Charles Darwin.

Down House
Downe
Kent
England

21st February 1841

Dearest Isabella,

How very kind of you to send me your recent publication, which Emma and I enjoyed most thoroughly and to the utmost. We have the greatest of admiration for your explorative endeavours and travels. You and young Henrietta really must come and visit us after our impending birth. We are to have a baby. And we feel certain it is our first girl.

Kindest regards,

Charles

Charles Darwin, FRS

Zoe manoeuvred the bureau back snugly against the wall and paused to imagine Isabella seated at it. She placed her hands on the wood grain as she hoped Isabella had once done. Then she looked at the shoes of her family discarded by the front door. She knelt closer and arranged them in perfect order. She imagined Isabella and Henrietta's shoes amongst them, and a hand on the door, and a man, yes a man, knocking on the other side. A big man he would be. And then she aligned Tom's trainers, which sat last in the row, redundant, and white as a ghost.

She stood, reached for the old front door and opened it. She felt the freshening wind of the night and looked to the plaque which confirmed the house had indeed belonged to the famous travel writer and explorer, Isabella Bird.

'It's okay,' she said aloud, 'I am here. I am Hennie.'

Oak Tree sat at the end of the pier. His heavy legs dangled off the end of the island as he watched the sea massage the stone below. He wondered who before him could have completed the super-human task of erecting thick pillars of stone in the water. And when? His mother told him he had been asking too many questions lately, but was it not normal, he wondered, to want to know more? They had argued again and now here he was, sitting in the place where he could be alone. The rusting metal ladder that disappeared into the sea had only two rungs showing above the bobbing tide; it looked like the stairway to hell. Tomorrow he was going to see a man go to heaven, and he would be part of that journey; so if there was a heaven then he decided there must be a hell. These thoughts made him feel full.

He loosened the black tie from around his thick neck; he

had never worn one before and wearing it now with the white shirt was a trial run for tomorrow. His mother had needed to borrow the shirt from his uncle Randy, such was the circumference of his neck. Oak Tree had been just days old when his mother had first struggled to get a garment over his big skull. He turned back to view the seafront and the main street; the quietness deafened him. When walking past the graffitied clock earlier, he had noticed it was still encircled by police tape; as though the clock-keeper had committed a crime worthy of *CSI*.

It was all too much to take in. Tomorrow he would start his apprenticeship with the island's undertaker. But he already felt too close to death. This was the first time he had ever felt this fullness. This was also the first day in all his seventeen years that he had produced a catch. Usually it was boredom that brought him here, but tonight, just when it mattered to him least, he had finally come up trumps: he looked down at the sad, dead seagull, his prize catch, which he had hooked earlier with the fishing rod he stored at the end of the pier. The clock chimed and Oak Tree counted eight strokes. He pushed his head backwards to take in the dark blue sky. The stars looked like diamonds stitched into cloth. Some were reflected on the black sea. He liked to look at the sky on nights like these, but maybe there had never been a night like this.

He had been wondering a lot recently about what lay above and beyond his remote island. He smiled, imagining there was nothing else out there but the whispering waves. He rearranged his fat bum on the stone wall. The buttons on his trousers were already burst; he was fishing in his suit tonight so that he would know how to wear it tomorrow. His mother had said he was eating too much. His friends often said he looked pregnant. He opened another packet of crisps but was startled by a movement below. The seagull flapped about on the ground and brought Oak Tree's fishing rod down with it. He noticed it only had one leg.

Oak Tree brushed the remains of the crisps off his suit. The seagull broke free from the rod and flew into the night, at first on a low trajectory several feet above the water but then, rising, it was lost to him. He watched the black space it had last occupied. That seagull now knew more about what was beyond the island than he might ever know. Oak Tree was glad it had defied him and was now free, already part of the future. If he looked hard enough he could see the future himself, bold as skyscrapers.

Early the following morning Dave the Grave was in his preparation room, which was in fact one side of his garage. In his capacity as a leading historical expert on the island, Dave had researched this space, and apparently it had long been considered a holding place of sorts, a waiting room for the dead, dating back to the nineteenth century and the big man Duncan Punch, *An Gnuis Dubh*. Dave had discovered this man Punch also made coffins, and built the town clock with his own hands. According to folklore, he transported dead bodies on his cart next to slabs of peat – all from this very place. Dave also suspected the man Punch had a hand in the fine wooden swords, two of which he had found buried behind an old bench that had come with the house, upon which he now placed his coffins and bodies.

He had almost completed the dressing of the body below him on his bench. Unusually, he did not feel fully in control. He had noticed how the body, although stilled in death, emitted a presence of mind as if still ticking. He knew this had been a man with brains, after all. The bruised legs and buttocks were stained and had required a good wash. The undertaker had long considered himself the keeper of the dead's secrets, of which this was just another. This occupational gathering of information, to which only he was privy, felt like a promise made to angels, a step closer to heaven. The banker man must have soiled himself in the final moment of life – when that terror was felt. Dave had used one of his own shirts to dress the corpse, and now stood in nothing but his underpants – he enjoyed being this exposed, this close, to the dead.

He was not unfamiliar with the nickname the locals had given him. Still, he imagined Shakespeare could rest safely. He moved through his house to the bedroom and looked out his own burial suit. The suit was not the type a civilian man might wear; instead there were details on the lapels and in the lining that distinguished him, and aided the higher functions of his job. There were times he considered his purpose was not to mark the end of life but to stage an occasion. Detail was everything. He had taken many of his burial practices to a new level as a result of a book he had acquired. As the stamp on it revealed, it had once been owned by the local school, but was now held by the island's undertaker, he being the incumbent. The handbook, entitled *Coming to the Gates of Death*, was bound together by yellowed tape. Its content charted the practicalities and emotions surrounding death, and had been handwritten by one Isabella Bird. He liked to think of it as the 'Book of Death'.

Dave put on suit trousers and a vest, and moved through to the kitchen to the iron, which had just reached the temperature for silk. Everyone must prepare to play a part, he thought, even the bereaved, and the graveyard was his stage. The creases would be important today, given that most of the island's community was expected to come out to see off the coffin, if not half the world. There was talk on the island of Sky and BBC camera crews arriving. All the more reason for him to keep Pluto well hidden from view – and that was his intention. 'You're a genius right enough,' Dave said to himself. He now felt more settled. On the day previous, when he had been fuelling up the hearse, the lads at the local garage had even reported a sighting of Rupert Murdoch. Despite his scepticism, Dave had conceded that indeed there were Murdochs on the island; it couldn't be denied as he had buried one himself, and well, it wasn't beyond the realms of possibility that the man Murdoch could have been a friend of the other famous man on the island, who was now a corpse and at this very moment lying on his bench, which he thought of as the dressing table.

Dave had not that long ago moved to the island from Glasgow, and his adopted community was proving slow on the deaths front, as compared with mainland tallies. It was a question of source numbers. Although things were improving – first there had been the very recent death of the old man Ivor Punch, a fellow Dave now wished he had known better in life, given his discovery of Ivor's lineage to the undertaker Punch, and also because Ivor's final request, delivered to Dave by Ivor's housekeeper, the lady Miss McBeth, had been one of honour, which was to be buried in his police uniform from this very room where his forebear had once presided. And now there was this corpse before him; although it could hardly be considered local. Still, he was at times thankful for the lesser-populated world over which he now presided, and felt sure that his decision to move to the tranquillity of the island had been a good one. It had brought challenges, though: on his way to one of his first jobs the hearse broke down due to a lack of spare parts and so he had to improvise with his everyday car, with the boot left open to make room. That was the same day he heard a mobile phone ring from inside the coffin. 'That will be God now,' Pluto had said with a nudge, having come along for the ride. Dave now chuckled at the memory as he looked out from his kitchen window to the wondrous view of the sun rippling along the sea like a kind of applause. 'Appropriate. Like heaven,' he muttered to himself. In his more poetic moments Dave thought of himself as the man with the keys to the Pearly Gates. So yes, despite the planning, it was often a job of the unexpected: on one occasion he had even been asked to cut a pacemaker from a dead man's chest, as a memento. 'A surgeon too,' he had proudly whispered to himself from above the gaping hole. Dave the Grave looked down to his polished shoes on which the overhead lights created little moons, and said: 'I'm Saint Peter, right enough.'

Now fully dressed, he walked back through to his garage that had once been the man Punch's workshop, and stood once again in the presence of the corpse. Just the day before, in life, this body had been a man of infamy; well, Dave thought, nothing was changed in death. He had never before taken so much care when polishing the brass handles on a coffin's side. It was the finest casket he had ever seen. He knew the man had money – the whole world knew; it was the first time Dave had ever been asked to close the lid on a Knight of the Realm. 'Sir Tom Bywater, right enough. Pleased to meet you,' meet you,' he whispered. 'I won't let you down.' It had been a sorry situation the previous evening when the man's wife and two small daughters had come to visit the body. English they were, of course, and heartbroken. Dave leaned his bald head down to the cherubic head, for he believed that all men return to the motif of the cherub, to smell the milky flesh; most of the man's scent had disappeared. Dave's grandfather had been a perfumer from France – that land where people looked like fish and were proud of it; and so Dave trusted the genetic heritage of his nose; had it not been flesh and bone he now prepared, it would have been scents in a bottle. On occasion, he believed he could in fact smell one of the island's dead awaiting his services before he even received the call. He looked up to check the clock; he had warned the new boy to be early.

The night before Dave had been unsure if the clothed body was in fact a little bare. It was a hard one to fathom. And that decision had left him with a dilemma: to apply a tie or not. This was a man who had been more accustomed to wearing a suit and so Dave had dressed him in one, but would a tie be a tad too Mafioso? He took some comfort in the realisation that he and Pluto's crime, their theft, was of a far smaller magnitude than the one presided over by this man Bywater.

'There,' he said, dusting the face of the body and straightening the parting in his blond, greying hair, 'you can't cause any more trouble to our pockets now.' He took a step back to admire his work.

'Handsome,' he said quietly to the suited remains, 'you're almost ready.'

All this thinking of money had made Dave the Grave

nervous again; he hoped Pluto could remain calm. He had better try out the coffin for size. So he drew a black sheet over the body, then turned to the open casket and climbed inside.

Oak Tree was on his way to the undertaker's house. The previous night, at the end of the pier, he had felt so relaxed beneath the stars, but this morning he was edgy and had cut himself shaving. *Bend your knees*, Dave had said on the induction he had received over the phone. Dave had said that the lifting technique for transporting a coffin needed to be exact. Oak Tree had practised by lifting the heaviest drawer in his house, which was full of his mother's library books. Now here he stood nervously by the undertaker's house, looping his tie around his fingers. He did all he could not to visualise the paleness of the dead body that he would soon encounter. He was a famous man they said – Oak Tree couldn't remember what for, but his uncle Randy had said what the man did for a job rhymed with 'wanker'.

Through the early morning darkness he saw a light on in the garage. Oak Tree walked slowly towards the light and then stopped and hovered like a moth. It was the earliest he had been up since the last Christmas tree hunt, a tradition of his uncle Randy's. He knocked at the garage door and waited for a response. There was none.

'Hullo?' he said in his deep, low voice, which added years onto him. He knocked once again. Still no response. Oak Tree pushed at the door and it opened. 'Eh, hullo?'

He ducked his head below the door frame and the first thing he saw was a black sheet covering something on a bench, and, up against the far wall, a coffin. He breathed deeply through his big nostrils and lifted his gaze from the coffin, which was the colour of the gym bench he had once collapsed at school.

'Make yourself at home,' said a voice.

'What!' Could Oak Tree have jumped on the spot he would have; his breathing sped and he felt drips of sweat run down his back. He turned around as quickly as his frame would allow but there was no one else in the garage.

'You're five minutes late. That'll come off your first pay packet. Are you at least in a tie?' Oak Tree didn't move.

'I'm in *here* lad. I like to do this; eh, I don't like to put a body in a coffin without first trying it for size myself. And I couldn't resist this fancy one. I've stayed in worse hotel rooms. Good aroma too.' Dave sniffed. It was best that he fashion a good reason for his unusual positioning, he couldn't possibly reveal the truth.

Oak Tree backed up to the garage door. *The voice was coming from the coffin?*

'We must get this one right,' the voice went on. 'Even though the funeral's happening elsewhere, on the mainland, we must get the body to the ferry, and with dignity. The world's eyes will be on our backs, and so we want to make a good showing of our island. I've been dealing with more layers of bureaucracy with this one than I have ink.'

'Hullo! Who are you?' shouted Oak Tree.

'Yes, this man made a menace of himself. Good lining in here for him, right enough. Nice support on the back too.'

Oak Tree heard a squeak and the coffin lid shot up.

'Fuck!' yelled Oak Tree, making a racket as he backed up against the corrugated door. 'Fuck! It's alive!'

'Christ, what a commotion,' said Dave the Grave, peering

his egghead out of the casket, 'anyone would think you'd seen a ghost.'

'I thought …' Oak Tree quivered, peeking his head back around the door frame.

'That's your first mistake, my lad – I do all the thinking here,' said Dave. He looked to the boy and gestured for him to come forward. 'Come back in. It's just as well people do not live forever,' he said, 'cause you'd be in deep trouble finding another job with a tongue like that. I'll have your mother wash your mouth out!' Dave propelled himself up and out of the coffin like a gymnast releasing from the parallel bars. 'Come!'

He noticed how the boy walked with his head down as though he'd perpetually lost something; he was in danger of missing the world. And he had quite a square skull, right enough.

Oak Tree didn't want to get too close. He hadn't slept for most of the night trying to prepare for the image of the body stripped of life. He was also mildly embarrassed by his shaving cut. But he had no choice now. He had made his mother proud by getting this job and he wanted to be good at it. He walked slowly towards his new boss.

Dave of course had spotted the blemish on the boy's neck but didn't feel this the time to make any consequence of it. Perhaps he never would. This, after all, was the lad's first body.

'Lay the tie on the man. He's still that – just,' said Dave. 'Take your time. Although I don't suppose you have a choice. I've seen dead bodies go about their work faster.'

Oak Tree stood at the opened casket. He wondered where the body was and then he realised. There was a funny smell like potatoes boiling. Dave gestured somewhat impatiently with the movement of his gloveless hand through the air towards the black blanket. Oak Tree's big eyes circled in their sockets and then he put out his hand but it wouldn't go all the way.

'Here!' Dave pulled the cover off the body in one movement, and despite the absence of a top hat, he made a magician's audience of the boy. Oak Tree's breaths quickened and became louder. He saw the serious purple lines as well as the bruising around the man's temples, which amassed under the skin like neon worms. Oak Tree's Adam's apple performed a somersault inside its toilet-papered bandage. He could not run. Here he was, the Coffin Boffin, as his friends had taken to calling him, at work. He brought a spare tie out of his pocket, a flailing thing with little life, and peered down at the pale dead head. He closed his eyes and slowly lowered the tie, which, thanks to his mother, already had the required loop, and held it above the head.

'Come on lad, the man could tie it faster himself. He's got a ferry to catch!'

'I dunno if I can . . .' quivered Oak Tree.

'You can lad; I too once had my first dead body. We are all virgins at the beginning. Even Quincy.'

Oak Tree nervously looped the tie around the head of the body. Dave the Grave watched how promisingly the lad moved the head up – gently, but commandingly; no doubt the boy would be surprised by its full, dead weight. Oak Tree moved back and just about opened his eyes.

'It was needed,' Dave said. 'The tie definitely finishes him off, if that cliff's edge didn't already. You know he was a faller?' Dave realised he was talking just as much now to the new help as he was to the version of himself from the night before, when he had wondered if such a statement around the neck was required, after the poor man's family had left the garage. They were to reconvene this morning at the ferry with the rest of the Bywater family, who would be travelling up from The South. Sad it was.

'Yeah my friends think he jumped,' said Oak Tree. 'I saw it on the TV with my parents. Not the jump.'

'We'll never know. It's possible to fall; certainly I've heard of a young local lass who fell from the exact same headland in the 1950s. She was never even permitted a resting box, the poor thing; she was taken by the sea they say. Of course, this was way before my time here. Anyway, both the man's arms were broken; I had a spare, good arm in the freezer right enough, but not needed in the end. He had enough to jump away from I suppose; the pressure of the world's banks in crisis for one. But ...' Dave put his hand on the body and Oak Tree grimaced, 'he is still a Knight of the Realm, I think. Strong ankles. And we'll do him proud. I'm sure some mainland cowboys would fleece his pockets, but ... we are professionals.'

Oak Tree smiled his large teeth back at Dave the Grave; his cheeks were flushed; he was thrilled to be included in this club and did now feel like a professional.

'Here. Help me load the cargo.' Oak Tree was just about able to watch the elastic limbs being manipulated as though the man was a drunk who would not wake up. He wondered if he would ever become comfortable with the workings of the dead.

'Yes. I'm sure you will lad; if you learn from me then you're learning from the best. I have no problem saying that.' Dave bent his legs at the knees and rolled up his sleeves. 'Right. To work.'

Dave took hold of the corpse under its armpits and directed with the jut of his forehead for Oak Tree to take the other end of the body. Oak Tree closed his eyes and wrapped his big swollen arms around the legs of the body behind its knees. He was glad he had practised using the drawer.

'Nice,' said Dave, looking up to the boy, 'you have a human touch, and a good back – the perfect combination. I suppose they named you well. Try not to fart. Some do in this position. Nerves get us all.' Dave looked down to survey the crease at the boy's bottom to make sure the trousers hadn't split.

Dave put the lid down on the coffin, and caught sight of the child's watch inside, which he had taken from the house where the dead man and his family had been holidaying. He had assumed it must be important and possibly belonged to one of the man's daughters. It was a nice addition. 'It still keeps time,' he whispered.

Oak Tree noticed that Dave the Grave didn't seal the coffin, and wondered why.

'There's a reason for that,' said Dave. 'It's important that a person be at ease with the consequences of their actions – even the dead; maybe, *especially* the dead. I like to let them breathe, for that to happen. And this one needs it more than most. The jury's still out as to whether he is departing for heaven or hell. I'm still waiting for instruction.' He wasn't in the business of making assumptions but Dave had an inkling that after thirty minutes under his stewardship the big lad had been upgraded from something resembling a thick woodland plant to something more approaching a man.

*

The undertakers made their way southwards in the hearse, along the scraggy coastline to where the more remote settlements on the moorlands sat below hovering hills. Further around the coastline, the mysterious rock known as The Looming was believed to lie. Touching the body and feeling the heavy weight of a lifeless head made Oak Tree realise that some things did not have a pulse, but still carried weight, and still meant something. He wondered why they were not heading in the direction of the ferry terminal, but knew better by now than to ask aloud.

The water's edge rocked at their side, clutching things to it. Dave was satisfied that all preparations had been adhered to. He had noticed a heavier foot than usual was required on the accelerator to propel this cargo. 'Aye. It's a posh, solid coffin,' said Dave, breaking his humming. 'If I didn't know better I'd swear the bastard had diamonds in his teeth. He could afford them.' He was making sure the boy was fully prepared for what was to come. He was not daft to the fact that a certain amount of adrenaline was necessary to see off a human shell, and for that, the boy would need nerves. 'He'll need a stiff back from us. Oh, and we have a stop, a slight detour, to make on the way.'

Oak Tree nodded. He looked at the deep creases in his flabby hands. He was feeling older. He was thinking how impossible it must be to know the exact moment when a body will decide to give in to these little acts of the ageing. Jumping from a cliff would do it, though.

'Not a man or woman alive can know the answer to that,' replied Dave.

Oak Tree turned as quickly as his big neck would allow. He wondered if he had in fact spoken aloud?

'But when enough of the changes occur the balance is tipped to death. And some work more at addressing that balance than others – the buggers in Hollywood and the like. And some fade away and others are remembered. This man will be remembered, if not for the best reasons.'

Maybe, thought Oak Tree, it is only the dead watching – which now included this corpse in the back – who know when that time will come. And it is their secret. He almost turned around to check.

'You might well be right there, lad,' said Dave assuredly, crunching through the gears, 'maybe there's a brain in that big overgrown skull of yours after all. Rest it for now though.' The lad's big frame was making gear changes tricky. 'We're almost there; we have our own homage to Hollywood to visit.' Dave chuckled to himself.

Oak Tree saw a deer run through the field next to them and wondered what it felt like to jump and run and float like a deer. Then he saw horses in the next field. He liked how strong horses looked; one had extra fat at the sides as though a baby horse was sleeping inside. Then the horse stopped running and spun round and round, chasing its own tail. Oak Tree thought how amazing it was to be able to do that. He had never noticed that before. It reminded him of the rogue seagull.

The two undertakers pulled up outside the house – fishing creels were stacked up one side. Pluto was sitting on the front window ledge, skimming stones unsuccessfully over his ragged front garden. For years this gangly one had chosen this perch to admire the sky, day and night. Dave smiled at the sight and killed the engine. He looked to Pluto and imagined that the stone had moulded the bum cheeks as much as they in turn had moulded the stone: this he imagined was the physical administration, affirmation even, of God's gradual work unseen. Dave then looked to his new recruit beside him in the hearse and hoped the boy was ready. He and Pluto had been looking for a solution to their problem and this chance was not to be missed.

'This, my boy, is Pluto,' began Dave, looking proudly ahead through the windscreen. 'He is none other than the former Chairman of our Island Historical and Archaeological Society, of which I am the other member, and new Chairman.' His address had come clumsily off the tongue, Dave knew it. He studied from afar his former Chairman's uncharacteristically serious face, propped as it was on his increasingly Coke bottle-shaped shoulders. Pluto appeared frailer to him and, like sunrise on those nights when he was fully concentrating on a body, his friend's fragility seemed to have happened without Dave even noticing it. He watched as Pluto skimmed his final stone and reached down to pull a small tobacco tin from a hole in the bricks below the window ledge. Pluto rolled a cigarette. 'You know, as a younger man he once tried to place a mouse in that hole during a hailstone shower, understanding that it needed shelter,' chuckled Dave to Oak Tree. 'Despite the other stuff, we can all learn a little humanity from that man. Less so on the banjo. And there's a form of intelligence. Although Bill Gates may beg to differ.'

Dave opened his door and said to Oak Tree, 'You'll wait here a minute lad; I need to have a chat with my planetary friend. He is in need of our help, and we of his.'

Oak Tree watched Dave the Grave progress towards Pluto's

house, which was elevated on the hill near the southern edge of the island. Dave looked as though he might clutch a cloud from the sky as he climbed the muddy driveway.

'To the nines, my friend. To the nines. You look a million dollars,' smiled Pluto.

'Aye well,' managed Dave, brushing Pluto's escaped saliva off his jacket.

'Is that the lad?' asked Pluto, looking beyond his friend.

'Yes,' Dave said, resting his body against the house; for ethical reasons he preferred not to look back to the hearse, because of what they were about to do. He was about to disrespect his profession and the dead, too.

'What a skull.'

'Agreed,' said Dave. 'My wing mirror on his side is all but redundant. I can forget the view. I hope he's capable, you know, and has the craft. The fool.' But Dave knew he had not said 'the fool' with conviction. He had said it with little force at all. It was as though his mouth wished the word to come out forcefully, but his gut, that place of knowing, the very base of his soul, would not allow it. He could feel his tie tightening around his neck. The two men stood for a moment. It was, Dave knew, a more delicate and innocent land on which they stood, and one they were about to corrupt.

'Does he know?' asked Pluto.

'No, of course not.' And then, more sombrely, 'And I'm sorry, Pluto. And for Mae-Li.'

'For what?'

'Well, given you took the money, with your own hands, the heat would seem to mostly be on you. I wish it had turned out differently. Our plan was almost foolproof.' Dave shifted his polished shoes nervously on the muddy track. He knew in truth there was no more suspicion on Pluto than there was on himself. Nil even.

'At least we have a solution, eh, *Chairman*,' Pluto said. It was still difficult for him to use the title for another.

'Aye, well. We had better get to work. Did you dig the hole already, out the back?' asked Dave.

'It's like the Chelsea Flower Show back there,' replied Pluto. 'Worthy of an archaeological dig, should we ever pursue one.'

'Is it deep enough?'

'For certain. I damn near dug myself to Bangkok and saved us the bother.'

'Good work. And we will. When you come back. I'm sure things will grow over – I mean blow over.'

'Yes,' mumbled Pluto. He looked towards the hearse. 'Will I fit?'

'The coffin?' whispered Dave. 'Yes, although it'll be tight; I wouldn't go tap-dancing in there.'

'No.' Pluto flicked away the failing stub of tobacco. 'Would it take the banjo though?'

'I'm sorry my friend. I better get the lad. You go inside and let's get this thing done as quickly as we can.'

'What does he think we're doing?' asked Pluto, the smoke still protruding from his mouth and catching in the wind, escaping to the inferior mainland, as he himself was now intending to.

'He has no clue,' said Dave. 'If we get the coffin inside, I'll explain that it needs a blessing from you – you know, a man of the sea thing ... Then I'll send the boy back to the car, we'll get the body out, bury him out back, and you jump in.'

'You're a magician,' tooth-grinned Pluto.

'The corpse's family are waiting at the ferry – and no doubt with a crowd,' continued Dave, wrestling with his code of ethics. 'I'll get you to the mainland, release you, and by then nobody will be any the wiser. You'll be half way to Asia with a hard-on by the time I get home. The new lad's lost in himself anyway. I can hear him thinking.'

'Okay. I'll see you on the other side, as it were. Oh,' he patted himself down, 'is this suit okay?'

'It'll do, my friend. The kneepads are unfortunate, but still. I would lose the new moustache though – it gets hot in there. Unless you're planning on a detour to Mexico. I've made you a vent. Give me two light taps if you're in any bother for breath.' And then Dave nearly smiled: 'It might even be worth it just to see the big lad shit himself.'

'That was kind, Chairman,' said Pluto.

Dave walked away and then stopped. 'But it troubles me.'

'What does?'

'This is the first body I have not properly, and professionally, put into the ground.'

'Well you *are* putting him in the ground.'

'Aye well. This was only possible because, together with the family, I managed to persuade the authorities, and they in turn the TV companies, that every man, despite his crime, deserves a modicum of privacy on his journey to his maker. But they'll have a field day at the pier.'

'You mean for me?' asked Pluto, swelling with pride. 'Then I should have washed my hair.'

'No, not for you.' Dave grimaced. 'You must be as good as invisible. Anyway. I'll kiss my ticket to heaven goodbye. Nothing surer.'

'Will you want the Thai fountain? I feel by rights it comes with the Chairmanship . . .'

'Eh, no. I'll decline, my friend. You'll need someone to keep guard while you're away.'

'Indeed. Well, I'll be careful not to get aroused in the box, I'm not sure there's room,' quipped Pluto. Then he bent down to replace the tobacco tin in the hole that was not sufficient to accommodate a mouse all those years ago.

After the three men had delivered the coffin to Pluto's front room Dave the Grave instructed Oak Tree to go back to the car. Twenty minutes passed and then Dave reappeared outside Pluto's front door and motioned to Oak Tree to come back in from the car. Dave made his excuses to the boy for Pluto being, apparently, holed up in the lavatory – often his associate could spend what seemed like hours in there, seemingly flushing the loo over and over again – and then the two undertakers – although at this point in proceedings Dave preferred to think of them as 'hearsemen' – came out of Pluto's house and opened the boot of the black vehicle. They surveyed the insides, making sure it was ready. Dave stole a glance to their surrounds to make sure they were not being watched and then returned inside the house. It was not long before he and Oak Tree re-emerged, this time more burdened. They struggled efficiently with the coffin to keep it level with the aid of a rolling device around which black straps from the coffin were tied. It was not their business to drop such a thing. That had never happened on Dave's watch, and he couldn't risk breaking his proud record now. He no longer measured this task in weight alone. It was all about technique, like weightlifting. He was no longer filled with re-morse; the adrenaline had taken over.

'As before,' rasped Dave to the boy, his eyes darting from side to side, 'he's a heavy bugger in the box so be careful, especially when we get to the pier, we'll have half the world's eyes on our backs.' He was introducing Oak Tree to this way of speaking of the dead in the present tense, as most others would do of the living. Oak Tree didn't speak. He hadn't the words during such an important task; he didn't have any reason to question or look back up at the house on the hill. One of the long straps had untied and was dragging along the ground. The two men settled and then levered the coffin into the back of the hearse. Oak Tree picked up the strap and replaced it around the casket. His initiative had been noted.

'Poor bastard he is,' Dave breathed to himself as he looked back to the house. Oak Tree didn't speak, but noticed that Dave's hands were muddied. 'Right. Let's get off to the waiting party. We're each of us meant for the work that we're at lad. Remember that.'

As the vehicle turned, the contents became obscured by the late-morning sunlight. The tyres released and finally gripped on the mud below. It was a cold day out of the sun's gaze, where Pluto's house remained, as if shrink-wrapped but barely protected by the lengthening shadows. Dave now felt free of the guilt pangs he had encountered in Pluto's back garden; he was never a man to do anything for one second longer than necessary. He could have his hearse fuelled with just one word – 'Unleaded'. He replayed the sight of Pluto's smiling face from inside the coffin, before he had closed the lid – how the skin on his friend's face had tightened with that one last inhalation of smoke to fully reveal those sharp cheekbones, his eyes like crawling insects. His friend was still blessed with a handsome face, despite the scars of a life on the drink, not to mention the impact of his recent misdemeanour.

Dave considered once again Oak Tree's angular movements and flashlight stares when they had moved the coffin. But it was history to him now. This was the glorious present.

The hearse completed its turn at the bottom of Pluto's land then disappeared over the brow of the heather-strewn hill. Oak Tree was now more at ease in the presence of the dead. He thought about the earthly remains inside the coffin. It was like trying to imagine the heart he had seen on the wall chart in biology class hidden within his own body.

Despite his years of experience, it was almost impossible for Dave to think of such a man as the famous banker from the global news giving way to mortality, far less decomposing – but now he told himself that it was happening in the boot of his very own vehicle. He had to believe that, so that others would. How quickly the mortal blow does strike, turning the present into the past; how instantly the tarnished skin is returned to a state unblemished: Dave had seen it many times before, but death always arrived at him as a new visitor.

When the hearse reached the main pier the local Minister was standing expectantly with the banker's grief-stricken family and some official-looking people clearly from the mainland. Dave saw that quite a crowd had gathered, which included John the Goat, and he presumed Malcolm too. The sight of Randy in his banking uniform pinched Dave's concentration, but he managed to keep his focus on the job in hand. Behind them were several outside-broadcast trucks. The hearse parked and Dave the Grave took a deep breath, then got out to open the rear door, which slowly relaxed in the direction of the sky. Oak Tree stood several paces behind him. Without the need for words, Dave the Grave continued to direct the younger undertaker through his virgin paces.

In years to come he hoped Oak Tree would similarly blood a new recruit or two, easing them into the responsibilities of the job. Dave motioned to the banker's family to come forward and lay their flowers; he was eager to follow every procedure as normal, and was keen for these procedures to be noticed; it was not often he had this audience and he was still a proud man, mightily aware he was also carrying the responsibilities of his entire profession. It would be a nightmare if anything went wrong.

Oak Tree straightened his long back and puffed out his big rosy cheeks; he now felt a new thing growing inside him and realised it was the Coffin Boffin. Dave nodded respectfully to the bereaved family and closed the back door of the hearse.

Inside the box Pluto smiled with pride and licked at his whiskers but kept his body perfectly still, trying not to breathe too loudly or think of Mae-Li. Back in his garden lay the mortal remains of a Knight of the Realm, no less. And soon flowers would grow on the man. It was going to be hard for Pluto not to tell anybody.

As for Dave the Grave, he would only confide in the dead.

15

Man Who Walks the Earth – II

'Of course, we're saying it was a fish bone,' said Mary McBeth. It was the day after Ivor's funeral. 'It seems the lies won't leave us. I'm sixty-six years of age and still they come.'

Jake nodded. He could see how especially pale she was.

'You know ... he was proud after all,' added Mary. She cupped her hands around her teacup. 'Only myself, Randy, and Dave the undertaker know the real reason he died. You know, the knife.' She gulped heavily and put a tissue to her mouth. 'Goodness. At least the undertaker did a nice job on him ...' Her voice broke.

'And now I know too,' Jake said. He reached for her arm.

'And now you know too. Indeed. Thank you dear.' Mary rubbed his hand and closed her eyes to compose herself. 'It was Randy's idea – the fish bone. They protected each other till the end.' She paused and shook her head. 'How was the bed?'

'It was perfect, thanks. Just what I needed.'

'Good.' Mary nodded. 'It stays made up for you. Always.'

'How is Randy taking it? I understand he found the body.'

'Oh, and the doctor. He knows too.'

'Yes. Of course.'

Mary stared at the photo of her and the teenage Jake on the

sideboard, taken not long after she returned to the island in the year 2000.

'Randy? He's bearing up,' she said, 'bit ashen as you saw for yourself yesterday. And there's been lots of drinking talk. I'm not sure about him wearing Ivor's old police badge with the bank clothes, but still. It's right he should have it. I'm grateful it was him who found him, you know ...' She sighed deeply. 'I don't expect Edna will be much help. But when he realises there's the prospect of more food for his stomach he'll be okay. He has his sister too, nice lass. Needs a shave of course.'

'His sister?' Jake smiled.

Mary closed her eyes tightly, refusing her impulse to laugh. 'Oh Jake you could always make me hoot. I'm so glad you came. And that you were there for the funeral. *He* would have been.'

'I'm glad you called – after sending the letter.'

'I wasn't even sure I had the correct address, to be honest. I had to call the orchestra number for it. I wondered if you were on tour. But I saw the Proms was on the telly and wondered ... I looked but couldn't see you.'

'I was at the Proms.'

'You know how I don't like the phone. They were very helpful. I didn't think you would ... you know ... still ...' Mary stopped.

'*Care?*'

'Well. I understand you didn't want your past following you dear, I understood that. Forgetting can be as important as remembering.' Mary puffed up the cushion on her lap. Then she put it back in position, perfectly in line with the others. She took up her cup again and looked to check the order of her attire, as though preening her feathers. Jake could see she was thinner. 'I should have written more to you lad, but, you know, it's not really my thing. I'm just glad I managed to put it all down in one go. I waited till he died, I promised him I would. But you deserved to know. It was our secret really, not yours. And it was taken over by his parents. Ivor's.'

'Yes, I'm getting used to the fact that you're my grandmother. He was my ... *grandfather*,' sighed Jake. 'I'm twenty-four, and now I know ...' Jake put a hand on each of his knees and rocked on his seat. 'Of course I care. I should have come back to see you more. And I'm sorry you had to call the orchestra.'

'Well, I didn't want to interrupt the playing, you know.' She paused. 'And so I've tried to protect you like one, a grandmother, when I was finally *allowed* to,' Mary said. 'Like a mother even. More than your ... *great*-grandmother ever was. Silly woman pretending she was your grandmother. Pretending she was me.'

Jake stared straight ahead.

'You left as soon as you could.'

'I did, I suppose.' Jake moved uncomfortably.

'Eighteen.'

'Yes.'

'I understand why you couldn't stay, lad. At least we had three years living together, until you left for the academy. We had that. He gave us that.'

'God?' questioned Jake.

'No. No. Ivor. Well ...' Mary's eyebrows jumped and she looked to the window. 'Of course the arrangement suited Ivor,' she went on, 'but still ... I know he wanted you to have a female influence, *my* influence.'

270

'We did have that time. We still do,' said Jake. 'I'll be here for you.'

'Even if I did have to be just the housekeeper from a few doors down to the rest of the world, to the island. It wasn't difficult, what with me having the skin of a ghost! I never gave you that.'

Jake smiled. He brushed his dark, hairy arms, which were even darker than normal from the London summer.

Mary watched his long, black eyelashes flutter as they used to. She could see the Celt in those at least. 'Do you remember when we used to watch the orchestras playing on BBC2 on Saturday night?' she asked.

'I do indeed. The Proms.'

'Those nights you would play your violin to me. So many times I wanted you to know the truth, but somehow the decision was taken out of my hands. But I'm so proud of you, lad. You did it – all the way to the Proms and the Royal Albert Hall, and all by yourself. You did it without any of us. And you're still so young!' Mary smiled. 'He was so proud of you. Even if he didn't know how to show it.'

Jake paused. 'I hope I got round to thanking you for sending me the violin, from before we knew each other?'

'You did lad. You wouldn't have known at the time, that I sent it. At least they let you have it.'

'Yes . . .' Jake nodded.

'Lucky that you never got the Punch rough hands . . .' Mary's thoughts returned to Ivor's parents. 'And Ivor's father? A truer shit never walked the earth. Excuse my . . .' Mary stopped.

Jake could see she was blushing; he had never heard her swear.

'Each night he willed his heart to stop just so that he could blame somebody else.'

'Even *he* said that – Ivor I mean – that his father was, well ….' Jake stopped. He didn't know how to swear in front of Mary. He recalled Ivor's stories from his youth of tending the doves in his father's dovecote, only to have to kill them off one by one. Ivor's letters had spoken of little else; or at least those letters Jake had received before he last moved.

'I knew what you meant. You're my blood. So you needed to know the truth – finally. I was ashamed, of course.'

'I'm sorry.'

'For what? You have nothing to be sorry for. You do know that they made me leave the island? I only came back when Ivor's parents were cold. Even in death they kept me away for a bit. Until Ivor arranged for me to take over their house a few doors down, and then for you to join me. But still.'

'I understood that you were on the mainland.'

'But it's not the same. I wasn't a native but I always felt *right* here. Ivor used to say that when you are an islander the isolation never leaves you. But it never left me either. Still, I was ashamed of myself back when it all happened. It wasn't how I was brought up.'

Mary took hold of another pillow for inspection. She removed and replaced each foot in her slippers. 'And as I said in my letter you deserve to know. We never married of course. I was too young when it happened, when Ivor and I … You know I wasn't that kind of girl. He was twenty-two, two years younger than you are now. And I was,' her voice gave way, 'just fifteen. And it all happened during one summer. That's when his folks packed him off to the whaling and I was packed off back to the mainland. My parents were embarrassed, my

272

father was the organist in the local kirk, by God – maybe that's where you got the music from my lad – anyway, and so they agreed the baby could go back to the island, to Ivor's people. Nobody wanted it, the baby – your father – except us: Ivor and myself. Over time he seemed to blame me more than anyone else. And then when I returned we came to an arrangement: me as housekeeper, and I suppose he was, well, The Clock. I wanted to marry him back when it all happened, I really did. Just one summer told me that. At least I can say that now he's gone.'

'You didn't want him to know when he was alive?'

'I don't know.' Mary frowned and sniffed deeply through her nose, becoming almost skittish. 'When you've had what you want denied you, well, you stop wanting altogether. You just are. Cooker, cleaner. My son was taken from me – twice.' Mary took a tissue from the sleeve of her cardigan. 'And then they tried it with you too.'

'The plane. My father,' Jake said, looking down to the carpet; it was the same carpet. They had never spoken about the plane. Jake wondered why he had said *my father* when it was so obvious to them both. It had been a long time since he last said it. Mary nodded continuously and wiped her eyes.

Jake noticed they were the same slippers she had always worn, and still in good order. He looked around the old front room: even in London, if he closed his eyes tightly, he could itemise the contents of this room. He could do that on any given day, on any given tube line, during any given rehearsal. He looked to where the scavenged Christmas trees used to stand, year upon year, with the same paper angel on the top. Could fragments of fir needles, of the past, still be on the carpet – from before? Hidden, like everything else. He wasn't sure if anything could last that long. He recalled the odour of resin the tree would bring into the house, and how it would fade as another Lockerbie anniversary, another Christmas, loomed. It was a part of the forest brought into their home, but released just a fraction of the scent he would experience in the woods. The deposited sap on the carpet would cling to the soles of his socks, as that night in 1994 had clung to him. He thought of the Christmas trees discarded in early January – naked, browned and bereft – tossed onto pavements and sidewalks the world over; in all the cities he had visited to entertain.

He looked at the painting – of a landscape he didn't recognise – that had always hung above the fire. Now he saw that there was something missing, something the painter could not capture. The trees were too static and the sheep did not look at home; it was as though the painter had added them as an afterthought in the hope of eliciting an emotional response. If the laws of physics were being properly observed, they should fall off the sloping hill. But now he wondered if that really was the function of art – to capture reality?

It was the wind; it was the wind which was missing.

'You know he was buried in his uniform?' Mary said. 'Silly bugger even took his truncheon with him. Randy said, "Well it got him into enough bother ..." If you know what I mean.' Mary rose and sat down again quickly, never more than several inches from the sofa.

Jake was embarrassed by her implication. This ageing Mary was a more liberated version of the one he had known before. But then, thought Jake, wasn't everyone? 'I suppose Randy would know about getting into trouble. They were quite a pair.'

'When I think about it now. He and Randy would go on their jaunts around the graveyards, one in bank uniform the other in police. For fun! Of course, the one grave Ivor longed to see he never got to. None of us have.' She pushed her neck forwards. 'Well at least Randy has another grave to get excited about now. Even Ivor's false teeth were, you know, handed to Randy, out of view, by the undertaker.' She shook her head. 'You know, I think Ivor actually resented Randy because he likes life. Or he certainly used to.' Mary turned incredulously to Jake.

Somehow Jake could not recall Ivor's teeth in his mouth. But then an image returned. 'His teeth were rotten, though?'

'Precisely. He had asked Randy to source him a new pair. Vain bugger. But when the moment came, well, apparently it didn't look like Ivor. That's what Randy said to me. He said, "Mary, it didn't look like Ivor." Poor man was crying like a baby when he said that. No – Randy loved him.'

Jake looked at Mary's suffragette-like hair, which, as always, was suspended in a great bun at her crown; and then to her bulging, goggle eyes, the heavy eyelids familiarly half-cocked, giving the constant impression of worry, of a woman carrying the weight of her thoughts. Only once, shortly after they had begun living together, did he witness through her open bedroom door the elaborate art of Mary tying up her hair. He had watched as she did this without a mirror; the well-practised labour of criss-crossing her hair as though she were working knitting needles through wool. It had occurred to him then that the removal of one hairpin could collapse the whole structure into flailing, unruly strands, and with it, Mary would somehow have ceased to be Mary. He recalled how in a letter Ivor had likened 'Miss McBeth's' choice of hairstyle to Taliban headgear. And now Jake thought about a sign he had seen at the beginning of his journey to the island outside a shop near his Camden flat. '*Hairdresser wanted, who likes hair.*' Several times since he had arrived back on the island, he had thought about the implication of those three underlined words. He thought of George Swan, now lying in his own allotted patch of London, who, as Randy did, 'liked life'. 'He liked his job didn't he?' asked Jake.

'Ivor?' said Mary. 'He took pride in the uniform, there's no question. How much law did he actually enforce? Well ... it depended how well you knew him, or, on how many of his Christmas trees you bought.'

'He was keener on the chase than the prize, perhaps.' Jake heard his voice; the English inflections were more noticeable now he was here. He wondered when he had started saying perhaps instead of maybe.

'Let's say Perry Mason can rest easy. Poor man in his chair.' Mary sighed loudly. 'I've seen them all, every episode. I used to bring him over his dinner just after it finished.'

'Perry Mason?' teased Jake, with a smile.

'No, lad!' Mary chuckled.

'Did Ivor know, about my dad? That they were father and son?'

'Of course. How could he not?' Mary blurted out a quacking sound. She put down the cup and replaced the tissue under her cuff.

'I suppose,' Jake said, shaking his head. 'Sorry, stupid question. I'm still, eh, getting used to all this.' He looked at her again to make sure she was okay. Then he woke his phone and browsed through pictures of Sophie. He wiped at his stubble and said: 'Do you miss him?'

'I miss – silly things ... I miss cooking for him every day. And making his bed.' Mary flinched, stretched out her arms and returned them efficiently, folded into her sides. 'Those Punches and their stubborn ... still heads. Well, you're one of them. At least that disposition is handy for a violin player.'

'No. I meant my dad.'

'Oh son,' Mary leaned forwards, 'I miss him more than anything. I never even really knew him; I even miss that. You understand he didn't know about me being his mother. He was gone before I could even–'

'Yes. He would have appreciated that. Ivor, I mean – the dinners,' Jake said abruptly. He looked to the photo on Mary's sideboard. His father was sporting an era-defining bushy moustache and wide lapels below his square, dimpled chin. He would have been in his late teens. Jake could see himself, the same black hair and sallow skin; he could see Ivor even, but his father was more handsome, and frozen in time.

'I took that from Ivor's house,' Mary said.

'Yes. I recognise it.'

'I'm sure he didn't – appreciate the dinners. Still ...' Mary wiped her hand over her forehead. 'We called each other Miss McBeth and Mr Punch till the end ... stupid really.'

Jake shook his head. It was a description as far removed from him and Sophie as he could imagine. As Mary turned her head he noticed the elaborate clasp in her hair was inscribed with the letters 'H.B.' He had never seen it before.

'And your father's girlfriend – your mother – an American, I never knew her of course.'

'I barely know a thing about her.'

'Rose she was.'

'And no one else seems to.'

'No. I know lad – that is very difficult for you. I've always appreciated that. As far as I'm aware there was no contact from America, we don't know if she had any family left. Maybe it was too difficult for them. An Italian name I believe... of course there's so many of them. But I don't believe she had many folks, at least that's how I understood it. Given my own predicament, I've always really felt for her. Both of us ... outsiders.' Mary's voice broke. 'It's a miracle you weren't on that plane ... You were here, but I wasn't with you.'

Jake sniffed slowly, deeply.

'Maybe that is something you might feel you can do now. Try to trace her?'

Jake nodded slowly and tried to force a thankful smile. 'I'd like that.'

Jake felt squeezed, as though he should leave the island as soon as he possibly could. This onrush of the past was alarming in a way he could not define; he hated to think about his parents and the plane, so he had trained himself not to. That was until he met the old lady in the graveyard and everything changed; until Ivor slit his throat with a knife; until now.

'I miss organising him,' said Mary.

'And fuck.'

'Jake!' laughed Mary. 'Goodness ...'

'I'm sorry.' His face had remained serious.

'You know he left me his house. So this one will need to be sold. You'll have all that, son. I'll move over to the other one soon. I'm just surprised I beat the chicks to it. That'll be yours one day too. It's mortgage-free. I suppose now he doesn't care who knows. Or everyone will just think I'm the world's best-kept housekeeper. Randy must have suspected something, he had to. But he never said a word. Ivor understood that. Even though they bickered he left Randy his prized sergeant's badge you know, and erm, his helmet . . .'

'I see.' Jake smiled broadly. Given Randy's reputation as a younger man, he wondered if that last offering carried additional significance.

'Maybe he'll get back out on that motorbike of his,' said Mary.

'Randy?' Jake then recalled the bike that was a fixture of his childhood.

'Yes. Ivor banned him from riding it, gosh, a while ago now. Randy wasn't getting any younger and he was never sober on the thing. And so Ivor banished it to Randy's garage. It was sad, Randy would still go in and sit on it. There – protection, once again. Oh,' continued Mary, 'and he left a cardboard box on the neighbour's door – Ivor. For the Polish lot.'

'What?'

'The chicks, in a box. The girl's to have the coop apparently. He had run out of dictators to name them for. So Communism lives on . . .'

Jake didn't know what else to say, and then he knew: 'He wrote to me.'

'He did?'

'Yes, until I moved. Although he could well have kept on writing, I suppose. It was mostly about his chickens.' Jake shook his head. 'He seemed particularly drawn to *Genghis Khan*; but I think Genghis was shy on the egg front . . .'

Mary returned his smile for the first time. 'Well, well,' she said, 'he wrote to you. He probably couldn't put it down in print, lad, the truth.' She looked down to inspect her yellow washing up gloves. Jake had seldom seen her without them.

Mary paused for thought. 'No,' she went on, 'I miss controlling him. That's it. I still have his engagement ring. I wore it yesterday, at the funeral.'

'Do you?' Jake turned eagerly to Mary and smiled.

'He didn't know that,' she said. 'I used to wear it here, but never at his place. You see, I never actually said "No". For all his training on the job he missed that one. Only a few doors separated the officialdom of our engagement, even after all these years. Well, it's over now of course. He thought I'd left it on the fencepost all those years ago.'

'He would have liked that. I think. And he would have appreciated what John the Goat did, at the funeral – the doves. I had no idea.'

'It was fitting. I'm glad Malcolm had the day off though; it could have been a bloodbath inside the coat.'

Mary grew more pensive then said: 'He never understood why you left.'

'He didn't want me to go. Then he quickly forgot about me or maybe I did him. He forgot that he once told me not to stay.' Jake thought back to that night he had shared with Ivor in the woods. 'Anyway. I think he blamed the violin more than anything, for me leaving.'

'Och, he blamed himself. He was hurt, but he would have seen it many times before, folk leaving. He even did himself for a time, goodness.'

'The whales ...'

'Well, you were never police material, he knew that. You were ...'

'I was ...' finished Jake, smiling, and then hacked away at an imaginary violin as if to provide confirmation.

Mary heard the notes. 'What I would do to hear you play

'...' she said, sitting forwards. 'I was there you know, in '98, at the memorial. I was in the town hall.'

'Really? I wish I'd known.'

'It was beautiful.' Mary closed her eyes. 'It really was.'

'Would you like to come and hear me play, in London?'

'Me?'

'You could bring your slippers ... there's somebody I'd like you to meet.'

'Goodness. My goodness.' Mary was briefly lost in the details of the imagined trip. 'Oh while I remember, love, you must take his letters. Will you want them? I've no idea what you'll do with them. Most days I would see him at the table scribbling away; if he heard me coming he would do his best to hide them, but I always saw him. The Magna Carta they probably aren't. Still, he was welcome to his privacy.'

'I'd be happy to take them,' replied Jake.

'Good. That's the right way of things. Anyway, if anyone asks here on the island – it was a fish bone.'

'Understood.'

'Not that he ever ate a fish from me that wasn't deboned first, but still. If the hat fits.' Mary got up and spun as if on rollerblades to the kitchen. She performed a brief and perfunctory clear-up of the debris in her sink. Jake walked through the door and propped himself against the wall as he used to as a teenager. He looked at their cups and saucers, now piled as dripping monuments to a lunch and a past revisited. He watched as she moved gracefully, wiping the lid of the bin, rinsing and folding the cloth, carefully laying a towel over the wet dishes, and flicking on the kettle again. As Jake heard the creaking element warm up, he wondered, was it simply the filling of things that was important? It occurred to him that Mary was reclaiming control over her domain, the way a lioness might on returing to the veldt. She removed the gloves to reveal her ring finger.

'I think it does fit Mary. Grandmother.'

'It was so damn far to fall,' Mary said, collapsing to her forearms on the sink. 'It was so damn far.'

The following evening Jake walked out of Mary's house just ahead of sunset and the falling dusk. He was to leave the island the next day, to return to the other world, to Sophie, Sibelius, the Proms. He passed Ivor's house, which he could see was now in mourning, silenced by drawn curtains. He could slip inside – he knew all the nooks and crannies – to become part of the mystery, but decided against it. He turned up the hill, past the sign that pointed tourists to Bloody Bay, and on to Transmitter Road. He kept his head down – he didn't want to see anyone, not even Randy. He looked to the dirt below for signs of dragged Christmas trees, those hostages of the forest from years before.

He arrived at the gate to the golf course, which was surrounded by rust-coloured bracken. He caught sight of the stone wall with spots of white moss that had always lined this pathway – he knew it was green moss turned aged and grey. This knowledge, his possession of it, would no doubt surprise his colleagues in the orchestra, not to mention Sophie. He had Ivor to thank for that. He walked up the hill and soon arrived at the Games field, situated on the flat plain of land in the heart of the course. He looked to the wispy hillside that acted as a spectator stand on Games days; it seemed naked without the bodies which would leave the grassy bank flattened for weeks thereafter. The messages on his phone now erupted like chirping monkeys. Apparently he had crossed some mythical border, and the signal had returned; from somewhere in the ether, people had discovered him, were trying to connect, to overcome geography with information. He apparently needed to know, must know now! The Proms my dear boy! The fucking Proms!

And there it was, what he had come for: the sandpit. Jake knelt down. He lowered his body as though he were about to perform a Muslim prayer, and kissed the dry, sandy earth. He rose to his knees and imagined the marks of his father's record-breaking body. Then he took a picture of the pit on his phone.

It was getting darker.

He had one more thing to do before he boarded the ferry in the morning. He walked discreetly down to the seafront. He looked out to where the fishermen used to work – and where some still did. He visualised those tribes of men, who marched in unison from village to village, a conclave of sorts given to optimistic thoughts of full seas and bulging creels, decorated in blue and yellow and orange oilskins pulled up high to their mysterious chests which protruded like the breasts of Ivor's chickens. If the orchestras and conductors he used to watch on TV were merely out of reach to Jake, then the fishermen were something else – they were untouchable, governed by the higher gods of the ocean. He hoped these warriors of the sea still marched as they once did.

He was standing at the post office on the seafront. The street was deserted apart from a few parked cars and their reflections on the water, which looked like giant, shimmering stepping-stones, leading somewhere else. At the far end of the old pier in the distance he spotted a large boy with a fishing rod cocked in the air, dangling his feet off the edge. Jake pulled out the pile of letters from his backpack. Earlier, he had put each letter in an envelope and searched online as best he could for the appropriate addresses. One by one he posted the letters of Ivor Punch – many to the White House, some to the UK Head of the soft drinks company SodaStream Ltd, several to the television entertainers Ant & Dec, one simply to Abdelbaset Ali Mohmed al-Megrahi, which he had labelled, in the absence of a Libyan address, 'c/o HMP Barlinnie, Glasgow'. And one to Kenny MacAskill MSP, Secretary For Justice, c/o the Scottish Parliament, Edinburgh. There was a release in letting go of them and watching them disappear into the box. There was one letter that was addressed to no one. 'Dear . . .' it read. He would need to bury that one in a special place. The clock chimed ten and Jake had the impulse to salute.

He stood silently in the shadow of the old town clock and licked the grains of sand from his lips. He needed to return to the pit.

16

To an Athlete who Died Young

What tense, the sea?

Two months later we are touching down at Washington's Dulles airport for the United States' National Humanities Medal ceremony. The Writer and I. When he said to me in the weeks following the invite, 'Alexander I want you to go to the ceremony with me,' I was truly surprised and delighted. And now we are here, surrounded by the embarrassed colours of the Fall. A representative from the White House is to meet us first on Capitol Hill for a drinks party. (Later, when I discover this unassuming man flew in only yesterday from the UK, and presumably, inevitably, over the Atlantic Ocean, this information, given my recent charge from the sea, makes me greet him as though he is Charles Lindbergh or a creature of oceanic wonder.)

It is a nervous affair, the pre-party, a bit like speed-dating but without even the prospect of a Presidential fuck, the Writer observes. I realise he is referring to the elephant in the room, President Clinton, with whom he is still fascinated. I nod my head, reassured. And then we are whisked away – there are two other notables who are to be honoured at the same ceremony, another writer and a musician – in case the first two turkeys are burnt, the Writer says, adding, with a slur – 'This turkey voted for Hanukkah a long time ago!'

And then, more quickly than I imagined, we are arriving at the security gates of the big house, and pulling up its leafy driveway. The house is smaller than it appears on *The West Wing*. I am privately embarrassed by my own provinciality, at the surreal recollection of an old lady whom I never met but whom I knew once lived on my island: *Cailleach Taigh Geal*, the Old Lady of the White House. And here we are, parked alongside those commanding white pillars, which rise like a family of miniature lighthouses. Our limo doors are opened and I am unbelievably, deliciously, given a ringside seat to the most powerful man in the world. *Call me skipper.*

We are led into a bland holding room, the White House Green Room. A very tall, officious and suited lady – who disappointingly is not C.J. Cregg – swings into the room with a clipboard. She explains, in a friendly yet unbending tone, that it is not official protocol for the leader of the free world (although she calls him 'The President') to meet any of the recipients, or to enter this room, before the ceremony. And then, just as she is making sure we have drinks and all we need, the door swings open and the most recognisable man on earth strides gracefully into the room in the way you would expect – with a slightly exaggerated overstep – and he is more handsome in the flesh than I expected. He makes a beeline for the Writer and, in that voice, announces loudly and deeply, the Writer's name.

The Writer doesn't miss a beat, rising more sprightly to his feet than I have seen him in a long time – and only I notice how his hands momentarily, instinctively, search for his dressing gown pockets. He returns the same tone of surprise:
'President Obama!'

And with that the two men shake hands and are

immediately jousting. But the exchange does not smack of two instantly recognisable people who have never met but who cannot avoid each other in a small room, insincerely pretending to be best of friends, or unavoidable rivals. A genuine warmth exudes from them; then Mr Obama explains they will talk more later, and goes on to work the rest of the room with equal vigour. But I can tell, because I have watched people my whole life, that he does so in a more functionary, on-message manner. It seems, the Writer announces to me – he who has documented and lived through the Cold War – that I am finally to get my Jewish mitts on the big red button!

My mind wanders, thinking of the pride that my grandmother, perhaps my literary originator, would have in me, were she alive to share this moment. I realise now that my own observational skills were first honed early in the morning on the seafront when Napoleon and I would watch my grandfather go about the preparations of *Eliza*. As I am sure other boys who grew up in the Western Isles did, and I hope, still do. I can appreciate now that the sea became us to him; it was our replacement. Briefly, I am there again. I can see it all played out before me: a series of facial ticks, the particular placements of oars and buckets, the loading of nets and creels. I am holding my nose to Napoleon's foul breath and, though I cannot see it, I can feel the presence of the small bible in my grandfather's chest pocket, somewhere below his deerstalker. And all this for the benefit of the sea. He knows it, my grandfather. I feel that old sense of danger, caused by my proximity to his. And then he is gone once again; and Napoleon too, who died in my grandmother's arms four years after my grandfather rowed off.

And now the tenses align: *God did love. God is love. God will love.*

I struggle to rejoin the present, stealing a downwards glance to check I am still wearing shiny black shoes and not knee-length Wellington boots. A thought enters my head – I must find a painter and decorator, back on the island, to maintain the words on the cliff. But, in truth, that may require an army of painters. And then mortality strikes – for who will ensure the upkeep after I am gone? Who will love? Who will paint: 'LOVE'? *Hours like cars collide*, she once said – my mother – or that apparition of her in 1976, seventeen years after her death. And now I too feel a collision of sorts, between the old and new. *I have to go back now*, she said in parting. Now I too must go back.

After the ceremony, during which the President proclaimed the Writer had 'chronicled the American experience from the streets of Newark', he is taken for a private meeting in the Oval Office. I sit outside, only feet from the President's two secretaries. Energetic, efficient people come and go (who, I am in no doubt, run much of our country and several others too, and are also in some larger way providing the same service as I do for the Writer).

The wine we had at lunch is beginning to catch up with me when I overhear a conversation which stops me in my tracks. For there must be a higher order of arrangement, these coincidences must be related to Charlie, my friend, my blood brother.

'Has this *Ivor Punch* gone through clearance?'

These words have been spoken by one of the secretaries into her bosom, which is propping up several letters. Her question intended for the ears of the other. 'It cleared the mailroom,' she adds.

The other secretary checks her computer screen. 'It's referenced under "Lockerbie",' she says. I flinch. She goes on, 'Looks like they couldn't find anything on him; no international record or previous correspondence. They want him to have it.'

'Okay, I guess we'll send it through,' sings the first. I watch as she leans to drop the letters into a basket marked POTUS. It is then that I realise the identity of the latter *him*. My confusion at overhearing this conversation, this mention of the man Punch – here of all places – merges with a general feeling of unreality surrounding the day's events. This feeling is, if not superseded, then matched, in fact dampened, by the illusion that this could be any office, in any town. It could even be the back room of a reasonably well-funded church.

But it is not. It is the gateway to the most powerful office in the land. And I recall how my grandmother once told me: 'Alexander, all men are ultimately flesh and bone.' It must have been one of those times when she was trying to nullify the extremes of my grandfather's behaviour; but really she only bolstered his mythology. I touch my own arm to reassure myself that this is real.

The Writer emerges from the room. The same suited, efficient lady accompanies him, no doubt with several more ticks marked on her clipboard. I don't have time to think more than, *It can't be, it cannot be, Ivor, the man I knew as the police sergeant from back home – can it? The Clock?* How many Ivor Punches can there be in the world? We are then politely summoned to walk with the lady, retracing our steps, back along the hallway on the State Floor that leads us to the chequered tiles of the Entrance Hall and along the line of red carpet. There, the woman says goodbye to us and we cross a line without noticing it. Suddenly we are out of the front door, to catch our breaths, to return to civilian life, to inhale the rest of the country and the waiting world. And – for me – to reacquaint myself with the familiar, rushing sound of the ocean. Despite his lifetime in the public eye, I can see that the Writer is permanently changed in some way. I realise what it is – this event, this official acknowledgement, together with the Writer's private knowledge that his final, published word is in the world – have conspired to make him realise he is free. The limousine driver scurries to open his door.

'Excuse me,' the Writer addresses our driver – 'can you hear the sea?' The Writer's lips purse, as though allowing those things, his words, to breathe.

The driver frowns and shakes his head.

'No. I didn't think so,' the Writer says, turning to me. 'It lives in the present Alexander,' he announces, before doing his best impression of Big Bird entering a limo.

I raise my head enquiringly. It is as though this nugget of knowledge has been assimilated in the confines of the Oval Office, perhaps over a tumbler of Scotch, as a direct result of the Writer's conversation with the President. But I know that is ridiculous, is not the case.

Given the significance of our surroundings, and the timing of his remark, I can only surmise that something has been unlocked in the Writer. Perhaps the decision of an esteemed man of words to give them up has bestowed on him the power to move the tectonic plates below another man. And that is to say nothing of the coincidence of overhearing that name from my youth, our island's very own Commander in Chief.

'And, as one born to the city, I prefer, on your behalf: "What tense, the *islander*?"' he adds, raising his boyish eyebrows. 'And now I can see *you* are present. And so it is too. The sea. In case you're wondering – that is my reasoning.' He looks at me impishly and I can see the precocious teenager in him once more; he is one of those enviable people who has been blessed with having the same personality, unchanged, all his life. And that consistency, that settled will, has enabled power. I wonder as I climb in alongside him if it is possible that when one man is granted freedom he can bestow it onto another. He is holding me up to the light.

So I'm asking you now if you can see the light, or is it just me? Can you see the light?

I can, skipper.

'I can still hear it – the ocean,' I say. 'I can still smell her.' *Charlie, my friend, can you hear it?* The *past sea. Can you let me go?* 'Mother, can you let me in?' I surprise, no, embarrass, myself, by realising I have said some of this aloud. It must be the mention of Lockerbie. Its effects.

Surely I never saw her on that night in 1976. I couldn't have. Why didn't she say, 'It's me'? Maybe Charlie and she did form a covenant of sorts. But I'll never know. Because twelve years later, my beautiful, charismatic friend Charlie was blown out of the sky from inside a Pan American plane high above the Scottish borders. He took my blood and our pact with him. He left me alone. And for the intervening twenty years, I have felt guilty for secretly appreciating that solitude, and my guilt increases when I wonder if she, Eliza, my mother, had some premonition when she told me to look after *him*.

And now here I am, sixteen years older than she was then. Up until the time of his death, Charlie Punch – for he was Sergeant Punch's brother – and I had never again spoken of her or of that night. And I never told him she had said to me, 'I know.' I realise he had taken my island with him too, if it wasn't taken before. And I must take it back. I must find Jake, the violinist, Charlie's son. Now more than ever.

'I know you can,' the Writer replies, in so doing bringing me back to the present, to America, and, sensing my confusion, he adds – 'hear the ocean.' And, never refusing an opportunity to force his tongue into his cheek, he adds with a beautiful, generous smile that fixes my eyes, 'Even though I haven't in fact written it.' His arms outstretch. 'And look around, there is no ocean in DC.' He smiles contentedly, marvelling at the light cascading on the buildings in his own land, which is now my island, my home, my present. I hear a clock chiming on the Hill, and it reminds me of the last time I saw my grandfather. I don't remember whether I looked to the old town clock, but I *heard* four chimes. And I wonder now, by disappearing forever on his boat, was my grandfather saying to me with actions instead of words, '*I'm useless on dry land, I need to be with her, in the sea. To send her back to you.*'

I cannot resist the temptation to run my hands across the fine leather seat below me, as Charlie and I once did not in a limo but in a Vauxhall Victor. Just in case, just in case. I turn to watch as the Writer shuffles to find comfort for his back, and listen as he hums something by Bach over the dulled rattle of the city. Next to this fidgeting, American, Jewish, angular mass of pride, relief and prominence – I *am* the sea.

'The Looming,' he begins, as we gather speed, his eyes widening familiarly, his tongue now searching for saliva. I assume it is a sign of his anticipation, relishing the prospect of these words on a page – were he to allow himself one final opportunity. His world has been built on words. I see his eyes are illuminated, his fervour building at the very notion of a worker going to the coalface, to a rockface, and of a man going to the sea, in search of the truth or the fiction we can live with. 'Go and write it, for Eliza, before I do.'

And so I did.

Acknowledgements

This book would not have made it this far without the instincts, guidance and Zátopek-like stamina of my literary agent, James Gill, at United Agents. Here's to the run going on, Jim. And f...

To my editor, Sophie Buchan, at Weidenfeld & Nicolson – both Ivor and myself could not have realised this story without your shaping, vision and 'Brocher' passion, and your complete care for the characters. Thanks to Rebecca Gray, Jennifer Kerslake, Craig Lye, Virginia Woolstencroft, Jo Carpenter, Dominic Smith, and all the team at W&N/Orion and Hachette Australia for all the work you do on behalf of these particular island folk; and to Edward Hodgson and all the team at UA.

Thanks to my uncles for talking of lasting jumps and perfect moments, to my cousin, Paul Kirsop, for planting the idea of mobile bank irregularities ...

I am indebted to a band of readers in different corners of the globe – you know who you are – who were brave enough to read not this book (because I kept this one a secret) but to cast their eyes over my formative works: your feedback is still greatly appreciated. I would like to acknowledge Rupert Davies-Cooke and The Original Writers' Group, London, for providing a safe platform for me to hone my early drafts. And

Atlantic for encouraging me, and in particular, something in these pages is owed to both my late grandfathers. Thanks to Rob Barlow for taking a rain-themed fact-finding walk with me to Bloody Bay on Mull, and for talking of the mighty St Kildans; and to Charlie Caplowe, Andy Prevezer and my music 'family'; and to Gordon MacIean, Tobermory.

Special thanks to my mum for her belief, which my late father provided too, who lives on with us – and who jumped.

Finally, I would like most to dedicate these pages to my wife Pam for all her love and support, and to our two beautiful daughters, for celebrating this, 'daddy's good news', with bigger smiles than my own.

THE
LETTERS
OF
IVOR PUNCH

Punch Paraphernalia

The Beginnings of Ivor Punch

I hoped one day I would become an author, as I did a songwriter. When I say I hoped, in reality I was willing to sweat blood and tears. But how did this happen? How did I travel from musician to author; islander to apparent mainlander?

I currently live in London but I was born and raised among a family of writers and storytellers in the Hebrides, namely on the isle of Mull, and so stories were always around me growing up, alongside music, as indeed was the beauty and the fury of the Atlantic Ocean. My songwriting developed through my teenage years and then later when my music – I have released seven albums to date under the guise of Mull Historical Society – started to take off, I found myself on tour a lot with time on my hands.

It was probably my late grandfather, Angus Macintyre, who provided the spark for all this. He was the bank manager in Tobermory, on Mull, and lived above the bank with my grandmother. He was a poet too, published for most of his life and still in print today. He would write serious, melancholic, comic verses about all sorts. Possibly his most often-recited poem is 'Islay Cheese', which was inspired by a story in our local bible – I mean, newspaper – the *Oban Times*. It was reported that the isle of Islay's cheese was having aphrodisiac powers in Italy – even with the nuns, and in the Vatican too. Everyone was at it. At least that was how my grandfather had it! My uncle, Lorn Macintyre, is also an author, so it was helpful for me to see my family doing it. And, as a musician, I've also enjoyed collaborating with writers, including Irvine Welsh and Tony Benn.

About three years ago I heard a voice in my head while sitting on a flight. I wrote down what I was hearing: '*Dear Mr Obama, There were six eggs in the chicken coop this morning, two more than yesterday and four more than the day before. It's official: you can tell your men the recession is showing signs of recovery.*' And I was off.

I wrote this voice down in the form of letters for a reason that was not immediately apparent to me at the time; some were written to President Obama, some to others. In these letters I suddenly morphed into an old man living on an island, a man called Ivor Punch, who turned out to be the island's retired police sergeant. He struck a nerve. I wrote more.

A whole cast of characters presented themselves around Ivor, some had secrets even his handcuffs knew nothing of. These were people from the nineteenth century, some from the present, some well-known, such as a visiting Charles Darwin, and the Victorian-era travel writer, Isabella Bird. And then I realised they had a shared story, and a kind of uniformity, despite their differences.

In Ivor's voice, and some of my other characters', I was keen to explore a notion I have that there is a global language: this thing that I've experienced of people on several continents, that despite their different tongues they often speak the same language. It's the shorthand delivery of speech, a certain directness often found in the aged and particularly prevalent in the humour and one-word character assessments of the Celts. Often that is a swear.

But why was Ivor writing to President Obama? In my songwriting I have always been drawn to the notion of

community, possibly because I come from a small, isolated one. I enjoy focusing on micro issues which I hope then tell a bigger, more universal, story: one to which we can all relate.

My own home, the isle of Mull, was, tragically, directly affected by the Lockerbie bombing: we lost one of our sons on the plane, and this loss moved me and I had always wanted to write about it. I transferred that loss to Ivor, and staged his first letter to Obama at the time of the international furore that accompanied the (eventual) release of the alleged Libyan bomber of the plane. And so Ivor writes because a man fell out of the sky, and he hopes the President can tell him why. Really, in a way Ivor is falling too.

This connection of my island to a world event allowed me to explore the theme of global community versus island community: I realise at the heart of the novel is the notion that an island life, an island community, can mirror that of a continent, or globe even. In that, maybe, the world can learn from the fabric that makes up an island.

I felt by pitting the two leaders together (one, the enforcer of the island's laws, the other, keeper of the free world) that this idea of island versus global could be explored even more.

The novel is also trying to explore the idea of equality and shared experience: and so, between the front and back covers, I have tried to present a world where, in Ivor's estimation, the President of Sodastream is on an equal billing to the President of America. But then we also discover that no one can breach the higher laws of the island's fishermen, with their singular eyebrows and maps of the seas confined within their heads.

But in my mind Ivor is not the novel's central character, the

island is. And it is run a close second to the Atlantic Ocean: an expanse of sea which as we know separates the two countries most affected by the bombing. And so this expanse became a character and provides a symmetry of sorts, because two of the island's sons leave the island, one to London, the other to the east coast of America (both destinations have attracted me). They go in search of themselves, to escape the past, but really they can't; there is still a part of them that remains on the island like the sheep's coat caught on the barbed wire fence. And so we discover the island travels. As it says better than I ever could on the back cover of my book, 'sometimes you have to leave home to know what home is'. And I have.

The myths and folklore of an island or small community are integral, and so there is also an element of the supernatural within the novel. When I was a child on Mull we were led to believe there was a Headless Horseman riding the peat bogs, and so I brought him to life within my book. Much of the Hebrides still have strong faith (Mull, less so), which was particularly strong in the nineteenth century: and so a certain Mr Darwin is then cast among this strong island Kirk, and comes face to face with said Horseman. This clash of science and religion was too good to refuse. This could be the island's revenge ...

This article first appeared in full in the Irish Times *as 'Mull of Colin MacIntyre: from stage to page' on 11 September 2015*

To get into character as Ivor Punch, Colin couldn't
resist sending some letters of his own

7th February

Ivor Punch

Dear Mr Punch,

Thank you for your recent letter.

As you are soon to celebrate your birthday, we would love to send you a bottle of
Cola as a gift.

Thank you very much for taking the time to write to us and for letting us know
how much you enjoy our product.

Yours sincerely,

SodaStream Worldwide Trading Company, 3 Francis Court, Fen Ditton, Cambridge CB5 8TE
Tel. 01223 378 153 Fax: 01223 293 167

www.sodastream.co.uk

Dear Ivor

Have a wonderful birthday.

We hope you will enjoy getting busy with the fizzy on this special day and for many years still to come.

Best wishes,

From all of us here at Sodastream.

A letter from Isabella Bird

Unlike Ivor Punch, the Bird sisters, Isabella and Henrietta, were real people. Isabella (1831–1904) travelled widely during her life, from Australia to the United States. She wrote letters to her sister, Henrietta, during her travels in the Rocky Mountains, which eventually became the book *A Lady's Life in the Rocky Mountains*. The book opens: 'To my sister Henrietta, to whom these letters are affectionately dedicated'.

In her final letter from the United States, written while she was on her way through the Wild West, she mentions the cowboy Jim Nugent, or 'Rocky Mountain Jim', the same Jim Nugent whom she mentions on page 141 of the novel.

This is an extract from her letter written from Cheyenne, Wyoming on 12 December 1873 to her sister, Henrietta:

I wrote to you for some time, while Mr Nugent copied for himself the poems 'In the Glen' and the latter half of 'The River without a Bridge', which he recited with deep feeling. It was altogether very quiet and peaceful. He repeated to me several poems of great merit which he had composed, and told me much more about his life. I knew that no one else could or would speak to him as I could, and for the last time I urged upon him the necessity of a reformation in his life, beginning with the giving up of whisky, going so far as to tell him that I despised a man of his intellect for being a slave to such a vice. 'Too late! Too late!' he always answered, 'for such a change.' Ay, *too late*. He shed tears quietly. 'It might have been

once,' he said. Ay, *might* have been. He has excellent sense for everyone but himself, and, as I have seen him with a single exception, a gentleness, propriety, and considerateness of manner surprising in any man, but especially so in a man associating only with the rough men of the West. As I looked at him, I felt a pity such as I never before felt for a human being.

My thought at the moment was, will not our Father in heaven, 'who spared not His own Son, but delivered Him up for us all', be far more pitiful? For the time a desire for self-respect, better aspirations, and even hope itself, entered his dark life; and he said, suddenly, that he had made up his mind to give up whisky and his reputation as a desperado. But it is 'too late'. A little before twelve the dance was over, and I got to the crowded little bedroom, which only allowed of one person standing in it at a time, to sleep soundly and dream of 'ninety-and-nine just persons who need no repentance.' The landlady was quite taken up with her 'distinguished guest'. 'That kind, quiet gentleman, Mountain Jim! Well, I never! he must be a very good man!'

*

Some months later 'Mountain Jim' fell by Evans's hand, shot from Evans's doorstep while riding past his cabin.

If you enjoyed *The Letters of Ivor Punch*, why not try these novels that inspired Colin MacIntyre?

Ask the Dust by John Fante

Hunger by Knut Hamsun

Gilead by Marilynne Robinson

Out Stealing Horses by Per Petterson

The Human Stain by Philip Roth

A Long Long Way by Sebastian Barry

Atonement by Ian McEwan

When Colin MacIntyre isn't writing he performs under the guise of the Mull Historical Society. He wrote 'The Ballad of Ivor Punch', which features on his 2016 album, *Dear Satellite*, to accompany his novel, and you can listen to it here:

bit.ly/1TSEYzX

Discover more from Colin MacIntyre by
downloading this free short story about a Burns
Night gone horribly wrong ...

Ewan should not
have accepted a lift to
Glasgow from The
Professor. He had
bought a train ticket,
had brought a packed
lunch – he had been
all set. All he had
needed to say was
'No'. Two letters.

Instead he nodded
his head gratefully
to The Professor's
kind offer. Now he's
driving down the ferry's
ramp, ready for the 96 mile (96.2, actually) journey
from Mull to Glasgow on Burns Night, sat next to
a bagpipe-playing, kilt-wearing, adulterous, foul-
mouthed Scot ... in the snow. Buckle up!

This free ebook is available to download here: bit.ly/1lCKdWr

Discover more ... Colin Mead ... by
downloading the ... next story ... in ... Night's
Night possibly ... too ...

... accept ...
... now found he ...
... robbers ...
... though it was ...
... had brought ...
... it was lying on ...
... all so. Almost had
... brow ... it was
... Not too ... after.

... Instead he nodded
... head gratefully
... he ... he endeavor
... and ... his lit
... as he ...
... run ... now ... too little ... s actually ...
from ... now on ... his Night's, at once
a bare ... One ... left ... warming ... He ... as, for
... in ... arm in the brow ... His ... she
... It ... all her brow ... for ... here and ...